PRAISE FOR SINS OF

Holy manicotti. From the delicious cover to the amazing story, this book deserves a million stars. Zoe balanced everything so incredibly well. The steamy times, family, drama, danger...all of it was so well written.

- Amy N.

Zoe Blake really brings her books to life for me. Now, add in that steamy, enemies to lovers, smexy vibes and its perfection! Every time I read Zoe's book, it ends up being a new fav!

- Heather B.

This was a page turner and a thriller. Could not put down the book until I finished.

- Siddhi

This book gave me all the feels!! It was sweet mixed with dark and savory, sprinkled with suspense!! The initial love/hate produces off the charts chemistry. Milana's hesitancy and Cesare's persistence creates a delicious push and pull that'll leave you wanting for more!!

- Maysen M.

SINS OF THE SON

A DARK ENEMIES TO LOVERS ROMANCE

CAVALIERI BILLIONAIRE LEGACY
BOOK TWO

ZOE BLAKE

Poison Ink Publications

CONTENTS

CHAPTER 1

MILANA

I stared with growing alarm as Cesare Cavalieri stalked toward me, his jealous anger palpable.

Before I could escape, his firm hand wrapped around my upper arm and wrenched my body behind him. He then stepped up to his cousin, Matteo. "Walk away."

Matteo's questioning gaze moved to me, then back to Cesare. "I didn't know."

Cesare ground out, "Now you do."

The moment Matteo left, Cesare turned his wrath on me. "Stay away from Matteo. Trust me. He's interested in just one thing."

I cocked my head to one side as I raised an eyebrow. "You would know."

Cesare stepped closer, the primal threat of his superior height and strength unmistakable. He had been working the grapevines all day alongside his father and brother. The heady masculine scent of leather, soil, and sweat still clung to his body. I stared at the steady pulse at the base of his neck and wondered if his skin would taste salty if I licked it.

As if sensing my illicit thoughts, Cesare moved even closer, his thigh brushing mine as he raised his arm to wrap his hand around my waist.

My eyes widened. With a gasp, I stepped back, breaking the spell.

He curled his fingers into a fist as he lowered his arm. His dark gaze moved from my eyes to my mouth. When he spoke, his voice was a low, sensual growl. "I'm tiring of this game you're playing, Milana. Either tell me what the fuck I did wrong so I can apologize or get over it."

I took a long sip from my wineglass as I glared at him over the rim before raising it high in the air and smashing it violently at his feet. "It will be a cold day in hell before I ever... *ever*... forgive you, Cesare Cavalieri."

I STOMPED up the limestone gravel path to the cottage on the Cavalieri estate.

My prison.

Technically, as far as prisons went, it was pretty posh.

The bedroom alone was bigger than my entire apartment, but that was not the point. I stamped my foot for emphasis, even though I was venting to no one but myself.

My foot landed on a stone the wrong way. My ankle collapsed to the side as the heel on my favorite pair of knockoff Dolce midnight black pumps snapped. I wrenched off my shoes and picked up the broken heel. If I ever laid eyes on Cesare Cavalieri again, I would throw these shoes at his head.

God! Why had I let him back into my life?

Oh, right, I didn't! He'd forced his way back into my life when he kidnapped me from my apartment and got me fired.

Bastard.

Although that was not really true, was it?

He was not a bastard.

That was part of the problem.

He was one of the exalted sons and heirs of the great Cavalieri fortune, practically a living god as far as most of Italy was concerned.

Tall, handsome, and rich, the man could probably get away with murder in this town and everyone would turn a blind eye because he was a Cavalieri.

Hell, he'd dragged me out of my apartment kicking and screaming, and not one person had rushed to my aid, the moment they saw whose shoulder I was slung over. Because in the village of Cavalieri, the Cavalieri men were kings.

Damn, damn, damn him.

Limping up to the cottage door, I rummaged for my key.

Not finding it, I dumped the contents of my purse out on the courtyard bench. Pushing aside shiny tubes of various shades of red lipstick, my compact, my mascara, the gold earrings I wore yesterday, the silver ones I wore last Monday, the onyx resin bangle I'd been looking for—which I slipped on my wrist—and a purple silk change purse filled with perfume samples, I finally found the cottage keys.

I unlocked the door and slipped my arm inside. My palm slid along the interior plaster wall, searching for the light switch. I couldn't enter until the light was on. Once the main room was flooded with a warm, welcoming glow, I opened the door wide and crossed the threshold. I rushed from room to room, turning on all the lights. Only then did the tightness in my chest ease.

Returning to the courtyard, I swept my arm over the bench and scooped all the items back into my purse which I tossed, along with my ruined heels, on the seat of a nearby chair before securing the door.

I sank to the floor and hugged my legs to my chest as I rested my chin on my knees.

What did I do now?

My best friend Amara was practically engaged to Barone Cavalieri, Cesare's father, and moving on with her life. Soon she would be married and starting a family. Not that I worried she would push me aside. We were ride or die girl-friends and always would be, but things were changing in our lives. It was time I made some changes as well.

Changes that didn't include being under the influence of the Cavalieris.

I'd only stayed for Amara's sake.

Now that she was happy with Barone, I could leave.

Cesare had made his intentions clear.

Especially after that kiss a few weeks ago.

And the kiss we almost shared tonight.

He not only wanted me… he wanted answers.

And *no* would not be one of them.

I tightened my arms around my legs as I tried to control the shiver that wracked my body at the terrible memories. As always, I silently berated myself for being so foolish. That was the messed-up thing about trauma. It didn't really respond to rational thought. I knew rationally that things could have been much worse. That because I fought them off, they didn't finish their intended attack, but still... the memories... the trauma... haunted me.

Being trapped in the darkness like that for hours and hours on end.

Screaming for help until I was hoarse.

Not knowing if they would return to finish what they'd started.

And it was all Cesare's fault. He was my friend back then.

He should have protected me.

But he didn't.

I didn't care if the rest of Italy's women thought he was God's gift.

I hated him and would always hate him.

Anger gave me renewed vigor and purpose.

I got up off the floor.

I hurried down the hallway, passing Amara's old bedroom.

The second I did, I backtracked.

I threw open the oak wardrobe's paneled doors. There were still several Gucci, Valentino, and Dolce outfits she hadn't moved over to the villa yet. Without a second's hesitation, I swept them all off their padded, pale pink silk hangers, then reached down and grabbed the matching shoes. I stretched my arm up to the top of the wardrobe and slung the purse straps to two purses over my neck and hustled out of the room.

She'd have wanted me to have them.

After depositing my new wardrobe items on my bed, I got on my knees and pulled my suitcases out from under the bed.

I could stay at Amara's old house and leave at first light. When I didn't show up for work, Cesare would come looking for me. Of that, I had no doubt. I needed to be long gone by then.

After I placed the suitcases by the door I went in search of a piece of paper and pen.

I knew if I called or texted Amara, she would race over and try to change my mind.

Worse, Barone would find out, which meant Cesare would find out.

And then they'd both get all over-the-top bossy about how staying in Cavalieri under their protection was for my own good, and how I was like a sister to Amara and therefore family now, blah, blah, blah.

Nope. No way. Not buying it.

I had vowed long ago never to let a man in my life, and I freaking meant it.

And that vow especially applied to Cesare Cavalieri.

I scrawled a quick note telling Amara not to worry, that I was fine, and that I would call her when I settled somewhere.

Snatching a handled basket from under the sink, I filled it with some fresh figs, a loaf of bread, some cheese, three bottles of wine, a bottle opener, a jar of plum preserves, and a bottle of sparking water.

After one last look around the cottage, I grabbed my purse and opened the front door.

Cesare was standing on the threshold.

His dark gaze swept from my face to the suitcases and back.

His brow lowered as his eyes narrowed. "Going somewhere?"

CHAPTER 2

CESARE

She backed away. "What are you doing here?"

I stepped inside, closed the door behind me, and leaned against it. "I'm here to finish our… conversation."

She clutched a basket filled with wine and food before her like a shield. "There's nothing to finish."

I looked around the brightly lit cottage, then down at the suitcases near the door. I inhaled slowly, trying to rein in the primal demons clawing inside my chest. There wasn't a chance in hell I was letting her leave. Whatever I had done that had pissed her off back when we were in school was in the past. I was a boy then. I'm a man now, an impatient one.

And I was fucking done waiting.

Milana had always been meant for me.

I knew it back then, and I knew it now.

No other woman came close to her.

She was the only one I wanted.

And as far as I was concerned, she was already mine.

If I were one of my male Cavalieri ancestors, the solution would be to simply carry her into the bedroom, spread her legs, and fuck her until she submitted to my will.

If she pushed what little patience I had left, that might still be the solution.

I reached between us, grasped the handle to the basket, and pulled. She resisted. I pulled harder. She wisely relented. I set the basket aside. "You see, that is where you're wrong." I stepped closer.

She backed away, placing a wooden spindle chair between us. She clutched the high back so tightly her knuckles were white. Despite her obvious tension, she faced me defiantly. With one elegant eyebrow arched high, she asked, "How many times does a woman have to tell you she hates you before you believe her, Cesare?"

I leaned on the back of the nearby sofa and crossed my arms over my chest, studying her. She really was magnificent. A fiery mixture of spirit, elegance, sass, and intelligence. My cock hardened as I imagined for the millionth time what it would be like harnessing that explosive mix of passions in bed. I'd probably have to restrain her just to get the upper hand. The idea had a great deal of appeal.

I rummaged through the basket and picked up one of the bottles of wine. I twisted my wrist so I could see the label, then chuckled. "*Vino Nobile di Montepulciano d'Abruzzo dei Cavalieri.*" I reached for the bottle opener nestled at the bottom of the basket. "You have excellent taste."

The little minx was lighting out of town with a five-thousand-euro bottle of wine… and she had three of them in her basket.

I flicked open the knife and sliced the wax seal as I watched her closely.

She tapped her foot. "What are you doing?"

I opened the silver corkscrew. "Opening a fine bottle of wine takes finesse. First, pierce the cork. Then slowly twist it in... deep." I matched my movements to my words, all the while never taking my eyes off her.

The pulse at the base of her throat beat a rapid tattoo against her soft skin as she stared at my hands.

I gripped the wine bottle more firmly. "Once you are fully seated, *deep inside*, that is when you use gentle *force* to get what you want."

Milana swallowed, her gaze staying glued to my hands as I tightened my grip on the corkscrew.

I yanked hard. The cork gave with a loud *pop*. Milana jumped and gave a soft cry.

She moved around the chair and would have made a dash for the door, but I shifted and blocked her way.

She stepped back.

I lifted the bottle to my lips and took a swig. Layered with hints of plum, smoke, and earth, I savored the wine's rich fruit flavor.

Milana crossed deeper into the cottage. "You need to leave."

"No."

"Fine. Then I'm leaving."

"No again."

"You can't say that."

"I just did."

"You can't keep me here against my will."

"Watch me."

"This is insane."

"I agree."

"Then let me leave."

I took another swig of wine. "No."

"I'll call the police."

"Do me a favor? When you do, remind Benito he owes me fifty euro from our last Scopa game."

She stomped her foot. "I hate you."

"No, you don't."

I set the wine bottle down and reached for the top button of my shirt. "And I'm going to prove it."

Her mouth dropped open. "The hell you are!"

I unbuttoned the first three buttons, drew the shirt over my head, and tossed it aside.

Milana extended her arm and pointed her finger at me. "Stop that! Stop right now."

I kicked off my shoes and reached for my belt buckle.

Milana swept up a pair of discarded high heels from the seat of a nearby chair and threw them at me. They missed their mark.

We circled around one another.

She tossed her head from side to side, looking for another missile to launch at me.

The blood pumped in my veins with heated excitement. Damn, this woman was never boring.

With what could only be described as devilish glee, she laughed as she picked up the open bottle of wine. She held it high.

I straightened my shoulders. My voice was low and stern.

"Don't even think about it."

She angled her arm back.

"I'm warning you, Milana. Put that bottle down."

"Are you going to leave?"

I narrowed my eyes. "No."

We stood there, facing off against one another, a clash of wills. Her arm trembled slightly. For the barest of seconds, I actually thought she was going to obey me.

Then the wine bottle sailed past my head, barely missing bashing my skull in.

It smashed against the white plaster wall. The green glass bottle shattered, splattering fiery ruby liquid all over the wall and down onto the floor.

After looking over my shoulder, I turned back to look at Milana.

Her face was frozen in shock, as if she were just now learning how glass bottles worked.

Her wide gaze then locked with mine. "Uh oh."

I whipped my belt out from its loops and folded it in my hand. "You're damn right, *uh oh*, babygirl."

She raced for the front door.

I beat her to it, flattening my palm against it so it wouldn't open when she yanked on the handle.

Abruptly she switched course and took off down the hallway that led to the bedrooms.

I was right on her heels.

She crossed the threshold of one of the bedrooms and slammed the door in my face. I tried the doorknob. Locked.

"Open the damn door."

"Vai all'inferno!"

Leaning back, I shoved my shoulder against the door, splintering the frame and breaking the lock.

Milana scurried to the other side of the bedroom. "This isn't funny anymore, Cesare."

I took two steps toward her. "I'm not laughing."

She squeezed herself into a corner. Her voice was high-pitched and fractured. "I mean it. Get out."

I was so close I could smell the spicy jasmine scent of her perfume. I kept my arms raised in front of me, approaching her as I would a wild animal, ready for either fight or flight at any moment.

She then did something I was not expecting.

She closed her eyes, tipped her head to one side, and let out a soft whimper.

My brow furrowed.

There was a fine line between hate and love, anger and desire, but this? Could this be fear?

My mind flashed back to that moment in her apartment over a month ago. It was so fleeting, I had passed it off as a figment of my imagination. There was a moment where I could have sworn she thought I was going to hit her. For all our heated banter, I thought she knew deep down I would never be physically violent with her, not in that way.

Something was fucking wrong.

There was no goddamn way I'd misread that situation. She responded to my kiss that day, to the feel of my hands. I knew she felt the same way about me as I did her, and it was only her stubbornness keeping us apart. I knew she was fighting the desire between us. I was not fucking wrong about that.

There was something else at play here.

I tossed my belt away from me onto the floor.

Gently running the backs of my fingers down her arm until I reached her wrist, I lifted her arm and pressed her open palm on my bare chest and waited a few moments, until I was sure she'd leave her hand there. I stepped closer until our thighs brushed. She hissed in a breath through her teeth, her body twitching in response.

I soothed her. "Shhh, *carissima*. I'm here." I reached for her waist and carefully wrapped my arm around her body until my hand was pressed against her lower back.

Fuck, she felt so small and vulnerable in my arms like this.

I just wanted to close her up in my palm and never let go.

She leaned in close... and sunk her teeth into my shoulder.

Her tiny fists flew at me, pummeling my chest. "Don't touch me!"

I snatched her wrists and wrenched her arms behind her back, easily securing them with one hand. "Listen, *la mia piccola gattina selvaggia*. I'm about to do a great deal more than *touch* you, so you better get used to the idea."

She pitched her torso to the left and right but could not dislodge my grasp.

I held her tighter. "Keep moving. I like the feel of your breasts pressed against my chest."

She immediately stilled.

She sucked air in through her clenched teeth. "I'm warning you, Cesare, let me go."

The corner of my mouth lifted. "You're warning me?" I leaned down and traced my lips along the soft curve of her ear. She really had the cutest little ears. I flicked my tongue over her earlobe before pulling it between my teeth and giving her a quick nip. My lips moved to the edge of her jaw. "So, what happens if I ignore your warning?"

She tilted her head back and away from my mouth to look up at me.

She had the most gorgeous lips. They were a soft pink, luscious and full. I especially loved how they formed an adorable pout when she was angry.

Her bright, intelligent eyes read my intent. "I don't want you to kiss me," she hissed.

I brushed her glossy black curls back from her face. "That's too damn bad," I growled.

I claimed her mouth. Christ, she tasted sweet. I twisted my fingers in her hair as I tightened my grip on her waist and stepped closer, pressing my thigh between her legs. I forced her head back and pushed my tongue in deeper. My head slanted, switching from one angle to another as I devoured her. I couldn't get enough of her taste or the feel of her in my arms.

The only thing that sliced through my fevered reaction to our kiss was the hesitant brush of her hand against my shoulder. I froze. Waiting to see if she was going to push me away.

The very moment her hand hesitantly wrapped around the top of my shoulder to clutch at my neck and pull me closer, she sealed her fate.

Refusing to break our kiss, I held her close and swung our bodies around, lifting her high until she was straddling my thigh. I placed one knee on the bed while bracing the heel of my palm against the mattress so I could slowly lower her down, not wanting to alarm her by covering her with my body weight right away.

As soon as she was prone, I couldn't resist pressing my hips down against the top of her thigh, to ease the pressure building in my cock. Cupping her jaw, I used my free hand to work the buttons of her dress, needing to see her breasts. I wanted to see if the color of her nipples matched her lips and if they tasted just as sweet.

Her hand covered mine, trying to stop me. "Cesare, wait...."

I shook her free and wrenched open the collar of the dress, exposing the lace edge of her bra and the top curves of her breasts. "Baby, I've already waited an eternity. I'm not waiting any longer to make you mine."

I kissed the top of her breast as my hand moved over her stomach to pull up the hem of her dress. My palm skimmed the warm skin of her inner thigh as I clenched my fingers over the hem of her silk panties. In my haste, I tore them off her.

"Cesare, please...."

I wedged my legs between her thighs as I tore at the zipper of my jeans. I placed open-mouthed kisses down the column of her throat. "Christ, I've waited forever to get inside this pretty pussy of yours."

I was a man possessed. My one thought was to get inside of her. I needed to feel her hot, wet heat clasped around my cock like I needed my next breath. I would not be denied. The hounds of hell could burst through that door at this very moment, and they would not be able to drag me from between this temptress's thighs.

Her head thrashed back and forth. "Wait...."

I circled the pad of my thumb over her clit as I pushed one

finger inside her slick entrance. A guttural moan escaped from deep inside my throat. My cock swelled and became painfully hard at the almost impossibly firm clench of her heat. She was so small and tight. I pushed a second finger inside and thrust as I twisted my wrist.

Her hips bucked. She reached down between her legs and pulled at my wrist. "Cesare, I can't do this."

I braced my forearm by her head and leaned over her, fisting my cock. "I'm sorry, *carissima*. You're so goddamn tight. This is going to hurt, baby."

I grabbed her wrists in my hands and held them to the bed as I pressed her deeper into the mattress with the weight of my body. I shifted my hips until the head of my cock was at her entrance.

Her eyes widened, "Cesare, n—"

CHAPTER 3

CESARE

I claimed her mouth the moment I thrust. My tongue speared between her lips as my cock pushed inside her body. Her pussy clamped down, resisting me. I was only halfway in. I pulled my hips back and thrust in harder. Her hips bucked.

I swallowed her scream as I was finally seated fully inside her tight heat.

I'd never felt such overwhelming pleasure in my entire life.

I wanted to thrust furiously and stay absolutely still and savor the glorious moment, all at the same time.

Finally, the beast in me won out.

I pulled back and thrust in deep. Again and again.

I released her wrists to wrap my hands around her jaw so I could tilt her head back and claim her mouth as deeply as I claimed her pussy.

I wanted to taste her heartbeat.

I wanted to swallow her every breath.

I wanted her only air to come from my mouth.

I wanted to feel the scrape of her teeth against my lips.

My mouth moved from her lips to her jaw and then to her cheek.

It was only when I tasted the salt of her tears that I reared back.

What the fuck?

Her eyes were closed. Her cheeks were stained with tears.

I leaned to the side on my right forearm and looked down between us.

Blood.

Goddammit. I'd really fucked up.

I was too big.

I knew she was tight.

I should have been more careful, prepared her more fully for my cock, instead of taking her like a fucking animal.

My brow furrowed.

There was too much blood.

Madonna santa!

A virgin.

Milana was a virgin.

It had never even occurred to me she would be. I mean, we were both twenty-four. This wasn't the Middle Ages, where women were expected to remain virgins until marriage.

My cock was still hard, deep inside of her.

I smoothed the hair back from her beautiful face. She was stunning, even when she cried. I leaned over her. "Milana, open your eyes."

Her eyelids twitched but remained closed.

"*Carissima,* don't make me ask you again."

She opened her eyes slowly. Dark, beautiful eyes, framed with thick eyelashes.

Eyes as icy and hard as black diamonds.

I tilted my head to the side as I watched her closely. "Why didn't you tell me?"

A cold tension settled over her face, as if she were raising a wall between us. With a rigid lack of expression, she said, "Because it was none of your business."

None of my business.

She set the trap.

And I took the bait.

I snapped.

I leaned down until we were nose to nose. "My cock is deep inside your pussy. I'd say it is my fucking business."

Her arm struck out to slap me. *"Vaffanculo!"*

I blocked her and wrestled her arm down to the mattress as she tried to writhe free and land her slap. "That's it, baby. You want it rough? Let's play rough."

The damage was done. She was no longer a virgin. It was far too late to be gentle and sweet. Besides, delicate words and kisses had never been our style.

I reached for the open bodice of her dress and tore downward, ripping it off her body.

Milana screamed and tried to roll out from under me.

All that did was give me a chance to unhook her bra. Her lush breasts spilled out. I pinned her beneath my body again and latched on to her right nipple, laving it with my tongue before biting down. Hard.

Her torso shot up as she delved her fingers into my hair, pulling equally as hard.

I moved my hips, pounding my cock into her tight hole.

I wrapped my arm around her body, planting open-mouthed kisses on her breasts and throat, increasing the punishing pace of my thrusts. Using my free hand, I gripped her under her knee and pulled her leg up close against my hip, wanting to go even deeper. I wanted every inch of my skin to be touching hers. I wanted her to feel my weight, to feel my dominance. To know who was in control now.

Her body rocked back and forth with the force of my thrusts. "Oh God!"

I growled as I pulled her left nipple between my teeth. "I'm going to make damn sure this pretty pussy is sore by the time I'm done fucking you tonight." I leaned on my side, taking her body with me, exposing her ass so I could give her several well-placed spanks as I continued to fuck her ruthlessly.

"Ow! Stop!"

"No."

I spanked her several more times as I thrust.

This wasn't making love. This wasn't even sex.

This was feverish, sweaty, primal, beastly fucking.

I rolled back on top of her and moved my hips between her thighs, reaching between us to tease her clit with the tip of my finger.

Her mouth opened on a moan.

"That's it, *la mia piccola gattina selvaggia*. Come for me."

I clenched my jaw as my balls tightened. I was so close, but I was determined not to come until she did.

I circled her clit with the pad of my thumb as I ground my hips down.

"*Dio santo!*" she moaned.

Her head fell back and she raised her knees to wrap her legs around my hips, pulling me closer. Her fingernails clawed down my back as she screamed her release.

I raised my torso, my arms fully extended, and threw back my head. I then thrust my hips forward and buried myself deep inside her before releasing my hot come with a guttural roar.

* * *

I COLLAPSED AT HER SIDE. Breathing heavily, I tried to catch my breath.

That was easily the single greatest experience of my life.

Milana had been a virgin.

A virgin.

I had taken her virginity.

She was now not only mine, she also had been no one else's, nor would she ever be.

Despite being utterly exhausted, I wanted to run to the top of the nearby mountains and shout it out to the world.

Milana was mine. All mine.

I was like a maniacal villain who had just achieved world domination.

This was what it truly felt like to know that the most glorious, frustrating, engaging, beautiful, intelligent, infuriatingly sexy, amazing woman I had ever known was now mine *and only mine*. The rush of possessive pride was invigorating.

It was all I could do not to jump up and start pounding my chest like a fucking caveman.

I turned on my side to pull her closer.

She turned away.

Before I could say anything, she flew off the bed and out of the room.

CHAPTER 4

MILANA

I ran across the hall into the bathroom and slammed the door behind me.

Shivering, I leaned against its cold, wooden surface.

The door vibrated violently with Cesare's knock. "Milana? Open this door."

I turned and locked it before backing away deeper into the bathroom.

It was the one modern indulgence of his brother Enzo's remodel of the cottage. He had combined several rooms to make an elegant, spa-like space. A thick, glass-walled shower the size of a walk-in closet dominated one end of the room, while a black, marble-topped island stood in the center, a crystal chandelier suspended above it. I reached under the island and quickly pulled a towel from the metal warming rack. Wrapping the warmed dark terry cloth around my middle, I stared in horror at the doorknob as it rattled.

Cesare called out again. His voice was terse. "Milana. I'm losing patience."

My head swiveled from left to right. There were no windows, just thick, frosted panes of glass to let in a soft glow of light. I padded across the cold tile floor to the shower. Leaning against a glass pane, I turned the brass knob to full blast. The shower nozzle above, as well as the six nozzles positioned along the sides of the shower walls, hissed as hot water sprayed into the chamber.

I stared at the door and waited.

Only after several minutes of silence had passed and the bathroom had filled with a comforting blanket of steam did I feel safe enough to drop my towel and step into the shower.

The hot water stung my sensitive skin. I adjusted the heat level and pushed my wet hair back from my face. I stepped closer to the shower jets and let the punishing stream of water pound into my flesh, a form of self-flagellation.

Looking down between my feet, I watched as the water swirled down the drain, grateful for the obsidian marble. If it had been white, I would have seen evidence of the biggest freaking mistake of my life going down the drain. I leaned my head back and let the water splash across my face.

I wasn't religious. My horrible grandmother had beaten any thought of a benevolent God out of me long ago. So it wasn't like I had been saving my virginity as some archaic blood sacrifice to my groom on my wedding night. It was just, after the betrayal of seven years ago, I had never allowed myself to trust anyone. Then there was the whole stupid trauma thing from that betrayal. I mostly had a handle on it. It was just at night, when it was dark, that it would sometimes get the best of me. No one wanted to sleep with a girl who woke up screaming for no reason.

I wrapped my left hand around my neck as I flattened my right palm over my opposite hip, hugging myself.

My lower lip trembled as I squeezed my eyes shut.

Of all the people...

Of all the stupid mistakes...

Why?

Why did I have to succumb to the man I hated most in the world?

The man I blamed for....

My eyes flew open.

I snatched the bar of soap from the brass dish. Not even bothering to lather it between my hands, I rubbed the bar against my skin. I needed to get his scent off me. I needed to erase the feel of his hands, his mouth, his... I rubbed harder with the soap.

How could I have responded to his touch? To the feel of him?

It made little sense.

Ever since the betrayal, I've hated to be touched.

I've especially hated feeling trapped.

And yet, only moments ago I had reveled in the feel of his hands restraining my wrists.

The weight of his body pressing down on mine.

Him holding me, trapping me with the force of his thrusts, caging me in.

I clenched my inner thighs as a shiver of awareness ran over my body even now at the memory.

I had not only responded like a fucking cat in heat, but the entire experience also made me feel strangely protected and safe. As if him taking control had somehow saved me from myself and my fears.

What. The. Fuck.

No. Fuck no. Absolutely not.

This is obviously some kind of psychosis.

I'm having a mental breakdown.

Cesare Cavalieri is the fucking enemy.

He betrayed me.

I hate him with every fiber of my being.

I lathered the soap and rubbed my hand between my legs, the slick remnants of our arousal a damning reminder. My chest tightened. I put the soap back and pressed my palms against the tiled wall, lowering my head between my outstretched arms. The water pounded down onto my back and sides. I turned the tap, making it even hotter, knowing I would regret it later when my poor skin itched and burned, but needing the scalding heat now. The shower hissed again as fresh steam rose around me, snaking around the glass shower wall to fill the bathroom with an impenetrable fog.

Everything was going to be okay.

I would lock this experience away deep inside myself with all the other pain. Tomorrow, I would wake up and put on the makeup mask I hid behind. No one would know. No one ever knew. That was how I liked it. That was how it had always been, and how it would always be.

I would put tonight behind me.

Tomorrow I would leave this place and forget all about it... *and Cesare Cavalieri.*

I lifted my head and whispered softly, "Like it never happened."

"But it did happen, *carissima*."

He appeared through the steam like a demon rising from hell.

With a shriek, I turned, my feet slipping on the slick, soapy, tiled floor of the shower. Before I could fall, Cesare captured me around the waist, pulling me flush against his naked body.

My hands flattened against his muscled chest. "What are you doing in here?"

His lips curled in just the barest hint of a smile before he brushed a strand of wet hair off my cheek. "Since from now on I plan to keep you *very* close to my side, you're going to need to stop asking me that question."

"The door was locked!"

He stepped forward, forcing me backward until my back hit the shower wall. "I had a key, something I fear I will need often in our relationship."

Our relationship?

He can't possibly be serious.

We are not now and never will be in a relationship.

Ever.

He towered over me as he spread his legs, pressing his erect cock against my stomach. He leaned down and moved his head close to my neck, inhaling. His lips brushed my jaw as he spoke. "It won't work, beautiful."

I tensed the muscles in my arms to keep from trembling. I didn't want him to know how much his nearness affected me. My eyes narrowed. "What won't work?"

He placed his right forearm high over my head as he leaned in.

I braced as I waited for the irrational claustrophobic-like fear to seize me deep inside my chest, cutting off my air and making my head swim. It didn't come.

Cesare used his left hand to grip my jaw, pushing my head back as far as the shower wall would allow. His fingertips painfully dug into the soft flesh of my cheeks. "Use all the soap you want. You won't get rid of my scent on your body. It's not just on your skin. It's deep inside that tight virginal pussy of yours."

I gasped.

His fingers tightened on my jaw, cutting my inner cheeks with the sharp edges of my teeth. He then drove his other hand into my hair, twisting his fingers into my short curls.

His mouth fell on mine.

He didn't kiss.

He laid siege, seizing power.

He dominated.

He controlled.

He claimed.

His tongue pushed between my lips and dueled with mine, not only tasting me, but once more devouring me. His head slanted to the right, then left, then right again, as if to keep me off-balance. His stubble scraped the soft skin of my lips and jaw as he ravaged and plundered. His hand slipped lower to grip my ass.

I squealed as I lifted onto my toes. The movement caused me to grind against his hard cock.

I hated how my body responded when he held me like

this. The way he leaned over me. The show of strength and power. It should have me raging. It should trigger a trauma response, but again, it didn't. I felt annoyingly safe. I was sure it was just some stupid, primal, cavewoman response, probably why they'd kept getting dragged around by their hair into caves to be ravaged.

My mind rebelled. He may not be triggering me, but I still hated him. I still wanted nothing to do with him. I fought, biting him.

His head reared back, and he flicked his tongue out to lick the bead of crimson which had formed on the plump center of his lower lip. The sound emanating from him started as a low vibration within his chest before erupting in a growl torn from between his clenched teeth. His dark eyes glowed with feral purpose as he gripped me tightly around the waist and lifted me off my feet.

I kicked and clawed at him to no avail as he carried me out of the shower.

He took several steps before placing me on the wide, marble island. It was hard not to feel like a virgin sacrifice to a demon god.

My wet body slid on the surface as I scrambled to get away from him.

He captured my ankles and pulled me toward him. My ass was almost to the edge when he wrenched my thighs open.

I stretched out my arms, trying to reach the brass, mirrored vanity tray full of perfume bottles. I pulled it toward me with my fingertips. The moment it was close enough, I grasped the nearest bottle and launched it at Cesare's head.

He lifted his forearm, deflecting it.

The bottle smashed on the floor, sending a sensual cloud of cardamom, vanilla, and jasmine wafting into the surrounding steam.

He reached over my body and shoved the perfume tray out of reach. He bent his head low between my legs, his breath hot against my cunt. "Careful, babygirl. I bite back."

My eyes widened. I tried to close my legs, but his wide shoulders prevented me. "No, I don't want you to...."

He flicked his tongue between the seam, teasing my clit.

My mouth dropped open.

He repeated the gesture, this time more slowly.

My body jerked.

Dio santo!

My fingers curled into my palms as I tried not to moan. I stared at the crystal chandelier dangling directly above me. Kaleidoscope prisms of gold and sparkling light that perfectly captured the explosion of pleasure and warmth radiating from my core at the touch of Cesare's tongue.

Cesare stared up at me, his dark eyes missing nothing. "Tell me, Milana. Am I the first man to taste this pussy?"

I turned my head, breaking his gaze. It was on the tip of my tongue to lie to him. It was bad enough that the arrogant bastard knew he had taken my virginity. I would not suffer the indignity of explaining to him how I never allowed myself to have a boyfriend or be touched in any way until now, because of my stupid trauma and trust issues.

His fingers dug into my inner thighs, almost bruising them. "Don't lie to me. Because if you say no, I'll be forced to track the man down and kill him."

"You're not serious."

"Say no and see how serious I am."

Porca miseria. He wasn't kidding. I pushed up onto the edges of my palms, trying to squirm away from him. My skin was still wet, so my body slipped along the marble top. Cesare easily pulled me back under his control.

Locking his gaze on mine, he leaned over my prone body and pushed one finger inside of me. Then two. "I'm going to ask you one last time. Has any other man licked your cunt?"

My cheeks burned from the intimacy of his interrogation. I clenched my jaw, blinking back the tears which threatened to fall. I couldn't force my lips to move. All I could do was give him a quick shake of my head.

The transformation that came over him was terrifying. He lowered his brow as his chest heaved. He bared his teeth as he ran his heated gaze over my body.

I shifted, preparing to flee again.

His fingers tightened, holding me in place.

He snarled one word. "Mine."

His dark head lowered between my legs as he pushed my lips open with his fingers. This time, he didn't lick... he feasted. My hips bucked as I clawed at the smooth surface of the hard marble, grasping for purchase. His tongue flicked, sucked, and laved at my clit until I was screaming for mercy. He showed me none, thrusting his fingers inside my pussy, opening me, preparing me. With his free hand, he caressed my hip, my stomach, then my breast, pinching my nipple.

My head turned from side to side as my shoulders lifted off the island with each delicate scrape of his teeth against my sensitive bundle of nerves. *Madonna santa!* No vibrator had ever come even close to this feeling.

The leashed power in his embrace, the threat of his control, the dominance under his hand, the feel of his tongue, the vibrations of his growls. They all played on my body like the strings of a fucking violin.

At that moment, I forgot I hated him. I forgot we were enemies. I forgot how badly I wanted to escape him. All I wanted was to pull him closer, to feel him deeper, harder, rougher.

A tremor raced over my limbs.

He squeezed my breast as he flicked my clit with the tip of his tongue. "Jesus Christ, Milana, come on my mouth, baby, so I can fuck you senseless."

I slapped the marble with my open palm as I pushed my hips up high.

Cesare grabbed my ass, his mouth against my pussy as I screamed my release. The light from the crystal chandelier seemed to shatter into a cascade of sparks as licks of fire coursed through my limbs. The blood in my veins beat a damning cadence in my ears as my entire reality shifted and tilted beneath me.

Before I could even catch my breath, he slipped his hands further up my back and flipped my body as if I weighed nothing, until I was over his shoulder, my legs dangling between his arms. Avoiding the shards of glass from the broken perfume bottle, he carried me to the still-running shower.

He grasped me around the waist and pulled me partly down. Wrapping my legs around his middle, he walked us under the scalding spray. The hot water hit my now chilled skin. My breath seized.

Cesare braced his hand against the wall as he shifted his

arm to support me under my ass. He leveled his gaze at me. "Hold on, baby, because I will not be gentle."

Before I could respond, he speared me with his cock.

I cried out, wrapping my arms around his neck, as his thick shaft pierced my delicate flesh to the hilt.

There was something twisted inside of me that wanted this, wanted the pain, wanted the pleasure, wanted the shame of fucking a man I hated.

He pounded into me harder and faster, using my body weight to force himself deep.

He nipped and flicked at my earlobe as he breathed against my ear, "I'll never get enough of fucking this sweet pussy."

Pride reared up my spine. "This is *never* happening again."

He slowed his powerful thrusts to push hard and deep, grinding his pelvis on my clit after each one, forcing gasps of pleasure from me. "Try denying me and see what happens."

What have I done?

CHAPTER 5

CESARE

*A*fter she came and I released my seed into her a second time, I finally let her body slide down over mine, relishing the feel of her silky skin. "Turn around."

"Why?"

"Do as you're told."

Her lower lip protruded in a pout as her brow puckered. "No."

I tipped her chin back. "Either turn around or get down on your knees. Your choice."

She flipped around so quickly her wet curls slapped me on the jaw. I reached for the shampoo and pooled a small amount in the center of my palm, then lathered it between my hands and delved my fingers into her hair.

She tried to look back at me over her shoulder. "What are you doing?"

I fisted her hair, keeping her in place. "Washing your hair." I massaged her scalp as I soaped her silky locks. I had always loved her thick, long hair and when I first saw she had chopped most of it off I'd hated it, but I was growing to like the cute chin-length curls. It suited her.

"I can do that myself."

I turned her back to face me, pressing her full breasts against my chest as I tilted her head back under the water spray. I ran my fingers through her hair, rinsing out the suds. My cock twitched. Damn, I was already getting hard again. Only a monster would take a virgin a third time in a row. I looked down at her upturned face. I ran my thumb over her full bottom lip, then cupped her shoulders.

Of course, there was always her mouth.

My erect cock bobbed up between us, brushing her stomach.

Her eyes widened as she tried to step back.

I tightened my grip. "You need to stop fighting me on this, Milana."

She needed to understand that the very moment my cock had entered her, everything between us changed. Everything.

"Fuck you, Cesare. Tonight was a mistake. One I don't plan on repeating."

She wrenched away and stormed past me, stepping out of the shower.

"Goddammit, woman. The glass!" I swept her into my arms before she hurt herself.

Navigating around the broken pieces, I carried her back into the bedroom and dropped her into the center of the bed. "Stay," I commanded with a point of my finger.

I returned to the bathroom to turn off the shower. I wrapped a towel around my waist and grabbed a fresh towel for Milana. Of course, by the time I returned to the bedroom, she had already scrambled off the bed and was halfway through the door. We collided in the hallway. I wrapped her flailing arms in the towel and lifted her high, carrying her into the bedroom. Again.

This time, I sat on the edge of the bed and tossed her naked over my lap.

"What are you doing?"

"If you are going to behave like a petulant child, I'm going to treat you like one."

I lifted my arm and spanked her left ass cheek.

Milana cried out.

I knew it was more out of shock than pain, although the pain was coming.

"How dare you!"

I spanked her right cheek. Then her left again.

Her legs kicked as she tried to bite my thigh. I increased the pressure of my strikes. Her skin, already rosy from the hot shower, now glowed a fiery red.

"Stop! Stop!"

I spanked her several more times, warming up to the task. "Are you going to behave?"

"Testa di cazzo! Bastardo! Ratto miserabile e infimo! Porco!"

"I'll take that as a no."

I spanked her ass cheeks several more times before moving to the tops of her thighs, enjoying the way her hips shimmied and squirmed over my erect cock.

"I'll behave!"

"What was that?"

"I'll behave!"

I let her climb off my lap. She scurried under the bedcovers, grasping the blanket high under her chin. "How dare you spank me like a child? *Pagano! Testa di cazzo! Ti odio ora più che mai! Se avessi un coltello, ti pugnalerei!*"

I reached for my discarded jeans, pulled them over my hips without fastening them, and left the room. I searched her escape basket for another bottle of *Vino Nobile* and opened it. Grabbing a single glass from the kitchen, I returned to the bedroom.

Fortunately, *la mia piccola gattina selvaggia* had learned her lesson, at least for now, and had stayed put in bed. I poured a glass of wine and set the bottle out of her reach on the bureau before sitting on the edge of the bed. I sipped it slowly, savoring the deeper complicated notes of dark pepper as I observed her.

Fuck, she was the most beautiful creature I had ever laid eyes on.

An almost unholy, possessive rush coursed through my blood.

She was all mine now. Mine.

La mia piccola gattina selvaggia vergine.

No man had ever touched her… and no man, but me, ever would.

After spending my entire adult life taking every precaution never to get a woman pregnant, tonight, for the first time, I had taken a woman bareback, without even a thought of putting on a condom. I actually hoped, no prayed, I had gotten Milana pregnant tonight. The thought of this amazing woman bearing my child made me want to tie her to the bed and fuck her until she truly conceived.

But first, I needed to get her to stop hating me.

"All right, I'm listening."

One perfectly arched eyebrow rose. "Other than 'get the fuck out of my bedroom,' I have nothing to say to you."

I took another sip of wine. "Why do you hate me so much?"

She crossed her arms over her chest. "You know what you did."

Something happened back when we were in school seven years ago. One day we were friends. I had hoped we would become more. Then she suddenly changed. She wanted nothing to do with me. She froze me out completely. If I even tried to approach her, she'd flinch as if I had struck her. It had pissed me off. I had asked Amara what was going on, but she swore she knew nothing, although I was never sure I fully believed her.

After that I gave up.

It was the greatest mistake of my life.

Stupid, pitiful, arrogant pride.

Like the entitled asshole she has often accused me of being, I got my back up that a village girl would snub a Cavalieri. God, what a fucking prick I was back then. I walked away from her. Then I did my best to avoid her over the years.

Avoided but didn't forget.

My brother's marriage had gotten me thinking.

It was past time I settled down, and no other woman would do.

No other woman remotely compared to Milana.

Her beauty. Her intelligence. Her fiery spirit. Even her incredible capacity for colorful cursing.

Milana wasn't a woman you fucked once and moved on from.

She was the type of woman you built a life with.

She was the type of woman you wanted to bear your children.

She was the type of strong, intelligent woman who would carry on the Cavalieri legacy while proudly standing by my side.

In Milana's eyes, I had a well-earned reputation for fucking and leaving women. Between that and whatever I'd done back in school to anger her so badly, it was no wonder she wanted nothing to do with me. The problem was, I wanted everything to do with her.

Milana was going to be my wife, whether or not she liked it.

I wasn't the type of man who took no for an answer.

I sighed as I swirled the red wine in my glass, watching the ruby liquid climb the sides and slowly drip back down. "I promise you I don't, but the past is the past. It was seven years ago, baby. We were teenagers then. You need to move on."

Something flickered behind her eyes.

Was it pain? Anger? Betrayal?

Fuck. Obviously, that was the wrong approach.

She turned her head to the side, avoiding my gaze. Her voice had a hard, clipped edge to it. "You got what you wanted. You can leave now."

I stared at the ceiling and counted to ten as I breathed deeply. This woman would try the patience of a fucking saint.

When I reached twenty, I tried again. "Have a sip of wine first."

She turned back to face me and snatched the glass from my hand. She then tipped it back, draining it. "There." She thrust the empty glass at me. "Now leave."

I shook my head. "You really have no respect for wine."

She leaned forward. Her blanket slipped to tease me with a glimpse of the top curves of her breasts. "And you have no respect for—" She clamped her mouth shut and clutched the blanket to her. Leaned back so forcefully, the headboard slammed against the wall. "Never mind. Just get out."

I wrapped my hand around her neck and pulled her close, forcing her to meet my gaze. "This isn't over. We'll talk more in the morning. Get some sleep." I kissed her forehead.

I rose and walked toward the bedroom door. As my hand reached for the light switch, her next words stopped me.

"I won't change my mind, Cesare."

I looked over my shoulder at her slight form tucked under the covers in the center of the bed. She looked so small and fragile in that moment.

Refusing to take the bait, I flicked the light switch off and closed the door behind me.

AFTER REFASTENING MY JEANS, I returned to the living room and cleaned up the shattered wine bottle. Tomorrow, I would send some workmen to paint over the stain and repair the bedroom door. Moving on to the bathroom, I cleaned up the remnants of the perfume bottle. I didn't want her to wake in the middle of the night and step on the broken glass.

I dumped the glass shards in the outside trash can, grabbed another glass of wine, and circled around to the shaded veranda on the side of the cottage. It really was more of an enclosed garden surrounded by wild rose and black-berry bushes, which gave the air a spicy floral scent. I inhaled the cool night air. The tightness in my chest eased. Nothing beat the beauty of the Italian countryside at night. The ethe-real tranquility of the azure sky as it darkened and glimmered with diamond-like stars. The low-pitched hum and whir of night creatures awakening. The crisp bite of the evening breeze, carrying with it the subtle scents of moss and citrus.

I took a sip of wine and stared at the fields of vines below. My legacy. Tomorrow, we would continue the grape harvest. Something the Cavalieris had done for generations. Reputa-tion, power, wealth, my family name. They meant everything to me. Yet, what had always seemed steadfast and solid now seemed hollow. What was the point of it all if I didn't have a family of my own? A wife, a child. The Cavalieri name stayed strong generation after generation and continued to build wealth because we didn't rely only on the eldest heir. The next generation inherited equally, just as we all equally worked the land side by side with our laborers to bring in the harvest. These vines were watered with years of Cavalieri blood, sweat, and tears. That was why they were strong.

I had a duty to my legacy, and to future generations, to marry a woman who would honor that tradition. Milana Carbone was that woman. Of that, I was certain. I just needed to have patience with her. Something I had always lacked, but for her I would try.

I refused to regret what happened tonight, only perhaps how it happened. Perhaps I should have been more gentle, more careful. I rubbed my neck as I smirked. I wasn't sure that would have worked, even if I had known she was a virgin before I fucked her. Back when we were friends, we'd always had a volatile relationship. It was one of the reasons why I adored her so much. Unlike most of my friends, she didn't give two shits that I was a Cavalieri. She'd tell me straight to my face when I was being an arrogant ass, then turn around and make me laugh until my sides hurt.

Fuck, I miss her laugh.

The truth was, I didn't just want Milana in my bed, or as my wife. I wanted my friend back.

But nothing with her was ever easy. If I was going to truly make her mine, she was going to make me fight for it, of that I was certain. Stubborn minx.

I flexed my shoulders. She should be asleep by now. I never had any intention of leaving. I just wanted her to settle in and fall asleep before joining her.

As I turned back toward the cottage, I frowned.

Her bedroom light was on. I knew I had turned it off.

Dammit, she was trying to run again.

I stormed back inside the cottage and down the hall, intent on stopping her. Apparently, the spanking I gave her earlier hadn't been enough to make my point. I swung the bedroom door open, prepared to confront her.

Milana was curled up on her side, asleep.

Strangely enough, not only was the bedroom light on, but the window was open as well, despite the October chill.

I walked over to the bed and stood over her sleeping form. I stroked her soft cheek, annoyed to feel her skin cool to the touch. Crossing to the window, I pulled back the cream gauze curtains, lowered the sash, and secured it.

I then turned off the lights and approached the bed. Pulling off my jeans, I slipped between the covers, naked. I wrapped an arm around her waist and pulled her close.

She shifted and murmured something in her sleep, but soon settled against me. Her hair was still slightly damp and smelled like lemon verbena shampoo. I hugged her more tightly to my body and closed my eyes. Soothed by the feel of her curves nestled close to me, I quickly drifted off to sleep.

Only to be awakened by her terrified screams....

CHAPTER 6

CESARE

*M*ilana shrieked and lashed out.

What the fuck?

"Milana?"

She thrashed about, tangling the blanket around her legs as her arms flailed.

"Baby, wake up."

Her body twisted from one side to the other before turning toward me. Her arm swiped at my face, her nails catching along my jaw. I grabbed her wrists and held them tightly against my chest. "Milana?"

She screamed again. The sound chilled my blood.

Her eyes were wide and sightless as her head kept whipping from side to side and she struggled to break my grasp.

I released her wrists and sat up, pulling her onto my lap and wrapping my arms tightly around her, pinning her arms to her sides. Pressing my hand to the side of her head, I pushed her cheek against my chest. She freed one arm and her nails clawed at my back as she continued to whimper and thrash.

After several terrifying minutes, she stopped fighting me.

For the barest of moments, she stilled. Then her entire body trembled.

I held her tighter, rocking her back and forth as I hummed a nonsense nursery song I remembered from my childhood.

Her breathing was still alarmingly ragged and uneven.

Fuck.

I didn't know what to do. I'd never felt so helpless in my life. Should I wrap her in a blanket and rush her to the villa? Maybe Amara would know how to help?

Just as I was lifting a blanket over her shoulders, she stilled.

Everything stopped.

The night became strangely quiet again, almost as if nothing had happened.

Even without looking at her face, I could feel that she was at least partially aware.

I leaned down and brushed the tangled curls away from her tearstained cheeks. "*Carissima*, talk to me."

She stayed silent.

I cupped her jaw and tilted her head back, searching her face in the dim moonlight filtering through the curtains. "Baby, I need you to say something." I kissed her forehead. "Please, Milana."

The shiver which wracked her body was so intense, I could hear her teeth chatter.

I snagged the blanket and wrapped it more firmly around

her shoulders before enveloping her in my arms, warming her with my body.

When she finally spoke, it was barely a whisper. "The dark. I don't like the dark."

My brow furrowed. The dark? *Cazzo!* The bedroom light. That was why it had been on.

Not wanting to leave her even for the few seconds it would take to turn on the overhead light, I reached over and turned on the bedside lamp, then returned to embracing her. "Shhh, baby. I'm here. I'm here."

I knew she was finally awake when she tried to pull away from me.

Her hands pushed against my chest.

I tightened my grasp.

She hunched her shoulders as she turned her head away from me. "Let go."

"Never."

Her head dropped and she sucked in a ragged breath. "Please."

That single word struck like a knife to my chest. It held so much tortured pain and desperation for such a small, pitiful word. Against my better judgment, I released her.

She swiftly scrambled to the other side of the bed, wrapping the blanket around her like a protective shield. Averting her face, she asked, "What are you doing here?"

I got out of bed and threw on my jeans. I ran a palm over my eyes as I released the breath I had been holding. "I thought I told you to stop asking me that question? I'm here because this is where you are. Milana, what the hell is going on?"

She wrapped her hand around the bedpost, clutching it so hard her knuckles were white. "It's none of your busin—"

I clenched my right hand into a fist as I closed my eyes. "I swear to God, don't you dare fucking say this is none of my business."

She whipped her head around to face me, eyes narrowed. It was a relief to see the fiery spark had returned to them, replacing her terrorized, sightless stare. "Just because we had sex doesn't mean you are now in my life and have the right to interrogate me."

Enough of this bullshit.

I grabbed her ankles and pulled, flattening her onto her back. Before she could react, I straddled her hips. The moment she raised her arms to strike out, I snatched her wrists and stretched them over her head. I then slid my body over hers, pushing my thigh between her legs, pinning her to the bed with my weight. "Listen to me, *la mia piccola gattina selvaggia*, because I'm only going to say this once. We didn't have sex. Sex is a meaningless biological function. We didn't even fuck or make love. There isn't a word for what we did tonight. The second my cock entered your body, I claimed you for my own. In that very moment, I knew you were my fate. You became a part of me, part of my blood. The fact that you were a virgin only reaffirmed it. You were meant for me, and only me. There isn't a single part of you or your life that isn't now my business. Do you understand me? You can run, bite, fight, yell, and scream all you want, Milana. It won't change a thing. You're mine now. Mine to take care of. Mine to protect. The sooner you realize that, the easier it will be for you."

"I'll never be yours."

"You already are. You just haven't accepted it yet, but you will."

She pulled on her wrists. "You arrogant, sonofabitch, prick..."

I tightened my grasp. "Skip to the part where you explain what happened tonight."

She let out a long, frustrated sigh. "There is nothing to explain. It was just a nightmare."

I lowered my brow as I stared down at her. "That was no goddamn nightmare. You were terrified and I want to know of what."

"Why?"

"Whatever has you so frightened, I'll take care of it."

Both her eyebrows rose. "You'll take care of it?"

My lips thinned. "That's right." She didn't need to know the details. My family had ways of dealing with problems that weren't exactly legal.

She tilted her head to the side, observing me. "So, what? You're now my knight in shining armor, come to save me? Come to slay the scary dragons that plague me at night?"

I knew she was being sarcastic. I knew this was her way of protecting herself. From me. From everyone. From the world. It was no secret she didn't have it easy growing up. Her mother was trash who'd slept with anything that moved in exchange for a drink or drugs. She abandoned Milana when she was a toddler. Milana grew up with her religious zealot of a grandmother, who seemed intent on punishing Milana for her mother's sins. It was anyone's guess who her father was, although the village gossips had opinions on the subject, none of them good. Milana had learned from a young age to fend for herself, to be independent. It would take time for her to realize she had me to fight her battles now.

A warmth filled my chest at the thought of being this beautiful creature's knight protector. "Just tell me who brought the fear to your eyes, and I swear to God, I'll see to it they never take another breath."

Her gaze hardened. "It's you."

The force of her words struck me like a fist. "What?" I could barely choke out the word past the bile rising in the back of my throat.

"You're the terror from my dreams."

* * *

Why do you hate me so much?

You know what you did.

CHAPTER 7

CESARE

The sharp edge of the blade sliced through the vine. I grasped the ashy, deep purple bunch of grapes in my hand and laid them in the basket at my feet. Moving down the row, I snatched at the next vine and aggressively sliced my knife through it.

"Damn, what did that vine do to you?"

I placed the grapes into the basket and turned to watch my father approach on horseback down a path between the vines. An icy mist hung low in the air, waiting for the sun's warm rays to burn it away. While it was better to harvest the grapes in the cool of the early morning when their sugar levels were at their highest, it was still several hours before dawn.

I sliced through another vine and added the bunch to the basket. "I couldn't sleep."

My father slid down from the saddle and pulled off his leather gloves as he approached me. "Anything you want to talk about?"

I glanced at him over my shoulder. His brow was lowered and creased with worry. I knew what he was alluding to. Enzo informed me of Renata's outburst a few nights ago. God, that wife of his was a fucking bitch. There wasn't a doubt in my mind that the trouble she'd caused with Dante Abruzzo's criminal enterprise wasn't the first or last fire we would have to put out because of her. Right now, though, her petty meddling was the very least of my concerns.

I bent and rested another bunch of grapes on top of the others already in the basket at my feet. I folded the knife I was holding closed and turned to approach Papà.

He had taken an old stainless steel thermos out of his saddlebag, along with two tin cups. As he unscrewed the cap, a waft of steam rose, sending the comforting rich, yet bitter scent of coffee into the air. Despite my inner turmoil, the corner of my mouth lifted. It was one of many things I loved about my father. Despite all our wealth, he still wore my great-grandfather's *Panerai Radiomir* watch with its worn leather band that had been replaced countless times over the years. Despite the fact that it no longer kept time and couldn't be fixed because it contained dangerous radium, he rarely took it off. And no harvest was complete without him riding around on his big black stallion with this scratched and dented thermos in his saddlebag.

He poured two cups and handed me one. I nodded my thanks and took a sip. We both stared silently out over the vast Cavalieri grape fields.

I rubbed my eyes. Fuck, I was tired. "Enzo told me, you know."

I could feel his gaze on me but continued to stare straight

ahead. "I just want to say that I feel the same way he does. I don't blame you for Mom's death. I was young, but even I knew how much pain she was in. And the medicine was no longer helping. It was horrible to watch."

He placed a hand on my shoulder. "I hope you understand. I never meant to lie to you boys."

I sniffed and looked into the distance, clearing my throat as I blinked back the tears that were threatening. "I know, Papà. To be honest, it was a relief to learn about what you did. I had felt guilty for being glad she died. She was just in so much pain, I wanted her suffering to end. It was comforting to know you felt the same and took control of the situation."

He squeezed my shoulder but said nothing. He didn't need to.

We drank our coffee in silence.

After several minutes, he asked, "So what has you out here so early?"

"I could ask the same of you. Honeymoon over so soon?"

His jaw tensed. "Amara has to say yes to the wedding first, for there to be a honeymoon."

My eyebrows rose. "She turned you down?"

He shot me a narrow-eyed look. "Not exactly. She won't even let me propose yet."

I smirked as I raised the tin coffee cup to my lips. "Good for Amara."

"Whose side are you on?"

"Yours, of course. I like Amara. Always have. Despite my earlier objections to the two of you getting together, I realize now she's good for you. It's also good for you to hear the word 'no' once in a while."

My father turned to face me as he patted his horse's neck. "Speaking of the word 'no,' how's Milana?"

I flicked my wrist, tossing the rest of my coffee onto the ground. "What have you heard?"

"Amara is worried Milana will leave for Rome to get away from you."

I flicked open the knife and ran my thumb over the sharp blade. "That's not going to happen."

I would be damned if I told him I'd stopped her from doing just that only a few hours ago. Or that I had her suitcases and purse locked in my truck and a security guard posted at the cottage so she couldn't leave again. After she tore out my guts with that admission last night, I'd left her in peace and spent several agonizing hours just sitting in the hallway outside her bedroom door until I thought I would go mad. I just kept turning over every memory, every moment, every conversation that I had ever had with Milana to try to figure out what I could have done to have traumatized her so badly.

Finally, I'd had to get out of there. The walls were closing in on me. I needed to be outside. I needed to breathe. So I posted a guard to watch over her and came into the fields. My sanctuary.

I could feel his hard gaze on me as I turned my attention back to the vines.

He sighed. "I love you, son, but there is absolutely nothing I won't do to make Amara happy. If you chasing after her friend upsets her…."

I gripped the knife handle harder. "I'm warning you. Stay out of it. This is between me and Milana."

He pushed on my shoulder to turn me to face him. "The hell it is. I'm still the head of this family, and as Amara's friend, Milana is under my protection."

I threw my knife to the ground and wrenched off my leather gloves, tossing them to the dirt as well as I approached him. "Seriously? I said the same goddamn thing to you not two months ago about Amara, and you told me to fuck off, so I suggest you take your own advice, Papà. Milana is my concern, not yours, and I won't have you interfering."

"Do I have to separate you two again?"

We both turned to watch Enzo approach.

I bent to pick up my knife and gloves. "What the fuck are you doing here so early?"

He pulled the thermos of coffee he knew would be in Papà's saddlebag out and fished for another tin cup. "I told Renata after the harvest I was dragging her to a doctor of my choosing whether or not she liked it."

Our argument quickly forgotten, I exchanged a knowing look with my father. We all had doubts about my brother's new wife's pregnancy. It wasn't just the fact that he somehow got her pregnant after a drunken night he could not recall; it was the fact that she was barely showing after six months. It didn't help that she refused to allow Enzo to join her on any doctor's visits, or even tell him the name of the mysterious doctor in Rome she insisted on visiting. Until now, he had allowed her to get away with it to keep the peace, but after the bullshit she caused with Dante Abruzzo, not to mention trying to frame my father by claiming he attacked her, Enzo had finally had enough.

I waited while my brother poured himself a cup of coffee and took a long sip before asking, "So, how did that go over?"

He winced. "About as well as you'd imagine."

Papà put the cap back on the thermos and tucked it into the saddlebag. "Is this going to become a problem?"

Enzo nodded without looking up. "Probably."

Clapping us both on the shoulders, Papà said, "Then we'll deal with it like we always do."

I raised an eyebrow. "With guns, money, and a disgusting amount of arrogance."

Papà grinned. "Precisely."

"Sounds like a plan."

"But first we need to get these grapes in and processed." Enzo looked up at the rising sun. "The laborers will be here soon."

Papà returned to his saddlebag and pulled out a map of the property. He unfolded it and pointed. "We cleared the fields to the west yesterday, but we really need to get to the ones to the south today."

I listened with only half an ear.

My thoughts on Milana.

Who brought the fear to your eyes, and I swear to God, I'll see to it they never take another breath.

It's you.

A normal man would recognize defeat and let her go.

But I was a Cavalieri. I had the money, power, and resources to force her to stay by my side until I could convince her we were meant to be. That whatever I had done, it was in the past.

And that was just what I planned to do.

CHAPTER 8

MILANA

I pasted a smile on my face and approached Amara. She had a clipboard in her hand and was busy checking in a busload of American tourists. For some strange reason, Americans actually paid the winery for the pleasure of helping harvest the grapes, as opposed to the other way around. Something about experiential tourism.

The moment she saw me, she handed me a second clipboard. "I'm so glad you're here. Can you help me—" Whatever she was going to say was cut off the moment she noticed the hulking man behind me.

Her gaze flicked from me to him and back again.

I broadened my smile, showing more teeth than any sane person would as I widened my eyes. In a strained voice, I said, slightly louder than necessary, "Of course, I'll help you. What do you need?"

Catching my silent distress signal, she kept her gaze on

me. "I need you to have each person sign out a pair of gloves and clippers."

I held up the clipboard, continuing to play out our strange pantomime. "Where should they sign?"

Amara gave me a tight-lipped smile before clearing her throat. "Let me show you."

She stepped close, her shoulder touching mine. Our heads bowed over the clipboard as she whispered, "Who the hell is that and what is going on?" before saying loudly, "Have them sign on this line here."

"Can't talk here. Wait for my signal," I whispered back and then tossed over my shoulder, "Sounds good."

For the next hour, Amara and I worked side by side, checking in three busloads of tourists who had come to the Abruzzo region for an authentic winery experience. Usually during the harvest, we were stuck in the village, with Amara working in the souvenir shop and me working the counter at Sal's leather goods shop. We had often wondered what it would be like to be a part of the real action up on the mountain at the winery.

As we checked the tourists in, I watched familiar faces from the village trudge past with their patched-up baskets and sharpened clippers. Cavalieri villagers still clung to the old ways. During harvest time, even the schools closed for the two to three days it took to bring all the Montepulciano grapes in. While some wineries had switched to more modern machinery for their harvests, the Cavalieris still insisted on hand harvesting. It was the only thing I admired about the family. Tradition still meant something to them. Harvest time wasn't just about them. It meant extra money for the village as well. From the workers who came to help, to the shops, to the extra tourism. If they switched to wretched machines, the mystique of ancient times would be gone and so would all that extra revenue.

After we had handed out the last of the leather work gloves and I had advised the tourists for the hundredth time to keep hydrated and not underestimate the power of the October Italian sun, I stretched my arms over my head and hazarded a quick glance over at my guard. He was lazing in a chair nearby with a half-smoked cigarette dangling from his beefy fingertips.

The moment he realized we were finished, he stubbed out his cigarette and rose.

Che due coglioni. Just my luck to get the one motivated guard dog.

I wrapped my arm around my middle and moaned loudly as I gestured toward Amara. "I think I'm getting my period!"

Amara wrapped her arm around my shoulders. "Oh no, is it bad? You should come inside the villa."

We both peeked at the guard as we took a few steps. He was following us with intent.

I moaned again. *"Dio santo!* Yes, I can tell it's *very* bloody!"

We peeked again. The guard grimaced and hesitated.

Amara nodded toward him. "You should wait here. She will need some privacy. We'll just be inside."

We hastened our steps. As we reached the shaded entrance to the villa, I let out another exaggerated moan for good effect. As we crossed the threshold, we raced over the smooth terracotta tiles to the nearest bathroom. We both went inside, and Amara closed and locked the door. Since the villa was massive and built for entertainment, this was one of the larger guest bathrooms meant for the women. It had an antechamber with three gold sinks set in pink marble, and beyond that, a small lounge containing white, tufted ottomans and two vanity tables with a selection of expensive perfumes, powders, and toiletries. If I weren't in such a predicament, I would have delighted in shoving at least one or two of the nicer bottles in my pocket.

I turned on the water taps to full blast just in case and then followed Amara into the lounge. We sat close to one another on one of the plush, circular ottomans.

She clasped my hands. "I was worried about you last night. I saw you and Cesare both leave the bonfire early. Did you two finally have it out?"

I hated the furious blush that stained my cheeks, wishing I still had long hair to hide behind. I tapped my foot as I rolled my eyes. "You could say that."

"Well, I saw him in the fields earlier, so at least you didn't kill him. That's... something."

I buried my face in my hands as I bent over to lay my head in my lap. "I had sex with him."

There was a moment of stunned silence. All I could hear was my own hot breath exhaling over my palms.

Finally, Amara spoke. "I don't think I heard you correctly. What did you just say?"

I groaned and repeated, "Iah ehh ex it em." My words muffled against my hands.

Amara slid to her knees in front of me and pulled my hands away from my face. "You had sex with Cesare?"

I nodded.

"Cesare Cavalieri?"

I nodded again.

"The man you swore you'd rather be dipped in honey, rolled in bees, and then tossed over a cliff than spend one moment in his presence? That Cesare Cavalieri?"

I got up and paced the small confines of the bathroom. "This is a disaster."

"What happened? Did you know it was him when you were doing it? I mean, you know, it was dark...."

I shook my hands out in front of me. "Yes... of course! Fuck!"

Amara stood and caught at my flailing hands. "It's okay. We're going to figure this out. Together."

I ripped my hands away from hers, turned, and paced away before pivoting to face her. "No, Amara. It will not be okay. Nothing is okay. Don't you see what they are doing? Don't you see what is happening?"

She frowned. "You're just upset. I get it. If he's anything like Barone, sex is a bit *overwhelming*. You saw me after I had sex with Barone for the first time. I literally ran away!"

"Amara, I have a fucking guard following me around! You think that's normal?"

"Yeah, what the hell is that all about?"

I took a deep breath. This was so not the time for any of this. I threw my head back and stared at the ceiling, trying to form the words. "You know the thing that we never talk about?"

Amara eyed me warily as she sat back down on the edge of the ottoman. "The thing that happened at school? The reason you hate Cesare?"

61

I swallowed past the dryness in my throat as I blinked back the tears that threatened. Already the walls of the bathroom were pulsing and vibrating. "Yeah, that thing... and the *other* thing we don't talk about?"

Amara tilted her head as her lower lip trembled. She knew this was a painful subject for me. She reached out and patted my forearm. "The nightmares?"

I nervously toyed with the thin, gold Gemini charm around my neck as I nodded.

Sometimes the most amazing thing about best friends was not what you told them, but what you didn't have to tell them. I'd never spoken to Amara about what happened that day. Never spoke about the almost-attack, the betrayal, or the lingering trauma and trust issues. And she never asked. Never pushed. She just gave me a shoulder to cry on and let me hide my pain behind a mask of laughter and makeup. And when the nightmares came, and I started leaving the lights on and needing the windows open, she never questioned it or made me feel silly or stupid or weak.

I swiped at a tear as my vision blurred. "I couldn't do it. I wanted so badly to be happy for you, and to just forget the past, but I couldn't. So last night I packed my bags, and I was going to leave for Rome."

Amara sprang up and hugged me tightly. "I knew it. I knew you were going to leave me."

I wrapped my arms around her middle and pressed my face to her shoulder. "I'm so sorry. I tried. You have to believe me, I tried, but I can't. I can't be around *them*. I can't be around *him*. It's too much."

She held me close and stroked my hair. "If I hadn't refused

to move into the villa with Barone, he wouldn't have worried about me being alone at the cottage, which only encouraged Cesare to take you there. I'm the reason you see them all the time now."

I scoffed. "'Take me there' is an awfully nice term for barging into my apartment, declaring it unsuitable, slinging me over his shoulder, and dragging me to the cottage *for my own protection.*"

Amara leaned back and gave me a weak smile. "But bonus, you get to share the awesome wardrobe Barone bought me." She then sighed as she hugged me harder. "This is all my fault."

I pulled away and stared at her. "No. None of this is our fault. It's *their* fault. Don't you see? No one is safe around the Cavalieris."

She paled. "Don't say that. I love Barone. He's a good man. I told you those rumors about him are not true. I mean, technically, some of it is true, but it's not like people think."

I sighed. How could I make her understand? "I don't doubt that you love him or that he loves you. It's *how* he loves you I have concerns about."

She blinked.

I had hit my mark.

She slowly shook her head. "No, Milana. Don't do this. I'm happy. For the first time since my mother died, I'm happy, and it's not his money or the things he buys me, it's him. I love him and he loves me. He wants to marry me."

"Have you said yes?"

She looked away. "It's not that simple."

"Yes, it is. If you love him, and he loves you, then it is that simple. Have... you... said... yes?"

"We've barely started dating!"

"Not the point."

"It's still too soon."

"Also not the point if you love one another."

Amara threw her hands in the air and stepped a few paces away. "Why are we talking about me, anyway? I thought we were talking about you and what happened last night and why you have a freaking guard following you around?"

I crossed my arms over my chest. "We are talking about you because we are both caught in the same damn trap. The Cavalieri trap."

She rolled her eyes. "There's no need to make things sound so sinister."

I raised my eyebrows. "Oh yeah? Do you know what happened to Rocco and Mario? Do you even know if they are alive?"

Before she could respond, I continued. "I'm not saying I give a shit about those two assholes and, truth be told, I'd be glad if they are dead because they had it coming. All I'm saying is, your stepbrother and stepfather had been beating on you for years since your mother's death and no one in this fucking village, including the police, gave a damn, until Barone Cavalieri suddenly showed an interest in you. And the very next day, they both disappeared."

"So? He's protective. That's supposed to be a good thing."

"And what about that guy he beat to a pulp for trying to kiss you?"

"That guy did a hell of a lot more than innocently try to kiss me."

"And again, I'm not saying he didn't get what he deserved, but what the hell, Amara? Aren't you just a little bit worried? I mean, Barone Cavalieri and his sons can do whatever the fuck they want in this country, and no one, not even the law, is going to stop them. That's what comes from having obscene amounts of money and power."

Amara inhaled a shaky breath as she hugged her middle. "What are you saying?"

I leaned against the wall, tipped my head back, and closed my eyes. My voice was deceptively calm and even. I knew I was talking in circles because I was worked up and upset and I had to make her understand. "Last night I packed and was halfway out the door leaving for Rome. Cesare stopped me. He told me I wasn't *allowed* to leave. That whether I liked it or not, I was staying. If he were anyone else in the world other than a Cavalieri, the idea would be ludicrous. *But he is a Cavalieri.* We fought bitterly. And then suddenly... we weren't fighting. I'm not even sure how it happened, but the next thing I knew, he was inside of me, taking my virginity."

Amara gasped.

I laughed without mirth, opening my eyelids just a slit to glance at her and then closing them again. "Yeah, I know I talk a good game, but I never gave up the big 'V,' not until last night. It's not something I ever wanted to talk about."

I curled my fingers into my palms, needing the comforting pain of my nails digging into my flesh. I kept my eyes shut, otherwise the walls might start closing in on me, and we needed to stay within the privacy of the bathroom.

"Then he was saying how I was his now, and that the past was the past, and that he would never let me go."

Amara cleared her throat. "Do you think that's possible? I mean, you used to be close friends, once. I even thought you guys were going to be more. I know you. There's no way you would have slept with him if there weren't *something* still between you."

That was the cruelest part of this whole mess.

Sex with Cesare Cavalieri was passionately intense and completely catastrophic.

I had wanted him, desperately.

My stomach clenched as vivid memories of the feel of his powerful arms holding me against him while his mouth roughly claimed mine flooded my mind. I remembered clinging to him, clawing him, licking him, biting him, needing to taste him, to feel his weight on top of me, inside of me. It was as if I had become possessed. My mind was not my own. It was strange. My hatred for him was still there, boiling on the surface, but it morphed into this twisted, darkly sensual energy. Like he was some sort of evil Svengali who had bewitched and charmed me into spreading my thighs for him when I had never been tempted to do so for any other man.

Last night had only confirmed what I already knew: Cesare Cavalieri was dangerous, and I needed to stay far, far away from him.

"Not after what he did. There is no coming back from that. There is no forgiving him. And I know I've never told you what happened, and I promise I will, soon, and trust me, you will understand why I could never forgive, but I can't get into it right now. We don't have time."

She nodded, understanding.

"I told him to leave, and I thought he did, but later I woke up in the middle of one of my nightmares and he was there."

"You haven't had one of those for ages. What did he do?"

"Nothing. What could he do? It's his damn fault I have them in the first place. I told him I hated him and that would never change."

"Is that why he has a guard following you around? Because he's afraid you'll try to go to Rome again?"

I pushed away from the wall and stepped closer to Amara. Fuck, I hated to do this to her when she was so happy, when she finally thought she had found a family. But we had been watching out for one another since we were little and both trapped in crappy home situations, and I would not stop now.

"When I woke up, Cesare was finally gone, but so were my suitcases and my purse with my wallet and mobile phone. He took them to keep me from leaving. Sound familiar?"

Amara's eyes widened.

I knew it was familiar because Barone had done the same damn thing to her.

I sighed. "And when I opened the cottage door, there was a guard posted there."

"Our situations are different."

I raised one eyebrow. "Are they? Can you honestly tell me you could walk off the winery grounds without Barone sending a guard to watch over you as well, 'for your own protection'?"

She didn't have to say anything. We both knew the answer.

I sighed. "They may look respectable to the rest of the

world, but the Cavalieris are dangerous men who aren't exactly used to hearing the word 'no'."

Amara laid her head on my shoulder. "What am I going to do? I love him, Milana."

I hated to hear the desperate sadness in her voice, but knew I had to use it as a warning to myself. Last night had been a terrible mistake, one I could never, ever, repeat. There was a fine line between love and hate, and Cesare had shown me how easily he could twist that line around my wrists, secure me to the bedpost, and then fuck me senseless until I found myself hopelessly in love with him. Trapped.

I rested my cheek against the top of her head. "Don't worry. I'll think of something."

CHAPTER 9

MILANA

$\mathcal{I}$ wasn't allowed to return to the cottage. Instead, late in the day, after the harvest labor had finished, I was escorted to Cesare's home. He lived in an annex attached to the larger villa by a walled-in courtyard. It wasn't so much a home as a lair. The one-story structure was made mostly of massive panes of shaded glass and natural beams of wood designed to blend into the mountainside and overlooked a private, heated pool created to look like a natural grotto. It was obnoxiously beautiful and an obscene display of his impossible wealth. I hated the fact that I loved it.

My guard ushered me through the door and disappeared. The interior was utterly masculine. All dark wood and natural stone. I inhaled the scent of pine furniture wax, cigar smoke, and leather. There was also an impressive number of bookshelves. Real bookshelves holding mismatched books with broken spines. Not those fake bookshelves you see in the homes of some rich people, with rows of perfectly matched, gilded leather volumes of titles they've never read. In the center of the lounge space was a table where you would expect to see an ornate chessboard carved out of some obscure and rare piece of Italian marble. Instead, a checkerboard was set up, ready to play.

I pressed my lips between my teeth to keep from smiling. Cesare had always loved checkers. It was such a silly, childish game. I remembered playing it with him when we were teenagers. I would refuse to say, "king me," instead insisting on "queen me." He would always oblige, often jumping up and making a big show of bowing to me whenever I got a queen. I ruthlessly suppressed the memory. That charming and sweet Cesare was long gone, if he had ever even existed.

Looking around the open floor plan, I spied my two suitcases and purse near the kitchen. They were sitting in the center of the space, deeper inside his home, like pieces of cheese inside a mousetrap. I resisted the bait, staying near the exit.

Movement in my periphery drew my attention away from my belongings. Cesare appeared from a side hallway.

My eyes narrowed as I clenched my jaw.

He must have come from the shower, since small beads of water still clung to his perfectly chiseled, bronze chest and abs. He had on a pair of black silk pajama pants which hung low on his hips. His head was canted to one side as he rubbed the edge of the towel slung around his neck over his wet, sienna brown hair. He padded toward me in bare feet over the gray slate tile. Dammit. Even the man's feet were sexy, which just wasn't right.

I arched one eyebrow. "It's not going to work, you know."

He mimicked my facial gesture. "What's not going to work?"

I gestured to him with a sweep of my hands as I sneered, "The whole casually sexy, wet billionaire, Fifty Shades thing you have going on here. It's not going to work."

He kept his sharp gaze on me as he lowered his head, intensifying his stare. He threw the towel to the floor and charged toward me.

I stumbled. Too afraid to turn and run, I kept moving backward until my body slammed against the wall. Cesare followed with his body. Placing his forearm high above my head and splaying his open hand on the wall near my face, he leaned in close, imprisoning me... but not touching me.

My arms and legs went numb as I struggled to expand my lungs enough to breathe. Delicious, traitorous heat pooled in the pit of my stomach. I could feel my heartbeat with every pulse through my veins.

Raw, kinetic energy crackled between us as his dark gaze moved from my eyes down to my mouth and back.

He moved his head closer. So close his lips were only a whisper from mine. I could feel the brush of his breath like a caress as he spoke. "Are you sure about that, *la mia piccola gattina selvaggia?*"

He pushed away from the wall and turned his back on me.

Through glazed, unfocused eyes, I watched him swipe his towel from the floor as he passed me and made his way into the kitchen.

I kept my palms flat against the wall for support. It was all I could do not to slide down to the floor and curl up into a little ball. I closed my eyes and took a deep breath, willing my heart to return to a normal, steady beat. *Santo inferno!*

Marshaling my anger like a shield, I shoved off the wall and stomped after him. "I want you to call off your guard dog."

He was standing next to an obsidian marble island, pouring two glasses of *Vino Nobile*. He lifted one up and tried to hand it to me. "I thought for a change of pace, we might *drink* this bottle instead of decorating the walls with it."

I crossed my arms over my chest, refusing to take it.

He placed my glass on the marble countertop and picked up his own glass, leaning his hip against the island. He crossed one arm over his bare midriff and studied me as he took a sip. "What's it going to take, Milana?"

"I don't know what you're talking about."

A small muscle in his cheek twitched, silently showing his growing anger. "Yes. You do." He slammed his wineglass down so hard I was shocked the stem didn't snap in half. He stalked toward me.

I circled around the island.

He followed. "I understand I fucked up seven years ago. Badly. I want a chance to make it right, so now I'm asking. What is it going to take?"

Moving around the island was making me dizzy, and the walls were closing in on me. I veered sharply to the right and pushed open the large, glass-paned door that seemed to slide on invisible rails as it glided open. It led out onto a glass-floored veranda that stretched partially over the heated pool grotto. I breathed in the warm, moist air as I focused on the soft rustling of the thick covering of leaves which concealed tree branches swaying slightly in the gentle breeze. It was like stepping into Eden.

"Milana?"

I turned, pressing my back against the metal railing. "I've already told you. There's nothing you can do or say that will change my mind about you."

He stepped closer to me.

I slid my back along the railing as I moved away from him.

His dark eyes narrowed as he studied me. He seemed to weigh his next words carefully. "Don't say that. Because if you say that, you are going to force me to take extreme measures to get what I want."

I gasped. "Are you threatening me?"

I was cornered. I had reached the end of the veranda. We were at the edge of the grotto where the craggy mountainside met a copse of trees just beyond the smooth rock edge of the pool. I looked over my shoulder. I wondered if I could hop over the railing and jump into the pool and swim to safety before he grabbed me?

As if reading my thoughts, he said, "I wouldn't if I were you."

He reached out and touched the Gemini charm that was hanging around my neck from a cheap, gold-plated chain. I had worn it for years. It was a sort of comfort talisman. He tugged on the charm and chain, pulling me to him.

"Think of it as a warning. Whatever monstrous thing you are accusing me of doing back when we were seventeen, I promise you, *carissima*, it pales in comparison to what I am capable of doing now. And trust me, babygirl, there is very little I wouldn't do to hold on to you now that I finally have you."

The shimmering lights from the pool were reflected as small sparks of white fire in his dark eyes, giving him an almost unholy appeal. He released his grasp on my zodiac charm and lifted his hand to caress my lower lip with the tip of his finger. "So I'm going to ask you, *one last time*, what is it going to take?"

In a panic, I blurted out, "A million euro."

The corner of his sensual lips lifted in a half smile. "Done."

Fuck. How fucking rich was he? I'd said the most ludicrous thing I could think of to get him to back off. I didn't think he would actually agree to it. I narrowed my eyes. "A day."

He grinned. "Fine."

Double fuck. Okay, he wanted to play? Let's play. "For one week."

"It's yours."

"And no sex."

"No."

I pushed out my chin. "No sex or no deal."

His gaze swept over me. "Fine, I won't fuck you, but you live here with me."

I shook my head. "No, absolutely not."

"Nonnegotiable. You also continue to work in my office by my side each day."

"Fine, but I want all this in writing and the money wired into a holding account."

"Consider it done."

"And if at the end of one week I still hate the very sight of you, you'll let me go and never, ever try to contact me again?"

He hesitated. That muscle over his cheekbone twitched again. Finally, he gave me a curt nod. "You have my word."

One week. I could do this.

I hadn't survived a terrible childhood and been forced to spend most of my teen years on my own by being one of those dumb bitches who put pride above practicality. I may hate the Cavalieris for all their money, influence, and power, but that didn't mean I hated money. Money bought freedom and options. With that kind of money, Amara and I could move to Rome and live in luxury.

He curled his hands over the railing, caging me in, brushing my stomach with his already erect cock. He lowered his head to skim his lips along the column of my neck before whispering in my ear, "Or, you could give in to me now." The tip of his tongue traced the curve of my ear. "Let me taste that sweet pussy of yours again."

I couldn't hold back the whimper that escaped my lips.

His right hand moved to grip my waist as his left wrapped around my neck. "I want to feel your thighs press against my head as you come on my tongue. Right before I thrust my cock so deep inside of you, you beg for mercy," he growled.

His hand slid up to clasp my jaw as he pushed my head back, partially bowing my body over the railing. His mouth moved over mine. "Give in to me now and I'll double the money."

I dipped under his arm and moved away from his grasp. "But that would make me a whore."

Taking his money while indulging him in his futile attempt to win me over was one thing.

Taking his money to sleep with him was another thing entirely.

He slowly turned to face me. His long, hard cock was evident through the silky fabric of his pajama bottoms. He rubbed his hand over his flat stomach before dipping his fingers just below the waistband as he watched me intently.

My cheeks warmed. Without thinking, my tongue swept out to moisten my lips.

A low growl vibrated through Cesare's chest. "Never call yourself that. We would both be getting something we want. Your mind may think it hates me, Milana, but your body wants me. Besides, I know how much you like pretty things. Think of all the designer shoes and dresses fourteen million euro would buy you."

I knew I shouldn't do it.

Taunting a man like Cesare Cavalieri was like taunting a caged animal.

It was worse than playing with fire; it was playing with fire while doused in gasoline.

Still, I couldn't resist.

I needed to wipe that smug, knowing look off his face. He needed to know my body responding to his touch meant he'd won a battle, not the war.

I propped my hands on my hips and cocked my head to one side. "Why would I need fourteen million euro? Your seven million will be plenty enough to land me a rich husband once I move to Rome. Then my new man will buy me whatever I want."

I knew the moment I said it I had crossed a line.

Everything became still.

The trees stopped rustling.

There was no more gentle lapping of water against the edge of the pool.

There was just a strange, unnatural... silence.

Cesare's lips thinned as he bared his teeth. "What the fuck did you just say to me?"

CHAPTER 10

CESARE

*T*he thought of my Milana with another man was enough to send me into a blind rage.

She turned and fled back into the house.

I paused a moment and took a deep, calming breath. She was lashing out. This was what I wanted, what I needed, I reminded myself. It was all part of my plan. The only way I was going to get her to let down her walls and tell me what it was I had done to traumatize her so badly all those years ago was if I kept her challenged and off-balance.

You don't break down walls with a light touch... you do it with great big stones.

Milana was not the type of woman to be swayed by soft words and soothing caresses.

Brute strength, sheer determination, and a tenacious will that outmatched hers were the only things she would respond to, the only things she would respect. I was certain of it.

ZOE BLAKE

The only way I was going to win was if I was more stubborn, more powerful, and more ruthless than her.

And make no mistake, in the end, I would win.

She would be mine.

When I finally entered the cool, dark interior of the house, she was standing near her suitcases, purse in hand.

There was a bright flush to her high cheekbones. Her chest rose and fell with each heavy, panicked breath she took. The movement pressed her breasts against the white silk of her blouse. I could just make out the barest glimpse of her white lace bra underneath.

Fuck, she really was the most gorgeous creature I had ever laid eyes on.

For harvest day at the winery today, everyone, including myself, had been dressed in their roughest attire, ready to get their hands dirty. Not my Milana. Despite spending all afternoon handing out grimy, leather work gloves and stepping around clods of soil and mud which fell from the bottoms of the grape baskets, she was dressed in a white blouse, a flowing black silk skirt that hugged her curves, and bright red heels, with lipstick to match.

She held her knockoff black alligator Gucci bag before her like a shield. "I don't want your money. It was never meant as a serious request. I... I... shouldn't have let it go this far. You need to just let me leave."

I cocked my head to the side as I observed her. "Remind me to ask my Aunt Gabriella to bring you a real Gucci purse back from Rome the next time she comes to the villa. What color would you like?"

80

"I don't want a fucking purse from you. I want nothing from you!"

I lifted my discarded wineglass off the kitchen island and drained the remaining contents. "You're right. I'll just tell her to bring one of every color."

Milana stamped her foot. "Cesare, you're not listening to me."

Taking a deep breath, I carefully set the glass down and turned to her. Closing the distance between us swiftly, I snatched the purse from her grasp and tossed it across the room. "Oh, babygirl, make no mistake. *I'm listening.*"

She shifted her stance to stand behind one of her suitcases.

"I listened when you said you were going to leave without giving me the one week you promised to allow me to make amends for my sins of the past." I grabbed a suitcase. Despite its weight, I lifted it high and threw it out of reach. It crashed against a sofa side table, destroying the sculpture on it.

Milana cried out and backed away.

I picked up her other suitcase and held it before my chest. "I listened when you threatened to use my money *to fuck another man.*" I threw that suitcase on top of the first one.

I stalked toward her as she backed away. Little did she know, I was directing her down the hallway which led to the bedrooms. "Believe me. I'm fucking listening. In fact, I'm trying very fucking hard *to listen* to both what you are and are not saying, otherwise I might get angry, and trust me, you don't want to know what happens if I let my anger take over."

I backed her into the spare bedroom.

Her head shifted left and right as she took in her surroundings and realization dawned.

I captured and held her gaze as I reached behind me to close and lock the door.

Her eyes widened. "What are you going to do?"

My shaft filled with blood as I watched her standing there. The soft, pale pink light from the setting sun gleamed through a nearby window, framing her body in a warm halo. She looked like an unholy Madonna, the very embodiment of sinful temptation. My cock hardened even further as I envisioned worshiping again at her altar.

The corner of my lips lifted. "Get on your knees."

For one short, blessed second, we just stared at one another.

Then all hell broke loose.

"I am not your whore, you arrogant prick bastard. How dare you think you can treat me like this! If you don't let me out of this room, I am going to scream until the fucking pope himself hears my cries."

As a relentless stream of cursing spilled from her beautiful lips, she reached down and took off her high heels, gripping them both in her hands like weapons. Already shorter than me, without her heels the top of her head barely reached under my chin. With her petite stature, she reminded me of an angry little Tinker Bell. All she was missing was a showering of gold glitter and stars around her. And just like Tinker Bell, I wanted to give her cute bottom a spanking to calm her down. I raised an eyebrow. The thought had merit.

She clutched one heel to her chest while raising the other over her head. "Don't you dare come any closer."

The corner of my mouth lifted. "I'm talented, but not that

talented. I'm afraid I'll need to be quite a bit closer for what I have planned."

"I don't give a damn what your plans are. I've already made it very clear to you. I want nothing—*nothing*—to do with you."

I sighed as I placed the flat of my palm over my abdomen. "And I've already made it clear to you, leaving me tonight is not an option. *One week.* You've given me one week."

She narrowed her eyes. "I've changed my mind. I'm leaving."

"That's too damn bad," I growled. "You're staying."

She inhaled sharply as she tightened her grip on her high-heeled weapon. "I don't care what I said. I'm leaving."

I studied her. "Only one of us is right. Care to guess which one it is?"

Her lips thinned. "I can name at least five women off the top of my head who would fall over themselves to spread their legs for you. Why can't you go bother them?"

"I don't want them. I want you *and only you.*"

"Cesare, I'm telling you right now. I hate you. I loathe you. I despise the very air you breathe. The very ground you walk upon. I wish nothing but hellfire and damnation upon you. Every cell in my body abhors the very sight, the very thought, the very existence of you," she declared passionately. "Last night was a mistake. A horrible, wretched mistake. One that I will regret for the rest of my life."

She was lying.

It was all there, like the mystery of a gorgeous painting to be studied and unraveled. The flush on her pale cheeks. The way her pupils dilated at the sight of me. The rapid pulse at the base of her throat. The way her eyes drifted to the right as she spoke, denoting deception.

"You're lying and I'll prove it."

She raised her shoe higher. "Don't you dare touch me!"

I chuckled. "Challenge accepted."

Her brow wrinkled as her gaze swept over me with suspicion. The grip on her high heel faltered. "What do you mean?"

"If I can prove you're lying, without touching you, you honor our agreement and stay for one week."

She hesitantly lowered her weapon. "And if you can't?"

"I'll let you leave, but first, you have to obey everything I say."

Her gaze swept over me again. It then shifted to the locked door behind me, the only exit, and back.

I knew how to get my girl to agree. I raised one eyebrow. "That is, of course, unless you know you'll lose?"

She inhaled sharply as her dark eyes glowed with fiery outrage. She threw the high heels onto the bed and crossed her arms over her chest. "Bring it on, Cavalieri."

God, she was magnificent.

I stepped so close, I could feel her breath against my skin. "Get. On. Your. Knees."

Her eyelids fluttered as she inhaled a shaky breath.

I waited.

My hard gaze zeroed in on her mouth as the tip of her tongue peeked out to lick her lips, giving her red lipstick a wet, glossy glow.

She slowly lowered herself to the floor.

I clenched my jaw, my shaft lengthening to a painful degree as I watched her kneel in such a subservient position.

Keeping my lust in check, I ordered, "Now, take off your blouse."

She hissed as she drew in a sharp breath.

I raised both palms up. "No touching... unless you beg me, of course."

Her eyes narrowed. "Hell would freeze over first."

Her fingers trembled slightly as she worked the pearl buttons. She slipped the blouse off her shoulders and down her slim arms. She had the most beautiful breasts, soft and full, the tops curving gently over the white lace edge of her bra. I wanted to pull one of her cherry nipples into my mouth and suck as badly as I needed my next breath.

She ran her gaze over my midsection, taking in the bulge of my cock through the silk of my pajamas. "You're not allowed to touch me," she warned again.

"Don't worry, babygirl. I'm a man of my word. I won't touch you."

I reached into my silk pajamas and pulled out my cock. "Eyes on me."

Her big, beautiful eyes looked up at me briefly, but then were drawn again to my thick shaft, which was barely a few inches away from her mouth.

I ran my hand slowly up and down its length. "Do you have any idea how many times I have fantasized over the years about having you down on your knees in front of me?" I kept my voice dark and low.

"I think about what it would feel like to push my cock between those pretty lips of yours. To see the stain of your red lipstick along my shaft."

Milana's breath faltered.

"I've thought about it so often, I can almost feel the sweep of your tongue across the head and the scrape of your teeth against the underside." I tightened my grip on my cock and continued to slowly rub it in rhythmic pulses.

She licked her lips again as she stared at the pre-cum glistening on the tip.

My breathing became harsh as I continued to taunt her. "The problem is, I wouldn't be gentle. My hand would grip the back of your head, twisting into your soft hair, holding you in place as I pushed deeper inside your small mouth, testing your limits. I wouldn't stop until I felt the tight press of the back of your throat squeezing the head of my cock."

Milana gasped.

I increased the rhythm of my hand as I stroked my shaft. "That's when you'd begin to struggle. The desire for air warring with your desire to please me. So I'd pull harder on the back of your head, forcing you forward onto my shaft. I'd push past your resistance, deeper into your throat."

I widened my stance as I shifted my hips slightly forward. "Your eyes would water, streaking your mascara down your soft cheeks. Your lipstick would be smeared all over your swollen lips as they stretched around my shaft, and in that moment, you would have never looked more beautiful to me."

I clenched my teeth as my balls tightened. "I would thrust harder, telling you what a good girl you were for deep throating my cock."

A faint whimper escaped Milana's lips.

"I would watch your eyes glaze over as you struggled to swallow *every thick inch* as I relished in the tight... wet... warm... feel of your mouth. Knowing the moment I came, I would be flipping you onto the bed, pushing my face between your thighs and feasting on your sweet pussy."

I sucked in a ragged breath through my teeth as I punished my cock with sharp, angry pulls. Harder and harder. Faster and faster. Moving toward a crescendo.

I watched Milana's hands move restlessly up and down the tops of her thighs as her eyes remained fixated on my shaft and the rapid movement of my hand.

"Open your mouth for me, baby," I growled. "Open your mouth and put out that cute little tongue of yours."

Milana's lips opened.

"Wider, babygirl. Let me see that pretty pink tongue of yours."

She opened her mouth wider, the tip of her tongue peeking out over her full bottom lip.

"*Brava ragazza.*"

I inched closer, still careful not to touch her. "I'm going to come in your mouth. And I'm going to watch my cream melt on your tongue before you swallow every drop like my good little girl. Do you understand me?"

Milana slowly nodded, as if mesmerized.

I threw my head back as I fisted my cock, pumping hard. I held my breath, my balls tightening, my thigh muscles clenching as my forearm flexed. The orgasm was so intense it was almost painful. I threw open my mouth with a roar, baring my teeth as come shot out from the head. Through narrowed eyes, I watched as thick cream coated her red lips and tongue.

She closed her eyes as I continued to come into her mouth

before lowering my shaft and shooting the last few spurts onto her glorious breasts, marking her.

For several seconds, all I could hear was the sound of the blood rushing in my ears.

When I could finally speak, I ground out, "Now swallow."

Milana blinked as if coming out of a trance. Her gaze shot up to me, towering over her. I watched as horrified awareness crashed over her features. She tossed her head sideways. Before she could spit my come out, I warned her, "Do it and I'll tie you to this bed and whip your ass raw with my belt."

She froze.

I tucked my still semi-hard cock back into my pajamas and went down on my haunches before her.

She kept her head averted.

I grabbed her chin and forced her to look at me. With the pad of my thumb, I swept a drop of come from the corner of her lips, forcing it between them, into her mouth. I leaned in close. "A deal is a deal, *la mia piccola gattina selvaggia.* Now be a good girl and suck on my thumb as you swallow my come."

She tried to close her eyes.

"Eyes on me," I barked out.

Her eyes sprang open, tears welling in them. The pressure of her lips and tongue against my thumb as she swallowed my come felt incredible.

There was no denying the sick satisfaction I felt at knowing my seed was now deep inside her belly. That the taste of me was on her tongue.

"If I reached between your thighs, I think we both know what I'd find."

A bright flush crept over her neck and cheeks.

I would not push her. We both knew I had won.

I kissed her on the forehead before rising.

She stayed on her knees, head bowed.

"Bathroom's across the hall. Why don't you take a nice, long, hot bath while I make us something to eat?"

She remained silent.

Unable to resist, I reached out and stroked the silky mink curls on her bowed head.

One week.

I only had one week to convince her to be mine of her own volition.

If I failed, God help us both.

Because she wasn't the only one who'd been lying earlier.

I had no intention of letting her go.

CHAPTER 11

MILANA

I waited until the sounds of pans clattering and cupboards opening and closing confirmed Cesare was in the kitchen before moving. Rising, I crept across the hall to the bathroom. After locking the door, I crossed to the mirror and stared in disbelief at my reflection. I looked like a complete wanton. No one would ever believe I hadn't just been thoroughly fucked, although Cesare hadn't laid a finger on me. My eyes were bright and slightly unfocused. My cheeks had a deep pink flush that stretched over my jaw and down my neck. And the tops of my breasts still glistened from Cesare's wet come. Even my lips were swollen from where I had bitten them to keep from moaning as I watched him vigorously masturbate in front of me.

I looked away and moved to turn the waterfall tap on in the large sunken tub. The bathroom fit the aesthetic of the rest of the house, with smooth, river stone tile and lots of natural brown and hunter green tones. I squeezed an overly generous amount of expensive looking bodywash from a black and silver bottle into the bathwater as the tub filled. Soon the air was permeated with the spicy scents of musk and sandalwood as waves of suds drifted over the edge of the tub.

I stripped off the rest of my clothes and slipped into the water, groaning as the soothing heat hit my tense muscles.

As I leaned my head back and closed my eyes, I thought again about what had just happened.

Madonna santa.

Never in my entire adult life had I thought for one fucking second that watching a man masturbate would ever in a million years be sexy. I'd always considered it something sleazy men did behind closed doors to porn or dirty magazines.

But. Oh. My. Fucking. God.

Watching Cesare's large, firm hand wrapped around his thick shaft and slowly moving up and down, up and down, had been positively hypnotic. And then the filthy things he'd said. It should have been a turnoff. It should have been absolutely offensive. It should have been....

Get on your knees.

My hand drifted over my stomach as my knees opened.

My hand would grip the back of your head, holding you in place as I pushed deeper inside your small mouth.

My fingers teased my clit. Circling the nub with the tip of my finger, I arched my back, lifted my hips, and opened my pussy lips further, feeling the rush of hot water over the sensitive skin. I bit back a moan as I increased the pressure on my clit.

I thought back to the intense look in Cesare's gaze. He didn't look at me with romance or love or even passion. There had been a raw, almost manic intensity to his gaze. As if he wanted to devour me, body and soul. I had this strange image of him wanting to claw inside of my chest just to feel my beating heart, to hold it, to claim it as his own. It was primal, macabre, fierce... animalistic.

That's when you'd struggle. The desire for air warring with your desire to please me.

I closed my eyes and threw my head back as I slid down in the tub, letting the water rise and lap at the edges of my cheeks. I breathed in the heavy, warm air as my fingers worked at a feverish pace.

I whimpered as my orgasm crested, just out of reach. I was so close. So close.

I thought of Cesare.

What would have happened if I had let him touch me?

Would he have forced his cock down my throat? Gagged me with it?

Oh God.

Or would he have started in my throat and then thrown me on the bed, on my stomach, to take me like an animal from behind? Pushing his big, hard cock inside of me as he pulled my hair and told me in that dark, gravelly voice of his what a good girl I was for taking his enormous cock so deep?

Fuck!

I bit my bottom lip so hard to stifle my cry as I came, I tasted blood. My hips shot up as my hand cupped my pussy, sending water sloshing over the edge of the tub, surely flooding the bathroom tiles. I couldn't muster the energy to give a damn. I was too lost in the best orgasm I had ever achieved from pleasuring myself, and it was all due to fantasizing about a man I hated more than the devil himself.

I raised my hands to wipe away the soapy water that had splashed on my face from my frenzied movements. I then braced my hands on the edge of the tub and attempted to slow my breathing, trying to focus as I opened my eyes.

And that was when I saw Cesare.

He was standing in the open doorway. The open doorway of a door I had, of course, locked.

A black silk robe hung open and loose over his chest and hips, doing nothing to hide his raging hard-on that was clearly outlined through his matching silk pajama bottoms.

His bare feet made wet, sloshing noises as he crossed the soaked bathroom floor. He tossed a folded pile of what looked like another pair of silk pajamas on the sink countertop, then turned to face me. At his much greater height, he towered over me. It was all I could do not to sink deeper under the sudsy water in a lame attempt to hide.

He placed a glass of wine on the tub ledge within my reach.

Leaning down close to my ear, without touching me, he whispered, *"Brava ragazza."*

Good girl.

I gasped as my cheeks burst into flames. The man really was a demon sent from hell... no... a *mind reading* demon sent from hell to torment me.

With a knowing chuckle, he picked up my discarded and now soaked clothes off the floor, turned, and left, closing the door behind him.

Uttering a humiliated groan, I sank below the water. Maybe I would get lucky and drown myself.

CHAPTER 12

CESARE

I leaned against the closed door and clenched both fists as I inhaled slowly, counting to ten.

It didn't work.

I still wanted to storm back into the bathroom, wrench her out of that tub, and fuck her until she screamed my name.

Jerking off had done nothing to ease the gnawing hunger I felt for Milana. Finally possessing her, learning I was her first —and knowing I would be her only—had unleashed a demon inside of me. I wasn't saying I condoned it, but I was finally understanding why some men chained women to beds. I was coming dangerously close to doing the same.

I needed to get a grip. I was playing a long game here. This wasn't for a quick fuck, a weekend of fun.

Milana was my future. She was going to be my wife. For that, I would have to show some restraint. I had no choice. I just wasn't sure how much longer I could hold out.

Dio santo!

The sight of her pleasuring herself with such abandon in my tub was one of the single most glorious things I had ever witnessed in my life. Knowing she was more than likely thinking about what had just occurred between us made it that much more pleasurable to behold. And that much harder not to join in. It had been worth it to hold back. It was proof I was getting to her. I was breaking through the massive wall of ice she had formed around her.

One battle at a time.

I was going to win this war.

The prize was too great for failure to be an option.

I made my way back into the kitchen to see about our dinner.

It was sometime later when Milana finally appeared. She cleared her throat, deliberately hanging back in the hallway area. She clutched at the lapels of the oversized robe she was wearing. "Where are my suitcases?"

I gestured with my head. "There is time for that later. Sit. Dinner is ready."

"I'd really prefer to put on some of my own clothes first."

I removed the pan from the stove and turned to face her. I shrugged. "I'm afraid that won't be possible."

I headed toward the table and ladled two portions into the dishes waiting there.

Milana gathered up the extra fabric of the robe and pajama pants pooling around her feet and marched into the kitchen. "What is that supposed to mean? What did you do with my clothes?"

I surveyed her from head to toe. She looked adorable in

my robe and pajama bottoms. They were, of course, way too large on her, so she looked like a little girl playing dress-up.

I placed the pan back on the stove and picked up the wine bottle. "Nothing nefarious. I know how particular you are about your wardrobe and knowing your clothes had been crushed in those suitcases all day, I thought the considerate thing to do would be to give them to the housekeeping staff at the villa to launder and press."

That she now no longer possessed a stitch of clothing beyond what I gave her was just a bonus.

She placed her hands on her hips. "You did this on purpose!"

The flaps of her too-large robe split open with the gesture and her beautiful naked breasts spilled out. My mouth watered at the thought of taking one of those cherry-ripe nipples in my mouth and sucking until her back arched and she moaned for me to fuck her.

With a cry, she grabbed for the lapels. "Do you *at least* have a pajama top?"

I spread my arms wide, enjoying how the movement brought her eyes to my chest. "Sorry. I don't wear them. Now, sit. Eat. Before it gets cold."

She wrenched the robe belt tighter as she grumbled a rather impressive string of curses under her breath regarding my questionable lineage, my various appendages, and, I believe, my ultimate destination once I shuffled off this mortal coil, before begrudgingly taking her seat.

I took the chair at the head of the table with her to my right. As I filled her wineglass, I said with a wink, "I made jugged hare with prunes and raisins. Although I didn't have

99

any of the traditional red currant jelly, so I hope you don't mind a plum jam substitute."

Milana stared silently at the dish.

I placed the cloth napkin on my lap before reaching for the closest platter and offering it to her. "Yorkshire pudding? I confess I did not make these. Rosa was kind enough to drop them off when she picked up the laundry. These are way beyond my amateur cooking skills."

She selected a pudding and placed it on her bread plate.

I picked up my knife and fork and ate with relish, pretending to ignore her silence and trying not to smile.

After a few moments, I turned to her with a raised eyebrow. "Is the dish not to your liking? I can prepare something else..."

She studied me for a second. She shook her head before picking up her fork. "No," she whispered, her voice hoarse and uneven. She cleared her throat. "No," she said more clearly. "It's fine."

I watched her closely. Her lower lip trembled slightly as she raised the first bite to her mouth. She then sniffed as her eyes misted. She turned her head and blinked several times before reaching for her wineglass and taking a large gulp to cover for her sudden display of emotion.

I continued to eat and pretended not to observe anything amiss.

When we were younger, Milana became obsessed with Jane Austen. It started with that one movie and moved on to the books and then other things, including British cuisine. Her favorite was *Pride and Prejudice*. I remembered because I caught humiliating hell from Enzo when he found me reading it one day. All Milana would talk about was that stupid fucking Mr. Darcy, and I wanted to know what I was up against.

It was probably a low, underhanded, dirty trick, but I wanted to remind her I knew her better than most people.

That we had history together.

That we'd had a connection once.

A friendship.

A friendship I hadn't forgotten, and I hoped she hadn't either.

I reached for my napkin and wiped the corner of my mouth before setting it aside. I leaned back in my chair and played with the stem of my wineglass. "So I hear from my office that you have become irreplaceable in the weeks that I was in Milan. It seems you have a true calling for real estate and property management."

Her lips thinned as she straightened her back and raised her chin. "Your point being?"

I sighed. "There is no hidden agenda in the statement, Milana. You saved me millions by catching that permitting issue two weeks ago. And from what I understand, two of my biggest building contractors now refuse to deal with anyone else in the office but you."

"Try not to sound so surprised. I was always smarter than you in school. I just wasn't born with a silver spoon up my ass, so I wasn't fortunate enough to have my daddy hand me a billion-euro side business to run when I became of age."

I leaned forward. Pushing my plate to the side, I rested my forearms on the table. "I'm doing my best to have a civil, professional conversation with you. That won't be possible if you start talking about placing things up your ass."

Her mouth dropped open. "That's not what I—"

My gaze lowered to her lips, then back up to her eyes. "Because now all I can think about is bending you over this table and watching that cute asshole of yours stretch around a silver metal dildo as I slowly push it inside of you while I fuck you from behind."

The robe she was wearing wasn't able to conceal how her nipples hardened into aroused peaks at my words. My naughty little girl liked when I talked dirty to her.

I stood and circled to stand behind her chair. I rested my hands on the high wooden back, careful not to touch her. "Would you like that, baby?"

I watched her chest rising and falling rapidly with her breath as her fingers nervously twisted the cloth napkin in her lap.

"You want a *daddy* to buy you a business of your own? Name any business you want, and I'll buy it for you."

I could practically feel the heat rising from her skin. "Answer me, baby. You name it and I'll buy it, but only if you thank me with that cute mouth of yours." I leaned over her and whispered, "It would be worth every penny to hear you moan, 'thank you... *daddy*'."

Milana sucked in a shocked gasp so quickly she coughed.

Who knew it would be so amusing to put such kinky, illicit thoughts into her pretty little head?

Milana's shoulders stiffened. "That's the problem with you Cavalieris, you think everything has a price."

I wrenched her chair around to face me. Placing my hands

on the arms, I rocked it backward, throwing her off-balance. "And you already named yours, didn't you, *la mia piccola gattina selvaggia*? A million a day."

"And it's still too low of a price to be forced to stay in your presence," she fired back.

I let the chair fall back into place as I took a step back and ran a hand over my face. This woman would try the patience of a goddamn saint.

I marched over to the refrigerator and opened the sub-zero freezer drawer and pulled out the bottle of homemade limoncello and the two port glasses I kept next to it. Holding everything in one hand, I stormed back to the table and grabbed Milana by the upper arm.

"What are you doing?"

"Come with me."

"Where are you taking me?"

"For once in your life, Milana, just shut up and walk."

I dragged her out to the veranda and down the short flight of frosted glass stairs which led to the concealed grotto level. Since the sun had already set and the temperature had dipped, steam rose from the heated water. I pulled her along the edge of the lit pool until we reached a padded, enclosed cabana.

I released Milana and placed the limoncello bottle and glasses on the table in front of the cabana. Milana immediately turned. "I'm going into the house."

I caught her around the waist and lifted her high before tossing her onto the wide, mattress-like cabana seat. "No, you're not."

I then poured us both a limoncello and handed one to her before joining her inside the cabana. We were shielded by a semi-circular enclosure of tightly woven, dark bamboo. Inside, the soft, beige, cotton-padded mattress was lined with countless large, blue- and green-colored throw pillows of various shapes and sizes. There was also a white and gray faux fur blanket for the chillier months.

It had a beautiful view of the gently lit grotto pool, and then just over the horizon, a view of our vineyards which seemed to stretch from here to eternity. I often came out here at the end of a long day for some peace.

I settled back into the pillows and stretched my legs out as I sipped my limoncello, while Milana insisted on keeping her back ramrod straight, tucking her legs to the side. Slowly, her shoulders relaxed as she took a sip of her drink and watched the back-and-forth sway of the water.

I watched her.

Without turning to face me, she asked, "Why did you cook… what you cooked for dinner tonight?"

I reached out to caress her back, but then curled my fingers into my palm before touching her. "You know why."

She set her glass down and turned to look at me over her shoulder. Her face was in shadow, so I couldn't read her expression.

She sighed. "I haven't watched that movie in years. It just wasn't the same after…."

She broke off.

After….

Always after.

Our entire relationship right now could be summed up in two words: *before* and *after*.

It was the *before* I clung to while I searched to solve the mystery behind the *after*.

I tensed, waiting for her anger. Every time I seemed to make progress, something would remind her of *after* and we would take two steps back.

It didn't come.

She had fallen asleep.

Milana's back curved as her head lolled forward.

Softly, so as not to alarm her, I placed my hands on her shoulders and eased her over to rest her head against my chest. I curved my palm over the side of her head, holding her in place. I released the breath I had been holding as the tension drained from my body.

Fuck, what I wouldn't give to stay like this, with her in my arms, forever.

I knew this was just an illusion brought on by exhaustion.

I had put her through the wringer the last twenty-four hours, not to mention all the chaos and activity at the winery because of the harvest wrap-up. Dinner tonight was probably the first decent meal she had eaten in days. Between that, the wine, and everything else, it was all too much.

Knowing it would get too cold for her out here, I gently shifted our bodies until I could lift her in my arms and carry her inside. As I walked down the dark hallway, there was the barest of moments when I thought to carry her into my bedroom. I wanted her in my bed, by my side, where she belonged, but I knew I needed to be patient.

With a resigned sigh, I carried her into the spare bedroom down the hall. The bed had already been turned down, so I placed her in the center and pulled the covers over her shoulders.

Not knowing how much light she would need, I turned on both nightstand lights, but clicked them down to a soft glow. The room was bathed in light, but not so much that she wouldn't be able to sleep. I then lifted the sash to the window. Frowning when a cool October breeze ruffled the curtains, I went to the linen closet and returned with a heavy quilt, shaking it out and placing it over her sleeping form on the bed.

I then took up position in an oxblood leather chair I had placed in a darkened corner of the bedroom earlier that day, just for this purpose. If she awoke from another night terror, I was going to be there for her.

I may currently be the monster in her dreams, but I was determined to become the knight who slayed them.

CHAPTER 13

MILANA

I awoke to the smell of espresso.

I sat bolt upright in bed and pulled the blanket up to my chin before hunching down against the headboard as I looked around the unfamiliar bedroom. I reached out and smoothed my hand over the pillow next to me. It was cool to the touch, with no indentations. I lifted the covers up and looked down. The robe I had been wearing last night was twisted around my legs and the impossibly too-big pajama bottoms had slipped low on my hips but were still on.

Still, I couldn't shake the feeling that Cesare had been in the room with me last night.

"Good morning, babygirl."

I peered over the top of the covers at the devil himself as he strolled in carrying two espresso cups. I blinked several times. *Santo inferno!* The man was a freaking Armani billboard come to life. He looked impossibly handsome this morning in a slim-fitting, soft gray pinstripe suit from their Manhattan collection. His usually unruly, dark brown, wavy hair was slicked back and his beard had been trimmed. Gone was the rugged laborer who had helped his family in the grape fields over the last week. He was back to being Cesare Cavalieri, billionaire property developer.

My stomach muscles tightened. I hated the fact that I found this side of his personality far more intimidating. Rugged, casual Cesare with his dirty denim jeans and rolled-up linen shirts was closer to the person he had been when we were friends. The Cesare I remembered from back when we would steal fruit from the piazza vendors in the village and eat it in the shade of the trees as we played checkers on a small, beat-up board he always kept in his backpack.

This Cesare was the man he had become.

The man after his betrayal.

The cold, heartless man who had ruthlessly tossed me to the wolves because I didn't fit into his arrogant, wealthy, elite narrative.

My shoulders stiffened as he got closer. The warmth in his eyes chilled as his gaze narrowed.

He set the espresso cup down on the nightstand by the bed. "I have an early meeting, so I am going to head in. I will send a car to come get you in one hour."

I kept my gaze averted. "I'm perfectly capable of driving myself into the office."

He placed a finger under my chin and lifted my head, forcing my gaze up. "To show you I am a reasonable man, I will allow you to drive yourself in exchange for a kiss."

"A kiss?"

He ran the backs of his fingers over my cheek. "A single kiss."

My heart beat so loudly in my chest, I was afraid he could actually hear it. I licked my lips.

His own mouth opened slightly at the gesture as he watched me intently.

I arched an eyebrow. "So one hour?"

Cesare lowered his arm to his side as he curled his hand into a fist. The veins on the top of his large hand bulged menacingly.

After several tense moments, his hand opened as he flexed his fingers, forcing the tension from them. "Yes, one hour. There is a dressing room off the bathroom. Your clothes are in there."

Without saying another word, he turned and left.

I jumped at the harsh sound of the front door slamming shut several seconds later.

I didn't take a full breath until I heard his car leave the gravel drive outside.

It wasn't until then that I realized the bedroom window had been opened and the bedside lights had been left on.

Since I didn't even remember getting into bed last night, there was only one explanation... Cesare.

LEAVING THE ESPRESSO UNTOUCHED, I padded barefoot into the bathroom and then through the door to the dressing room. I couldn't suppress an ugly twinge of jealousy. Although it clearly was decorated for a man with dark wood, low lighting, a large, black leather bench down the middle and only one floor-to-ceiling mirror in the corner, it was what I had always wanted. A dressing room just for my clothes.

I sort of had one in my old apartment, but it hardly counted when you had to convert your only bedroom and sleep on the sofa to get it.

I stepped inside and ran my fingertips along the soft wool and cashmere bespoke suit jackets that hung on elegant, polished wood hangers on racks that were inset into the wall and lined with emerald green wallpaper. Each inset even had its own recessed lighting. In the middle of the room a wide bureau was positioned along the wall, topped with various colognes, a boar's head hairbrush, and a massive wood and glass display case with nine super expensive watches that were slowly turning in unison. One of those watches probably cost my entire year's salary at the leather shop.

I closed my eyes and inhaled the spicy, masculine scent of his cologne and imagined what this room would look like if it were mine. It would smell like Chanel perfume and be decorated with ivory crown molding and robin's-egg blue paint with bright, buttery yellow accents. And I would have an elegant chandelier that looked like wildflowers with green crystal leaves. It would cast tiny rainbows of light that would reflect off the gold-framed mirrors that would be in each corner. I sighed. Perhaps one day.

I spotted my wardrobe neatly pressed and arranged on the right side of the dressing room. It was strange to see my dresses and skirts next to Cesare's suits, as if we were a married couple.

In a fit of pique, I slid my hands between our clothes and spread my arms wide, separating the hangers so they no longer touched.

I surveyed my options. I needed something that would look extremely professional, but also sexy and alluring. The trick was, it couldn't look like I was *trying* to look sexy. My lips twisted in a smirk. I was going to show Cesare who truly had the upper hand in this twisted game he insisted we play. I refused to think, for even a moment, that I was trying to attract his attention. The idea was ludicrous. I hated him as much... no more... than ever. Yesterday was merely a moment of weakness brought on by exhaustion and too much drama and upheaval.

I took a deep breath. I would be better prepared today.

That I wanted to look my best meant nothing. I always wanted to look my best. It certainly didn't mean I was softening toward Cesare Cavalieri.

I rifled through my wardrobe until I selected the Valentino dress I had "borrowed" from Amara. It had long sleeves and a pleated silk skirt with a deceptively demure neckline. The gathered fabric around the V-neck gave it a conservative look, but if I moved in just the right manner, *someone* paying careful attention would realize it was actually cut fairly low. It was also in Valentino's signature red, which would match my lipstick perfectly.

I went in search of my lingerie. I found it in a second tall bureau with numerous thin drawers meant to hold ties, scarves, and other accessories. As I pulled out each drawer and finally found my black lace bra and panties, I paused as my fingertips traced their delicate, scalloped edge.

Had Cesare stumbled upon this same drawer this morning when he was getting ready?

Had he reached out and touched the black silk of my panties?

Had he fantasied about ripping them off me?

Warmth pooled low in my stomach as my inner thighs clenched. I inhaled a shaking breath. What the hell was that? What did I care if he touched my underwear?

With a huff, I snatched the panties and bra out of the drawer and got dressed. I only had less than an hour to do my hair and makeup before the driver arrived.

* * *

ALFONSO ROLLED up in Barone's Fiat 124 Spider Lusso. He lowered the passenger window and called out, "I'm impressed. I can't say I would have pegged you for being the type of woman to be on time, Signorina Carbone." He followed it with a good-natured wink and a smile.

I leaned down to the open window and rested my forearms on the doorframe. "Years of getting the paddle from my nonna for being late to Mass will do that to a girl. Any chance I could convince you to give me the keys to my old Fiat and you could just tell Cesare that you were too busy to drive me in?"

Alfonso frowned. "That old deathtrap? No, signorina. That car has earned its rest. I've done all I could with it. Maybe we should let it die."

I pouted but wasn't ready to give in just yet. I turned my face up to the morning sun, knowing its beams would accentuate the glimmer of gold highlighter I'd brushed on the tops of my cheeks to nice effect, and batted my eyelashes. "What if I agreed to drive the new Fiat Cesare got me?"

He rolled his eyes. "The one where you keyed *Vaffanculo* and a crude drawing of a penis on the hood? I haven't fixed your... artistic expression of appreciation for his gift just yet."

Oh right, I forgot about that. Probably wouldn't strike the right professional tone I was going for, to roll up to work with "fuck you" and a cock drawing keyed in my car.

Before I could apologize, he waved his hand at me. "And you can forget about winking your eyelashes and giving me those sweet looks. I'm far too old to fall for such pretty girl tricks."

I sized him up. Afonso wasn't that old. I'd peg him to be about sixty-five years. And there was no denying he was a handsome man in that *hello daddy, I've been a bad girl* sort of way. Especially if you liked the whole man who works with his hands, rough mechanic aesthetic. I averted my gaze, letting out a dramatic sigh. "That's a shame. I was just telling *Gabriella* how you've been an *absolute sweetheart* to me, trying to fix up my beloved car, and always being so helpful."

I glanced up from under my eyelashes to see if I had hit my mark. A possible romance between Alfonso and Gabriella was one of Amara's and my favorite topics. We had spent many nights at the cottage speculating over a bottle of wine whether there had been an illicit affair in the past that had gone wrong, or if they were star-crossed lovers who had been kept apart by fate. It was obvious by Alfonso's protective looks and Gabriella's blushes that there was something between them. Just as it was equally obvious that neither was acting on it.

In fact, it almost seemed like Gabriella was going out of her way to flaunt her young lovers in front of him, just to piss him off. That's why I was convinced they'd had an affair that had gone wrong, and she was getting back at him. Amara was convinced Alfonso's pride and standing as a staff member would never have allowed for it. She was certain the two had never even kissed. Either way, getting them together had become a bit of a pet project.

Alfonso snapped his head forward and gripped the steering wheel. "Nice try, Signorina Milana, now get in this car before I get out and strap you into your seat myself."

I raised my hands in surrender. With a huff, I yanked on the car door handle and got into the passenger seat. "Boy, I see the bossiness isn't reserved for just the Cavalieri men. It extends to their staff, too."

Alfonso cast me a quick, sidelong glare as he rolled up the window before throwing the car into gear. We raced along the country lane that would bring us down the mountain and into the village. As soon as we neared the outer lanes to the main piazza, I asked Alfonso to pull over.

At his concerned look, I patted his upper arm. "It will take you forever to turn around in the narrow one-way streets and get back to the winery. I'm perfectly capable of walking to work from here."

At his continued stoic look, I leaned over and gave him a kiss on the cheek. "You worry too much."

I then got out of the car.

Before I could step away, he rolled down the passenger window again. "Have Cesare call me if you need a ride home."

My chest tightened. Cavalieri Winery was *not* my home. It would never be my home.

I pasted on a forced smile and waved, showing that I heard him. He waved back and drove away.

Carefully navigating the uneven, gray cobblestone pathway in my high heels, I made my way down the narrow street toward the open piazza. It was still early, but signs of life were stirring. This was my favorite time of day, when the tourists were still in bed, and it was just the shopkeepers and residents out, heading to work.

I passed the pizzelle bakery and inhaled the warm, buttery-sweet scent of fresh *pizzelles* being taken off the waffle irons.

Two elderly women dressed in out-of-fashion dresses faded from repeated washings, white aprons, and clunky but serviceable black shoes, swept their front steps as they complained about their husbands. The sun was already shining off a display of gleaming jars of regional acacia, chestnut, and wildflower honey from one shop and the shelves of confetti almonds, *torrone* nougat, and *ventricina* salami stacked between racks of Italian postcards in another.

I only just managed to get out of the way in time before two heavy shutter doors swung open with a bang. The insides of the doors were laden with plate racks displaying the traditional Abruzzese ceramic *centrotavolas*, bread plates, with their distinctive circular cutouts. Each was hand-painted with the *Fioraccio abruzzese* floral design. A bright and cheery display of the wildflowers and herbs of the region resulting in a burst of yellows, pinks, blues, and greens depicting poppies, cornflowers, daisies, wild roses, rosemary, and thyme. Upon seeing me, the male shop owner apologized profusely and tried to get me to come inside for a coffee and a brioche with jam, but I waved him off.

After a few more steps, the space opened onto the main piazza, which was already a hive of activity. The old men with their fedoras and canes were already taking up residence among the benches that lined the square as they engaged in animated conversation over the latest political scandal or football match. They nodded appreciatively and called out compliments as I passed. It was typical Italian male behavior, to be expected. I would have been disappointed and second-guessed my outfit if I hadn't gotten a reaction.

Since a few tourists from the wine harvest had stayed on to enjoy the village's ambiance and shops, there were the typical souvenir scam vendors setting up their stalls. One had watercolors of the Abruzzo region displayed on easels with used brushes set nearby for effect, as the man who claimed to be the starving artist played on the sentiments of the visitors to charge exorbitant amounts for mass-produced art he bought on the internet. Another featured a small table of knockoff honey that was priced significantly below the legitimate regional product for sale in the nearby stores. Not to mention the reject *Fioraccio abruzzese centrotavolas* that were not good enough to sell for top price.

As I neared the offices, I was delighted to see the red, green, and gold metal cart of the roasted chestnut vendor setting up. It was a sign the end of autumn and the coming winter season was upon us. I loved the slightly charred, sweet caramel scent of the chestnuts and the cute little red and white striped bags they sold them in.

I looked wistfully down the lane that led to Sal's leather shop. Like the other shopkeepers, right about now, he would be opening the doors and dragging out various displays to capture the attention of the last of the tourists for the season. I hadn't been back since Cesare had dragged me out and given me the job at Cavalieri Property Management. Cesare had assured me he had loaned one of the winery staff, at his expense, to help Sal through the rest of the tourist season in my absence. I hated to admit that was a gracious gesture on his part. At the same time, it was the very least he could do, given the fact he'd basically forced Sal to evict me!

I blinked back the sentimental tears that threatened to ruin my makeup. Maybe after work, I would grab a few bags of roasted chestnuts and swing by the shop for old time's sake and visit with Sal and his family. I knew he would be proud to learn of how well I was doing at my new job. He had always said I was meant for better things than his little souvenir shop.

I took a deep breath and raised my gaze up to the Cavalieri building. Walking through the piazza was the reminder of my old life that I'd needed. I could do this. One week. I had a plan. I had a future career ahead of me.

And I would be damned if I let Cesare Cavalieri deter me from it.

CHAPTER 14

MILANA

The Cavalieri Property Management offices were in a sixteenth century building off the main piazza in the village, between the courthouse and the church. The lower portion of the building was reserved for retail shops and restaurants for the tourists. The second floor had various lofts and apartments. Our offices were located on the third floor, while Cesare's office took up the entire fourth floor. They also had offices in Rome and Milan. However, since the village was the Cavalieri family seat, this was the primary headquarters.

I loved working here. As much as I adored Sal and would be forever grateful to him for giving me a job and an affordable place to live, there was no future in working as a shopgirl.

I had ambition. I wanted to make something of my life. I wanted to have a purpose, and it wasn't to be someone's wife and mother right away. I wanted a career first. I wanted to erase the stain my mother had left on my name. For years, I had dreamed of the moment I would come back to this village triumphant. A successful businesswoman from Rome, with money and designer clothes. I would breeze into the piazza and the old biddies would ask, "Who is that?" and someone would say, "That is Milana Carbone, she is a big deal now. *She's someone.*" I would have so much money and success, they would no longer dare say, "That's Milana Carbone, that slut's bastard daughter."

Shaking off the bitter memory, I stepped inside the dark interior of the building. Since nothing in Italy was modernized unless it had to be, there was no elevator, but I didn't mind. I took the beautiful, carved, central marble staircase to the upper floors. Enjoying how my black, patent leather high heels clacked on each step. There was just something powerful and boss bitch about that sound that I just loved.

I FELT Cesare's gaze on me the moment I entered the office.

He was across the room, greeting a pair of gentlemen who had arrived for a meeting on a project he was starting on some land the family owned in Tuscany.

As the men continued to talk with him, he raised his head and stared directly at me. Even from across the room, I could see his eyes narrow as his jaw clenched.

I grabbed the Gemini charm around my neck and nervously ran it along its gold chain, immediately second-guessing my plan for today. Maybe I should have just come to the office in sackcloth with no makeup on instead?

Shaking off the feeling, I met his glare by flipping my hair and turning my head away.

Despite my starting as a senior assistant, I quickly rose to the level of junior project manager of several important development projects once Cesare's cousin Matteo, who had been in charge of the office in Cesare's absence, realized my intelligence and skill. I would not ruin my progress by letting Cesare intimidate me.

Ignoring the heat of his stare, I greeted the new receptionist, Liliana, and asked for my messages. I frowned as she slammed her laptop shut and covered it with a notebook before handing me several neatly written notes. Before I could comment on her odd behavior, Matteo approached. From his intense glare in her direction, it was clear he'd seen Liliana's strange actions as well. I would let him handle it. I had enough drama in my life without borrowing more trouble. Besides, I liked Liliana. I certainly would not be the one to get the poor girl into trouble by ratting her out for something that could be perfectly innocent.

Matteo was holding two steaming, white porcelain cups. As had become our morning routine, he handed me a latte macchiato. He took a sip of his own caffè latte, and murmured under his breath as we walked into the main office together, "Couldn't you have done us all a favor and fucked him at least once? Because now I'm going to have to go through the hassle of throwing him out a window."

I smiled as I blew on the frothy milk foam of my preferred morning coffee drink. I guess Cesare was in a less than agreeable mood.

Before I could take a sip, a large hand gripped the mug and pulled it from my grasp.

Cesare was standing before me.

My heart skipped a beat at his sudden nearness.

His gaze moved between Matteo and me. "Milana already had an espresso *in bed* this morning." His intended meaning and message to Matteo clear.

I simmered with rage as my gaze quickly cast about to see if anyone else from the office had overheard his arrogantly outrageous claim. I snatched the mug back with such force, milky foam spilled over the edge onto my fingers. I took a quick step back to make sure none spilled on my dress or shoes. "Actually, I don't *like* espresso." I turned to Matteo. In my most saccharin voice, I said, "Thank you so much for my latte macchiato. *You always seem to know just what I need.*"

Before either man could respond, I hastened to my desk. For the next hour, I kept my head down, working on the latest permit proposals for Matteo's afternoon meeting. When I was finished, I gathered up the files and crossed the office floor.

I forced myself not to turn and look at the massive, glass-walled conference room where Cesare was currently holding court. Besides, it took my entire focus to remember how to walk. My legs were so stiff from nerves, I was deathly afraid I was going to trip and go head over high heels, humiliating myself in front of the entire office. Taking a deep breath, I exaggerated my step, swinging my hips as I pushed my chest out.

Feigning confidence I didn't feel as I strutted to Matteo's office.

I could feel Cesare's gaze on me with every step.

Since Matteo's door was open, there was a direct view from his office into the conference room where Cesare was sitting. I moved to stand beside Matteo, who was seated at his desk.

Leaning over lower than was strictly necessary, knowing it would cause my neckline to gape open and give a peek of my black lace bra, I said, "I have the permits you requested."

Matteo turned. His gaze went from the file to my cleavage, to my face, then to his open doorway.

He sprang from his chair and stormed over to his office door. He slammed it shut and stalked back toward me. "What the fuck do you think you're doing?"

I feigned innocence. "What are you talking about?"

"Let's get something straight. Cesare is my cousin, but I'm still only a man, Milana."

My cheeks warmed. Matteo had been nothing but friendly and professional toward me from the start. It wasn't right to use him to get back at Cesare.

He ran his hand through his hair as he paced. "Are you out of your goddamn mind? I thought you were too smart to play stupid games like this."

Before I could apologize, he continued. "You have no fucking idea how much danger you are in. You may have known Cesare the boy, but you don't know the man. You need to understand—"

Before he could continue, there was a deafening crack, then a spray of wood splinters as his office door was kicked open.

I backed up as Cesare stormed inside.

He didn't say a single word.

It was more terrifying than if he had shouted curses at me.

With focused ferocity, he stepped toward me.

Matteo grabbed his upper arm from behind. "Calm down, cuz. She knows it was a mistake."

Cesare kept his intense gaze on me. *And only me.* "Not yet, but she will."

Shrugging off Matteo's grasp, he reached for me.

Snatching my wrist, he dragged me forward and then over his shoulder.

Matteo tried one more time to save me. "Cesare—"

"This is the last fucking time I'm warning you, Matteo. Back. Off. She's not yours. She's mine."

Despite my cries, he carried me out of the office, and there wasn't a single person who dared Cesare's wrath to save me.

CHAPTER 15

CESARE

I was losing my goddamn mind.

The need to possess and control this woman was driving me mad.

Despite her screams and kicks, I carried her up the hidden back stairs to my private office. Not that it mattered. The entire fucking office had seen me carrying Milana out of Matteo's office, but I was far too pissed off to give a damn.

The very second I'd glimpsed her beautiful black-lace-covered breasts and knew my cousin was catching the same view, it was all I could do not to pick up my conference chair and toss it through the glass wall that separated us.

I didn't need to be concerned with any of my staff calling the authorities.

They knew better than to interfere in my personal business.

I kicked the office door shut and tossed her onto the black

leather sofa in front of the fireplace before turning and locking the door.

Milana sprang up and confronted me. "How dare you treat me like this!"

I ripped off my suit jacket and pulled at my tie knot. "How dare you put your tits on display for another man," I growled.

"For your information, I was doing no such thing and even if I was, it's none of your fucking business. You are not my man! You will never be my man."

That was fucking it.

I had had enough.

I reached for my belt.

Milana backed up. "What do you think you're doing?"

I unbuckled my leather belt and whipped it off. I folded it between my fists as I stalked toward her. "Giving you the punishment you've been begging for from the moment you sauntered through that door this morning."

Her eyes widened as she raised a hand up to ward me off. "You stay away from me."

I stalked closer, cornering her.

"I'll scream," she warned as her back hit the tinted, arched, glass windows that surrounded my office.

I lifted an eyebrow. "I hope you do. How else will I know if you're in pain or not?"

She gasped. Desperate, she attempted to bolt past me for the exit.

I stretched my arm out, catching her around the waist. Hauling her struggling form up against my chest, I fisted her hair and pulled her head back onto my shoulder to whisper in her ear, "I am not a patient man, *carissima*, you should have thought about that before you tested me today."

With a swipe of my free arm, I sent the contents of my desk crashing to the floor.

Using my grip on her hair, I bent her over the edge of the desk.

She tried to rise.

"Bend back over that desk, or so help me God, you won't like where I whip you next," I warned through clenched teeth.

Milana sobbed. "You promised no sex. You promised. You broke your word. I'm leaving. I'm fucking leaving, Cesare."

I flipped the back of her dress up. "The hell you are. I'm not going to fuck you, Milana. I'm going to punish you. I'm going to whip this impertinent ass of yours so red you'll think twice before flirting with another man." I wrenched her panties down to her upper thighs. "You're mine now. Do you understand me? *Fucking mine.*"

I raised my arm up high and brought my folded leather belt down across both her ass cheeks.

Milana's back arched as she raised up on her forearms. She cried out from the impact.

I spanked her with the folded belt again. And again. Her ass cheeks glowed a bright cherry red as her sleek thighs trembled with each strike. She looked so fucking sexy bent over my desk with her panties between her legs and her black high heels still on. Her ass warmed from my belt. My cock throbbed painfully in my trousers.

It took all my restraint not to pull it out and sink deep into her tight heat. Fuck my promise. I had the money and power to force her to stay by my side, regardless. If I broke my word, she would have brought it on herself by flashing her tits at my cousin. She should have known better than to try to play such a foolish game with me.

She needed to understand this wasn't a fucking game to me.

The stakes were too high.

I placed my hand on her lower back and held her down as I belted her ass several more times. "Say that you're mine, Milana. Say it."

"I'll never be yours," she choked out between sobs.

"Dammit, woman," I raged.

I pushed my belt between her thighs and rubbed it along her pussy. When I pulled it free, the black leather glistened with her arousal. I stood behind her, rubbing my erect cock against her punished ass as I fisted her hair and pulled her head back. I held the belt before her face. "Try to deny that you want me. Try to deny that you want this. Go ahead, deny that you like being forced to bend to my will. That you secretly crave a man who is stronger and more stubborn than you are."

"I'll never be yours," she repeated.

With a roar, I turned her around in my arms and curved both hands around her neck just under her jaw, pushing her head back. I trapped her body against the desk with my own as I leaned in, towering over her slight frame. "Stop it. Do you hear me? Stop saying that," I ground out, my hold on my rage slipping.

Her perfect eyeliner was smeared from her tears, her cheeks flushed from crying. "I hate you, Cesare Cavalieri, and *I'll never be yours.*"

My hands slid up to grasp her skull as my thumb swiped across her lips, smearing her crimson red lipstick across her cheek.

I couldn't keep the tortured anguish from my voice.

My brow lowered as I gazed down at her defiant, tearstained face. "Why? For the love of God, just tell me, Milana, what did I do to earn such hatred from you? Tell me so I can fix it."

"You can't buy your way out of a betrayal. You know damn well what you fucking did, and I won't live through that humiliation again, not for you or anyone, so you can just *fuck off.*"

I couldn't take it one more moment.

Not her hatred.

Not her condemnation.

I grabbed her by the back of the head and smashed her mouth against mine, as if I could stop it all if I could just stop her bitter words. Wrapping my arm around her waist, I lifted her against my body, forcing my tongue inside her mouth. I swallowed her screams as her small fists hammered at my upper arms, but still I held her tight as I walked her backward toward the sofa.

I shifted my head to the right, then left, devouring her mouth. She fought back, biting my lip. The taste of blood only spurred me on further. I dropped her onto the sofa, my body following hers down, pinning her.

I ripped her panties off as I moved between her legs. Shoving her dress above her waist, I pushed my face between her thighs.

"Get off me!"

Ignoring her cries, I pushed my tongue between her pussy lips. At least this between us was honest. At least this she couldn't deny. I tasted the truth of her arousal on my lips and clung to the promise of heaven while I drowned in the hell she was putting me through with her denials, secrets, and fierce resistance.

Her hips lurched up.

I palmed her ass, feeling the heat of her punished skin as I squeezed her cheeks.

She cried out in pain.

"Be a good girl, or I'll get my belt again."

She finally stilled.

Using the tip of my tongue, I searched for her clit. The moment I felt it, I swirled my tongue around, then flicked it.

Milana moaned as she tossed her head back and forth.

I squeezed her punished ass cheeks again as I increased the pace and pressure of my tongue, knowing the mixture of pleasure and pain would drive her wild.

I groaned against her pussy, knowing she'd feel the vibration. "Jesus, baby, you taste so good. I could feast on you all day."

I shifted one hand to place two fingers inside of her. I thrust them back and forth. Her hips bucked.

"That's it, babygirl. Ride my mouth and fingers. I want to feel you come on my tongue."

Milana whimpered as her hand reached down to grasp my hair.

I scooped some of her arousal onto the edge of my tongue and swirled it around her clit, around and around, increasing the pressure but not touching that small bundle of nerves. Teasing her.

Milana tightened her thighs against the sides of my head. I knew what she wanted.

Leaning back slightly, I let her feel my warm breath on her pussy. "Say it. Say what I want to hear first."

"Damn you, Cesare."

I thrust a third finger inside of her. Fuck, she was tight. I took pity on her. Knowing she would deny us both her climax rather than say she was mine, I commanded, "Say you want my mouth on your sweet pussy. Beg me to make you come."

Milana arched her back as she pushed her fingers between her legs.

I grabbed her wrist. "Don't make me tie you up. Now say it."

She tried to close her eyes.

"Eyes on me, babygirl," I barked.

Her eyes snapped open. "I want your mouth," she whimpered.

It was good enough.

I clamped my mouth on her pussy and sucked and laved at her clit until she was clawing at the leather sofa seats and screaming her release. And when her breathing had barely returned to normal, when she thought she was too sensitive for more, I showed her how wrong she was by making her come a second time.

It was for purely selfish reasons. I needed to make sure she had no more energy to fight me when I pulled her onto my lap. I held her close as her head lolled on my chest. I could feel her heartbeat still racing beneath my fingertips where they rested just above her left breast.

I closed my eyes and leaned my head back.

I wasn't even sure who'd won that battle.

I knew I had come dangerously close to letting my anger slip its reins.

I knew deep in my heart that Milana and I were fated to be together.

Fuck, I really needed to get us to the other side of this mess.

Somehow, someway, I needed to break past her walls before we ended up killing one another.

Or someone else.

I tilted her chin up and looked down at her.

Her gaze was still slightly unfocused when she opened her eyes to look back at me.

I stroked her cheek and smiled at her fondly. "If you ever try something like that again... with Matteo or any other man... I will put a bullet between their eyes. Do you understand me, babygirl?"

Her eyes widened.

"I need you to say that you understand me, Milana."

She swallowed. "I understand you, Cesare."

I kissed her on the forehead. *"Brava ragazza."*

CHAPTER 16

MILANA

I climbed off his lap and moved to the other side of the sofa. Sinking into the cushions, I raised my knees to my chest as I wiped under my eyes in a vain attempt to clean up my smeared mascara without a mirror. "You broke your promise."

Cesare rested an arm along the back of the sofa.

In that moment I wanted to scratch his arrogant eyes out. He didn't have a hair out of place. He looked as devastatingly handsome and put together as he did this morning. I, on the other hand, probably looked like a slut who had just been bedded by the boss. I looked like my mother. So much for breaking free of my family's reputation and becoming someone to be respected and admired.

I blinked back tears, dismayed to see the smudge of red lipstick on the back of the hand I'd just rubbed over the side of my mouth. "I have to go."

Before I could rise, Cesare placed a restraining hand on my raised knees. "Don't move."

He stood and glared down at me. "I mean it, Milana. I think we both know you've tested me enough for one day."

I lowered my head and nodded.

He strode over to a door partially hidden in the paneled decor of the office. I listened to the sound of running water before Cesare returned with a dark cloth in his hand. He sat near me. I tried to take the cloth away from him, but he held it back. With a sigh, I lowered my arm. He tipped my chin up and gently wiped the cloth across my lips and face, cleaning the lipstick off my cheeks. He then wiped under my eyes.

He caught my gaze and winked. "Still achingly beautiful, with or without makeup."

I ran my hands through my short curls to try to tame the tangles in an effort to cover my nervousness.

Cesare placed his hand on my knee. "Open your legs."

My mouth dropped open. "No, I'm fine."

"Do as you're told," he ordered.

Not wanting to risk another punishment, I opened my knees barely a hand's width apart.

Cesare took me by surprise by grabbing one of my ankles and yanking. He stretched my legs over his lap. My hips slid along the slippery surface of the leather cushion so I was now in a prone position, half lying down. He flipped my now hopelessly wrinkled dress up and placed the warm cloth between my legs.

Embarrassed, I sucked in a breath and held it as I stared up at the ceiling.

"Milana, look at me."

"No, thank you."

"Baby, that wasn't a request."

I lowered my gaze to his. As he tenderly wiped away the evidence of my arousal, he said, "I didn't break my promise."

My eyes narrowed. "You said no sex. If I stayed for one week, you said you wouldn't force me to have sex. You broke your word."

Cesare tossed the cloth aside and wrapped his hand around the back of my neck. He pulled me up until my mouth was barely a breath away from his. "I never promised no sex. I promised not to fuck you. I promised not to sink my cock so hard and so deep inside your pussy you forget to breathe. I promised to torture myself with fantasies of what it will feel like to bend you over, spread your ass cheeks and take your other virginity. I promised to wait to fill your belly with my seed until it swells with my child. But I never promised no sex."

Good God.

The ferocity and passion with which he uttered those words was both terrifying and annoyingly arousing. There was something undeniably intriguing about commanding the intense attention of a powerful man like Cesare Cavalieri. Intriguing and dangerous.

Wait, did he say he wanted to get me pregnant?

I broke free of his grasp and shimmied away until I was able to stand up. I had to hold on to the sofa back, because my knees were too unsteady to trust they wouldn't buckle. "I'm not having your baby, Cesare. Ever."

Getting pregnant with a Cavalieri baby would be the end of everything. He would forever have power over me. There would be no escaping him. Through my child, he would be able to control my entire life, my every movement—where I lived, who I married, where I worked. It would be a nightmare.

Cesare stood. It was clear from the tension in his shoulders and the small tic above his cheekbone I had made him angry again.

I held my breath as he stepped close. He stopped when he had almost passed me. We were shoulder to shoulder when he leaned in close and whispered, "How do you know you're not already carrying my child?"

My hand went to my abdomen.

He strolled back to his desk. He picked up his phone and pressed a few buttons. "Cancel the rest of my appointments today and reschedule that meeting I left... early."

He then picked up his belt, swiped the cloth down it to remove the humiliating marks of my arousal, and buckled it after threading it through his belt loops. As he shrugged back into his suit jacket, he said, "I'm going to get the car. Wait a few minutes and take the back stairs down and meet me outside."

I thought about arguing, but what was the point? It wasn't like I was going to go back to my desk and face the embarrassment of everyone around me knowing the boss had just fucked me in his office. Not really, but they didn't know that. Take the back stairs, like a whore slinking out.

"My purse is at my desk."

"Leave it. There's nothing in it you need."

Nothing I needed. Just my phone, I.D., money. Of course, nothing he'd think I'd need. I swiped at the tear on my cheek.

Dejected, I sat on the sofa arm and stared down at my clasped hands.

It was over. My dream of Rome, of a career, of showing this village I was not like my mother.

Sins of the mother are doomed to be repeated by the daughter.

Hadn't my grandmother spewed that venom at me countless times when I was a little girl? I looked down, way down to hell, where that woman surely was rotting.

Well, Nonna, you got your wish.

Appearing to not notice my silence, Cesare continued. "It will still be here tomorrow when we come into the office."

I shook my head. "I'm not coming back."

He grabbed his car keys and crossed to me. He stroked my cheek. "We'll take the afternoon off and return tomorrow. You can finish the permits for the Tuscany property then. I'll clear it with the boss," he said with a wink.

"Do you honestly not get it?"

His brow lowered. "Enlighten me. You insisted on keeping this job. I agreed, and you used it to make me jealous. Despite that, I'm letting you return to it. Now you say you no longer want it, so what am I missing, Milana?"

Fuck. When he put it that way, I sounded like an unreasonable shrew. "Never mind. Go get the car."

He held me by my shoulders. "Fuck the car, tell me."

"It's fine."

He sighed as his thumbs rubbed circles on my upper arms. "I can stay like this all day."

I had a flashback to when we were seventeen. He used to stand like this and rub my shoulders just this way when he knew I was upset about something, but stubbornly didn't want to tell him. Usually it was something my grandmother had done, or something nasty another classmate had said about my mother. Somehow, he always got me to tell him in the end.

There was the time when we were sixteen and Cesare practically put Tito Genovese in the hospital for spreading the rumor that I was a whore, because I had turned him down when he asked me out. I frowned. I had forgotten about that. Cesare had been in a rage. He had torn the school apart, looking for Tito the moment he heard the gossip. The only reason Tito was even alive today was because I was worried Cesare was going to actually kill him and I ran to get Enzo.

It took Enzo and two of his friends to physically pull Cesare off Tito. There was an enormous scandal in the village and cries for Cesare to face jail time that were, of course, quickly hushed up with Cavalieri money.

How could I have forgotten how Cesare had always been so protective of me?

It made the attack that happened later when I turned seventeen that much more confusing.

Could I have gotten it wrong?

Maybe Cesare hadn't betrayed me?

Maybe it hadn't been him who set me up... who sent those boys to....

No... I know what they said.

I know what I heard.

They said very clearly that Cesare had sent them to teach me a lesson.

I shook off the disturbing memory. I had enough trouble in the present without borrowing more from the past.

Cesare leaned down to meet me eye to eye. "Tell me." The dark command in his voice was unmistakable. Matteo had been right. There was no trace of the boy I once knew, only the dangerous man I was playing with fire by defying.

Deciding I had nothing to lose by being honest, I told him. "I wouldn't expect a *Cavalieri* to understand, but this job meant something to me. I had a purpose, real responsibilities. I was getting respect. I was no longer the unwanted bastard daughter of a druggie slut."

His jaw clenched. "No one has ever dared call you that within my hearing."

I broke eye contact, not wanting to see the pity in his gaze. "Yeah, but I haven't been under your protection for a very long time, Cesare. Not since—I've been on my own for a long time and small-minded people can be cruel."

"Whose fault is—" He bit off whatever he was going to say with a curse. His eyes narrowed. "You're under my protection now. And everyone will show you respect, or they'll answer to me."

I laughed. "Oh my God, you're not serious?"

His brow furrowed.

I shook my head. "Damn. It must be so fucking nice being a Cavalieri. Seriously, what color is the sky in your world?"

"Think you can answer without the sass, or should I take off my belt again?"

I sighed. "What do you think is happening down in those offices right now?"

"Well, hopefully, they are doing what I pay them to do."

"Wrong. They are gossiping about how Milana Carbone is just like her whore of a mother. How I'm fucking the boss. They're probably saying that is how I got promoted so quickly. Never mind all my hard work, or that I'm better at this than most of the people here and freaking deserved that promotion. They are overlooking all my accomplishments in this office over the last month and assuming I did it all on my back! They're saying I'm just a gold digger hoping to land a rich Cavalieri son. Just like they were saying back in school. And who can blame them when you *fucking broke down a fucking door and carried me out of the office over your shoulder?*"

He threw his head back and stared up at the ceiling as he let out a frustrated groan. "Dammit, Milana. You know that was not my intention."

"Who cares? The damage is done. I can't go back there! No matter how good of a job I did, they would always put an asterisk after it. Milana Carbone fucked her way to the top. Sins of the mother and all that." I threw my hands up. "You know what? It doesn't matter. I was leaving this place after a week, anyway. And now I'm just plain leaving."

My plan had been to transfer to the Rome office, but that was sunk after what had just happened. And I certainly wasn't taking a freaking cent from him now. I didn't give a hot damn if I was cutting off my nose to spite my face. Our stupidly foolish and dangerous deal was off. I had my pride.

I covered my eyes with my hand. "You can't expect me to stay after this. I will be humiliated throughout the entire village. The very thing I had tried to avoid seven years ago is happening anyway," I cried.

It's like I'm caught in my own traumatic nightmare, but I'm awake.

And just like seven years ago, Cesare Cavalieri is to blame.

The walls wobbled and weaved as everything went out of focus for a second. I pressed my hand over my heart as if that would stop the overly rapid beating which was making my head swim. My chest tightened as I struggled to expand my lungs.

Cesare placed his hands on either side of my face. He stared deeply into my eyes. "Milana, baby, focus on me. Focus on my voice."

I blinked as the edges of my vision darkened. "You betrayed me. Again," I whispered. "You got what you wanted in the end."

Fuck, I hated this.

The lack of control.

The vulnerability.

I didn't like anyone seeing me like this, let alone Cesare. The more upset I became, the more the room spun. I felt like I was rolling down the side of a hill. Everything was just becoming a flashing, chaotic blur of color and lights. I squeezed my eyes shut, but it only made things worse as a wave of dizziness made my body sway.

His powerful arm wrapped around my waist and pulled me tight against him, his other warm hand staying on my cheek. "Milana, eyes on me. Listen to my voice, babygirl. Focus on me."

Obeying his command, I opened my eyes and zeroed in on the dark intensity of his gaze.

The authority in his voice.

The touch of his hand.

The strength of his embrace.

It was all like an anchor in a storm.

The panic receded.

I sagged in his arms, feeling lightheaded. He picked me up and carried me over to the sofa. He sat me down and crossed to the other side of the room. I hated how cold and lost I felt without the warmth of his arms. He quickly returned. Lifting me onto his lap, he cradled me like a child.

Feeling as foolish as a child for my panic attack, I closed my eyes and tried to bury my face in his shoulder.

He nudged my head. "Open your lips."

I opened my eyes instead.

He was holding a bottle of amber liquor up to my mouth.

I shook my head. "No. I don't want that."

"I didn't ask if you wanted it."

"You never do," I grumbled.

"You're just begging for my belt again, aren't you, little one?"

Giving him a deliberate pout first, I opened my lips. He poured some of the fiery liquor in my mouth. It hit the back of my throat and I coughed and choked.

He took a long swig himself and then held it up to my mouth again. "Another sip."

"It burns."

"Good. Another sip."

"I really hate you."

"We've already established that. Open your mouth."

I obeyed, and he tilted the bottle, forcing more of the horrible liquor down my throat.

As much as I hated the fiery taste, it did warm my stomach and chase away the cold, shaky, clammy sensation.

He set the bottle aside and rubbed my back in slow, soothing circles. After several minutes, he stroked my hair. "Feel better?"

I nodded.

"Good. It's time to go."

I rose and took the hand he held out. As we left his office, I expected him to turn to the right toward the hidden back stairs. Instead, he turned left toward the main stairs that led to the third-floor offices. "Wait. We need to go right."

He pulled me along, grasping my hand. "No, we're going left."

"But that leads downstairs to the main office."

He glanced at me over his shoulder. "I know," he growled.

CHAPTER 17

CESARE

I knew.

I finally knew.

I didn't know all the details, and I was sure there was way more to the story, but I knew the start.

I didn't know who was responsible. Yet. But I would.

At least I finally knew what had turned her against me seven years ago.

How could I have been so fucking blind?

I had always known how sensitive Milana was about her mother's terrible reputation. Some piece of shit must have found out I was planning on making Milana my girlfriend back when we were seventeen and got to her first.

They are gossiping about how Milana Carbone is just like her whore of a mother.

I'm just a gold digger hoping to land a rich Cavalieri son.

Just like they were saying back in school.

I will be humiliated throughout the entire village.

The very thing I had tried to avoid seven years ago is happening anyway.

While part of me was surprised such stupid gossip would cause a strong woman like Milana such trauma that even years later it still gave her night terrors, I had to be careful not to judge. Even back as an idiot teenager, I was aware her grandmother had made her home life hell because of the choices her mother made.

Not unlike my own life had been made difficult because of the rumors claiming my father murdered my mother. It was one reason why we had become friends in the first place. Two people bonded by the scandals of their parents. All that, plus her grandmother's viciousness and my perceived betrayal and rejection, had somehow gotten twisted into one traumatic event in her mind.

Still, it made little sense.

It was like I was finally seeing the complete picture but it was hazy, like I was viewing it through a fogged window. There had to be more to this, but I was certain I was at least on the right track.

Whether or not she realized it, Milana had finally shown me a crack in the wall she had built around herself.

And I'm about to take a sledgehammer to it.

Milana pulled back on my grasp. "Cesare, I don't want to face those people."

I winked at her. "Trust me."

She tried to dig her heels in. "You are literally the very last person on the face of the earth that I would ever trust."

Fuck, that hurt.

I turned abruptly on the stair landing and pulled her

against me. I wrapped my free hand around the back of her neck. "I know, baby. And that's my fault. And I'm going to do something about it. Starting now." I gave her a hard kiss on the mouth and turned to pull her down the last flight of stairs.

I walked into the main area of the office and called out, "I need everyone's attention."

"Cesare, what the hell are you doing?" she whispered harshly.

"Hang up your phones. I want your complete attention."

Milana yanked on my arm as she tried to leave. I pulled her back and anchored her to my side.

"First, I want to apologize for the scene you witnessed earlier, but when you hear our news, you will know why I was eager to get Milana alone as quickly as possible."

Milana stepped on my foot with her heel. Grinding my teeth as I ignored the pain, I reached down and cupped her recently punished ass cheek, squeezing it. Hard.

She gave out a squeak of pain and lifted her heel off my toe.

I gave her a warning look before turning my attention back to my staff. "I want you all to be the first to know, Milana Fiorella Carbone has done me the very great honor of agreeing to become my wife."

Milana immediately struggled in my grasp.

I tightened my grip on her. For a little thing, she was surprisingly strong when cornered.

A confused silence fell over the staff as they exchanged looks. Then Matteo gave out a shout and began to vigorously clap. The staff followed his lead, with several of them standing up. A few started to cheer and whistle, although it was mostly the men. The women remained seated.

A few approached to shake my hand and offer their personal congratulations.

Milana pasted a wide smile on her face and said through clenched teeth, "I'm going to kill you."

I shook the hand of a longtime manager and friend and clapped him on the back as we shared a laugh.

Milana nodded as he then turned to her and congratulated her. "Thank you." She then whispered to me under her breath, "I'm going to slip a knife between your ribs and kill you dead."

Another well-wisher stepped forward and shook my hand. "She's quite a catch."

Milana smiled wider, her jaw tight as she murmured, "Seriously, I couldn't hate you more than I do at this very moment."

I moved my arm to enclose Milana's shoulders as I pulled her against my chest. "Yes, I'm a lucky man." I kissed the top of her head.

Since Milana could be unpredictable when cornered, and that was putting it mildly, I cut off any further felicitations and hustled her out of the office and down the central marble staircase. A sharp October wind greeted us the moment we exited the building.

I turned to Milana with a frown. Shrugging out of my suit jacket, I draped it over her shoulders.

She immediately tried to push it off. "I don't want your coat."

I wrenched the coat back into place and yanked her to me by the lapels. "I've got news for you, *la mia piccola gattina selvaggia.* From this point forward, you not only get my coat, you get my name... my protection... and if I get my way... soon my baby."

Her eyes flared with rage as her beautiful lips opened to fire back a retort.

Before she could respond, I wrapped my hand around the back of her head and pulled her mouth to mine. My tongue pushed past her lips, tasting the whiskey I'd forced down her throat moments earlier. Using the jacket to shield my movements, I cupped her breast in my free hand. My fingers pushed back the neckline of her dress, searching for the warmth of her skin. It was all I could do not to tear the damn thing off her, even though we were standing practically in the middle of the piazza.

Milana whimpered as I deepened the kiss. Her hands gripped my shirt as her tongue swirled around mine. No matter how angry she was at me, she couldn't hide her body's response to my touch, my kiss. It might be a dirty trick, but I wasn't above using every weapon at my disposal in our little private war.

I was fighting to win.

When we finally broke free, we were both breathless. I pressed my hand to her cheek and rubbed my thumb along her bottom lip. "When I get you home, I'm tying you naked to my bed and fucking this beautiful mouth of yours until you beg me to come on your tits. Then I'm going to lick your pussy until you come at least twice. And that's just to get you warmed up," I said with a wink.

Milana took a step back. Her dark eyes blinked up at me as if she were shaking off the remnants of a dream.

I reached for her. She leaned back, just out of reach.

I could see it happening. The wall of ice crystalizing in her gaze.

Someone from above shouted down, "Save that for the honeymoon!"

I looked up and gave a wave to the exuberant employee, who had poked their head out of the window to witness our kiss. Berating myself for allowing something so private to be witnessed, I wrapped my arm around Milana, pulled her close to my side, and hustled her around to the side of the building where my Alfa Romeo Giulia Quadrifoglio was parked in a private lot.

After opening the passenger door and helping her inside, I got behind the wheel and put the car into gear, racing away from the center of town toward the winery.

Cavalieri land.

My home.

My sanctuary.

Home field advantage.

Milana hugged her arms around her middle and sat silently.

I was so alarmed, I briefly considered heading directly to the villa instead and pleading for Amara's help but decided against it. If Milana needed someone, I wanted it to be me and no one else.

Still, I was worried.

Whether Milana was spitting mad with her claws out or curled up in a little ball feeling vulnerable and scared, the one thing you could count on was *la mia piccola gattina selvaggia* always still had some fight in her. I had never seen her with nothing to say. Ever.

I just needed to get her home. She was in shock from my announcement, but she'd warm up to the idea and realize all I was doing was hastening the inevitable.

It wasn't like I hadn't warned her repeatedly that she was now mine, and that I had no intention of ever letting her go. She had been fooling herself if she thought I was actually going to let her waltz out of my life at the end of the week.

Out of the corner of my eye, I saw Milana lean forward and pull the visor down.

She stared at her reflection in the small mirror for several seconds. I watched as she lifted her arm to run her fingertips over her now kiss-swollen bottom lip. She then touched the corner of her eye. "My makeup's all rubbed off," she said. Her voice was eerily detached.

I looked at her, then back at the road. "You don't need makeup, *carissima*, you are just as beautiful without it."

She cocked her head to the right as she continued to stare at her reflection. In that same disjointed and strangely calm voice, she continued, as if I hadn't spoken. "I never appear in public without my makeup on. People will talk. They'll know."

I frowned as I reached over and laid a hand on her left knee, squeezing it gently. "I don't understand, baby. What will they know?"

Although she turned to look at me, it was like she was staring right through me. "That I'm trash. That is what Nonna used to say. A respectable woman ensures she looks presentable at all times. Always. No excuses."

Milana looked down at her wrinkled dress. The dress I'd hopelessly crushed with my body when I'd pinned her to the sofa earlier. Her small hands looked pale and fragile as she tried to smooth the wrinkles out over her thighs. "As Nonna would say, only trash would appear in public looking like she just rolled out of some man's bed."

Her words couldn't have hurt more than if she'd physically kicked me in the stomach.

Bile rose in the back of my throat as my stomach clenched and twisted. The horror of her words settled on my chest like a damning weight. All those times I'd scoffed when she accused me of being an arrogant Cavalieri who, through my own privilege, couldn't possibly understand the reality of what she was experiencing and she had been right.

Like a fucking egotistical prick, I rushed in, assuming I could fix all her problems by simply gracing her with the Cavalieri name, not thinking about how I could make things worse. How it would look for me to hastily announce our engagement to staff, not family, with Milana looking every inch like I had fucked her sideways up in my office, instead of a formal, respectful announcement with close friends and family. By trying to salvage her reputation, I had actually shown her the ultimate disrespect and callous disregard.

Fuck her grandmother. If she were still alive, I would strangle that bitter old woman with my bare hands and relish in watching her take her last fetid breath on this earth, knowing my girl would never again have to hear her lips spew such vile hatred.

Milana pushed the visor back into place. "It's fine. Everything will be fine. It's better this way. People will know you weren't serious about us being engaged." She sniffed as she raised her chin. "They'll know it was all just a joke."

I flexed my fingers and gripped the leather steering wheel harder as I pressed my right foot down. The car surged forward, taking the next curve at a dangerous speed. The car fishtailed on the limestone gravel, but quickly regained its traction.

Milana cried out as she gripped the side door handle for purchase.

I edged the car faster.

In less than a minute, we roared past the villa and into the drive of my home. I barely waited for the car to come to a complete stop before I was tossing the parking brake on and throwing the door open. I stormed around the back and opened the passenger door.

Milana sat there frozen.

"Get out of the car, Milana."

"I want you to take me back to my apartment. My actual apartment, not the cottage."

"No. Get out of the car."

"Fine, then take me to the cottage."

"No. Get out of the car."

"Then I'll stay at the villa with Amara."

"Wrong again. Get out of the car."

Still, she didn't move. As I was reaching in to drag her out, Amara came running. She must have been waiting for us to drive up. Goddamn it. Word traveled fast in this damn village.

Milana ducked out under my outstretched arm that was resting on the top of the car door and raced toward Amara.

Amara called out, "Is it true? It can't be true. Is it true?" But as she and Milana got closer, her mouth dropped open. She lifted her skirt and sprinted the extra few steps to enfold Milana in a hug. Taking in Milana's uncharacteristically disheveled appearance, she exclaimed, "My God, what happened to you?"

Amara cast an accusing look over Milana's shoulder at me as she closed her arms protectively around my woman. "What the hell happened to her, Cesare? What did you do?"

The fingers of my right hand curled into a fist as my jaw clenched.

Amara was a friend.

A good friend.

A longtime friend… of both Milana's and mine.

I liked Amara.

My father loved her.

But that would mean nothing if she didn't release Milana and let me handle this.

My voice was clipped and hard as I responded to Amara's questions. "Yes, it's true. Milana and I are getting married as soon as I can make the arrangements. And no, nothing happened to her. Now, if you don't mind, Milana and I have several things we need to discuss."

While I was talking, Milana was shaking her head vigorously. "No, it's not true. We're not engaged. It was just a… a joke."

I never thought it was possible to actually both hear and feel your blood boiling in your veins, but in that moment, that was precisely what I was experiencing. If I wasn't physically holding Milana in my arms in the next two seconds, I wouldn't be held responsible for what happened.

Amara stepped in front of Milana, as if to shield her from me. "Don't tell me nothing happened. Look at her!"

I took several steps toward the huddled women. If I had to rip Milana out of Amara's arms and drag her into my house, then that was precisely what I was going to do. But I would be fucking damned if I was just going to stand here and be forced to explain myself or my relationship with Milana.

My father appeared up the pathway from the processing building where he must have been supervising the sorting of the grapes.

His brow lowered. *"Che sta succedendo qui?"*

Amara answered without taking her eyes off me. "I'm taking Milana into the villa with me."

My gaze narrowed. "The hell you are," I ground out.

My primary concern was for Milana.

Her silence was terrifying me.

I needed to hold her, to assure myself she was okay.

Amara may be her closest friend, but I was Milana's soulmate, whether or not she accepted that fact.

I was her man, her protector.

I'd failed in that role in the past.

I would not fail again.

Papà looked between us both. *"Dolcezza,* step away. This is between Cesare and Milana, let them sort it out."

I nodded briefly toward my father, acknowledging the show of respect and trust. I knew, because of her connection to Amara, he was concerned for Milana, but he also knew, as his son, I wouldn't hurt her.

Amara shook her head as she reached her arms back to hug Milana. "No. He can't have her."

My father and I exchanged a look before we both stepped forward in unison. He flanked the left as I flanked the right, caging the girls in.

Papà reached down and gripped the heavy buckle of his belt. "I'm going to give you to the count of three to obey me, Amara."

At the same time, I circled around, keeping my gaze on Milana. "Babygirl, I am not a patient man. Now, we both know how this is going to end."

Amara's head swiveled from left to right, trying to keep us both in her sights. "Milana was right, you Cavalieri men are just a bunch of bullies."

The corner of my father's lips lifted as his head lowered. "One."

Milana finally spoke up as she stepped out from behind Amara. "Cesare, it's over. This whole thing has gone way too far."

I flexed my fingers, itching to grab her. "Two."

Amara and Milana exchanged a sidelong glance.

I caught my father's knowing look.

We knew our girls. We knew precisely what they were silently planning.

The very next second, both girls bolted.

"Three."

CHAPTER 18

AMARA

I grabbed Milana's hand and ran hell for leather for the stables.

Alfonso was in there.

He was loyal to a fault to Barone and his sons, but he had a soft spot for Milana and me.

Maybe we could persuade him to hold off Barone and Cesare until....

A powerful band wrapped around my middle and wrenched me backward.

Milana's hand was ripped from mine.

"No! Milana!" I screamed as I struggled against Barone's grip.

My hair fell over my face as I was flipped over his shoulder. I tried to push up against his back with one arm and shove the thick cascade of hair out of my face with the other so I could see what was happening, to no avail.

I could hear Milana cry out.

I called her name again, but it was cut off by the slamming of the villa door.

Barone carried me up the stairs to our bedroom.

My teeth jarred as he placed me on my feet and then stood before me, legs spread, arms crossed over his chest.

It was obvious... he was pissed.

But so was I.

I squared off in front of him, uncaring that I looked like an angry mouse shouting at a bull elephant. "Let me pass."

"No."

My brow furrowed as I raised my voice. I knew I was courting danger, but I didn't care. "Milana is the only family I have, and I will not let him hurt her!"

Barone's eyes narrowed. "Wrong on multiple counts."

I clutched at my stomach as tears coursed down my cheeks. "I can't do this."

Barone uncrossed his arms and took a step toward me. His voice was harsh and low as he bit out, "Exactly what can't you do, Amara?"

I backed up a few steps, fear and nerves twisting my insides even harder. "I'm so sorry. I love you, Barone. You know I love you, but I can't. Milana needs...."

Oh God. This wasn't happening. Fuck, this wasn't happening. I wasn't about to tell Barone I couldn't marry him. I started breathing in short, rapid gasps to try to force oxygen into my lungs. I didn't know what to do. I loved Barone with my whole heart. The idea of not marrying him, of possibly never seeing him again, physically made my heart ache.

But Milana was my family. True family. The kind you chose. The kind who always had your back, no matter what. I could never live with myself if I abandoned her. How could I call myself a friend if I chose a man over her, if I chose my own happiness over hers? Especially after she'd tried so hard to set aside her trauma and feelings of fear and hatred toward the Cavalieris, for my sake.

And look what it had gotten her.

The startling image of her running toward me, looking disheveled and traumatized, was shocking and disturbing. And now she was with Cesare, going through who knew what, probably living through an absolute nightmare. And it was my fault. All of this was my fault. If I had just stayed away from Barone, none of this would have ever happened.

I sniffed as the tears ran over my lips. "Milana needs me. I have to get her away from here." I swiped at my cheeks and mouth with the back of my hand before choking out, "I can't marry you."

Barone just stood there and stared at me.

The agonizing silence stretched, filling the room.

I stiffened my arms to try to stop my body from trembling. "Barone? Did you hear me? I can't marry you. I'm so sorry."

His wall of a chest expanded as he took a deep breath. Then, without saying a word, he turned and walked slowly toward the door.

I stared at his back before crying out and crumpling to the floor. Covering my face as grief more powerful than I could possibly have imagined ripped all the warmth and energy from my body with every step Barone took away from me. I knew in that moment that I would never, ever, feel whole again. It wouldn't just feel like a part of me was missing. That was too mundane and trite of a sentiment. No. It would feel like a part of my soul had been savagely ripped from my body only to be clawed and shredded to pieces before my eyes.

Through my gasping sobs, I heard the bedroom door close and knew, without having to look, that he was gone.

Then I heard the unmistakable sound of the door lock sliding into place.

Startled, I looked up.

Barone was standing in front of the locked bedroom door, unbuckling his leather belt as he kicked off his heavy work boots.

My vision was blurred from tears. I had to blink several times before I understood what I was seeing.

He whipped off his belt and set it aside, but still within reach. "First, Milana is *not* your only family. I am your family now. *We* are your family now."

He unbuttoned and shrugged out of the hunter green, cotton twill outer shirt he was wearing, the sleeves stained a deep purple from lifting crates filled with Montepulciano grapes he'd been sorting all day with his men. "Second, any fool can see that Milana loves Cesare. And my son certainly must love her, or he wouldn't be going through all this trouble to keep her."

I opened my mouth to object.

He raised an eyebrow as he tossed his shirt aside, leaving him in a long-sleeved oatmeal-colored thermal shirt. "I don't give a damn about what happened in their past. Whatever it was, *the two of them* will sort it out."

I rose on my knees. "He hurt her!"

Barone drew his thermal shirt over his head and tossed it

onto the floor next to the outer shirt. "I'm sure he did, just as I'm equally sure that Milana is going to make him pay for it. Figuratively *and* literally."

Dammit. Why did he always have to do this? Why did he always have to be the voice of calm, stupid reason? Why did he always have to sound so rational and smart... *and freaking right?*

If I looked past Milana's protestations and viewed her relationship with Cesare through a more objective eye, like Barone was, I could almost see what was happening as *foreplay*. I meant sure, Cesare was being a big bully and telling her she couldn't leave and all that, but Milana was the strongest, most resourceful person I knew. If she wanted to leave, truly wanted to leave, she would have found a way to leave.

Hell, knowing Milana, if she really hated Cesare as much as she claimed, I really wouldn't put it past her to be capable of killing the man in cold blood. Look how she'd attacked Barone when she thought he was attacking me. She seemed all pretty and glamorous, like she wouldn't lift a finger for fear of breaking a nail, but in reality, she could be straight up mafia at times.

Maybe Milana wasn't in danger after all.

Maybe I had overreacted.

Maybe I had allowed my fears for Milana and my anxiety about the big changes in my life with Barone to spin into a great big, out of control snowball of drama and doubt.

Maybe....

I looked up from my position on the floor.

Barone was a few steps away, looking like an angry Roman

god who had been forced down from Mount Olympus to deal with a stupid human.

He flicked open the top button of his jeans. "Now that we have my son and your friend's love life settled"—he raised an eyebrow— "what was that about you... not... marrying... me?"

I leaned back on my hands as I tried to slide backward on my ass. "I just meant that... well...."

He stalked toward me. "I think there has been some confusion, so let me clear a few things up for you."

He reached down and fisted his hand in my hair, pulling me to my feet and wrapping his other hand around my throat before walking me backward until the backs of my thighs hit the bed. "I'm not *asking* you to marry me."

He reached both hands into the collar of my blouse and wrenched downward, tearing off the buttons. I fell back onto the bed as my blouse hung in tatters, exposing my lace-covered breasts. Barone quickly followed, straddling my hips. He undid the remaining buttons on his jeans and pulled out his fully engorged cock. It looked thick and menacing as he wrapped his hand around the shaft and slowly, methodically, stroked it. "I'm *telling* you. You're marrying me."

I swallowed past the rising panic that was closing my throat.

He looked down at my prone form. "Lick your lips."

Without even a thought of disobeying him, I licked my lips.

"*Brava ragazza.* Now, open your mouth for daddy."

A fresh tear escaped from the corner of my eye as my

lower lip trembled. "Please, Barone. I'm sorry. I didn't mean to doubt you. To doubt us."

He caressed the side of my face as he brushed my hair back. "I know, baby. And I know taking my cock deep into your throat frightens you, but I need you to do this for me."

I nervously licked my lips again as I nodded. Sucking on his cock this way frightened me. He was just so big and strong and domineering.

Barone leaned in close. His dark gaze bore into mine, showing me how angry he still was at my outburst. "I need you to get my cock nice and wet, because the moment you do, I'm flipping you onto your stomach and fucking your little asshole raw so that you never, ever, try something like this again."

My vision flooded with tears.

Barone stroked my cheek. "Now open your mouth and take your punishment like a good girl."

I opened my mouth slightly but couldn't open it any further. Fear had paralyzed me.

Barone helped by clasping his hand under my jaw and pressing his thumb and fingertips into my cheeks, forcing my mouth open. The moment it did, he lifted his hips and pushed his thick cock past my lips. My tongue swirled around the turgid length as my shoulders jerked. He pushed in deeper. I gagged, my hands pushing against the tops of his thighs.

"Use your tongue, babygirl. Get me nice and wet."

I struggled to obey him. The edges of my teeth cut into the underside of my tongue, wedged as it was beneath his hard length. Spit oozed from the sides of my mouth as he thrust in and out.

Then, without warning, he shifted to the side and flipped me onto my stomach, pulling my hips up to raise me halfway onto my knees with my face still pressed into the bedcovers. He then pushed my skirt up over my hips and pulled my panties down.

I tried to quell the rising panic as my asshole puckered and tightened with anticipation of the pain of his brutal entry.

A wave of relief washed over me when I heard the bedside drawer open and felt a glob of sticky, cool gel slide between my ass cheeks. He would not fuck me without lubricant after all.

He pried my cheeks open as he growled, "That was the only mercy I'm going to show you, *dolcezza.*"

The head of his enormous cock pressed against my hole. Despite my resistance, he pushed forward past the tight band of muscle. There was a rush of painful pressure as he slid inside my tight passage.

"Ow! Ow!"

Barone spanked my right ass cheek. "Where's my cock?"

I whimpered.

"Where's my cock?"

"In my ass."

"Why?"

I moaned as he thrust in a few more inches.

"Why?"

"Because I was a bad girl."

He pulled back and then thrust in to the hilt.

I cried out as my body rocked forward and then back onto his cock.

Barone fisted my hair and pulled me up fully onto my

hands and knees. He thrust in and out of my ass several times. His balls slapped against the lower curve of my ass as he bottomed out each time.

"Oh God!" I moaned.

He spanked my ass again. "What do you say?"

"I'm sorry, daddy."

"Louder," he growled as he fucked my ass harder.

"I'm sorry, daddy," I cried out.

He reached under my hips and pushed his fingertips between my pussy lips. I was already embarrassingly slick. His fingertips teased my clit, swirling and flicking, until I thought I would go mad. I pushed back on his hips, needing the pleasurable pain, needing the fullness, needing the kink, needing him.

Barone knew just the right moment to pull my hair and spank my ass as he increased the pace of his thrusts before returning to pinch and flick my clit. I screamed his name as my thigh muscles clenched and my back arched with my release. It was so intense, sparks and stars swam before my eyes as I deprived my body of oxygen by forgetting to breathe.

I collapsed forward onto the bed.

Barone's muscular forearms were braced on either side of my head as he continued to thrust several more times before spilling his hot come deep inside my ass. He stayed buried to the hilt inside of me for several heartbeats before pulling free and falling to the side. He wrapped his arm around my waist and pulled me into his chest as he kissed the top of my head.

I spread my hand over his heart, taking solace in its strong, rapid beat.

After several minutes, when we had each gotten our breath back, Barone placed a finger under my chin and lifted my head up to meet his intense gaze. "Tell me you didn't mean it."

I could see the hurt in his eyes.

I reached up to cup his cheek. "I didn't mean it. I love you."

He covered my hand with his own and shifted his face to kiss the center of my palm. "Say it again."

"I love you."

"Again."

"I love you."

He tightened his arms around me. "Never scare me like that again, *dolcezza*."

A frisson of fear spiked through my heart. "I won't. I promise."

He pressed his lips to my forehead. "You need to understand, babygirl. It's not just that I love you. It's this constant raw, aching need to be with you, to protect you, shelter you, to provide for you. Now that you are in my life, there is not a moment, a second, a heartbeat, that I'm not concerned about your welfare and happiness. At times, it is all I can do to allow you out of my sight."

He then rolled on top of me. Bracing his forearms on either side of my head, he gazed down at me. "I frighten even myself to think what I would be capable of, if something should ever happen to you, or if... you should ever seriously try to leave me."

My heart was beating so fast, I could feel it in the back of my throat. I needed to accept that loving a man like Barone Cavalieri came with certain conditions. One of them was, no matter how good his intentions, no matter how loving his words, there would always be an almost sinister edge to everything he said and did. It was inevitable. I could never take something a man with his amount of power and money said lightly. "Nothing is going to happen to me, Barone."

He kissed the edge of my mouth. "And you are going to be a good girl and marry me."

I closed my eyes as he kissed the underside of my jaw. "And I will be a good girl and marry you," I moaned, as I repeated his words.

The man may terrify me, and I may have doubts, and Milana may be right about him being overly controlling, but he was also passionate, loving, protective, supportive, and caring. I'd never felt safer or more loved in my entire life than I had in the time I'd known Barone. When I told him I couldn't marry him, the grief I felt was so instantaneous and overwhelming, I truly thought I might die from it.

For better or worse, I loved him.

My eyes sprang open. I tapped on his chest with my finger. "Wait. This better not count as your marriage proposal."

CHAPTER 19

MILANA

Cesare wrenched my hand from Amara's.

I turned, swinging my fisted hand in an arch. I missed.

Cesare snatched me around the waist and lifted me off the ground. I cried out as I clawed at his forearm. It was no use. His grip was like iron. Anchoring me to his side, he carried me across the drive and down the path to his house. The moment we were inside and he let me go, I turned on him.

"You've gone too far this time, Cesare."

Without saying a word, he wrapped his hand around my upper arm and dragged me down the hallway leading to the bedrooms.

The moment we passed the spare bedroom, I dug my heels in. "Don't you dare take me to your bedroom, Cesare!"

Even though I'd had the place to myself this morning, I'd resisted the dark, magnetic pull of his bedroom despite knowing it was just a little further down the hall from mine. I had this insane fantasy that the moment I crossed the threshold, iron bars would suddenly slam down, trapping me inside for all eternity, like a princess from a cautionary fairy tale.

He pulled me into the darkened room.

I jerked out of his grasp and backed away as I searched the room for an exit. It was no surprise that a massive king-size, four-poster bed dominated the room. What was a surprise were the bookshelves lining the walls on either side of it. They ran from floor to ceiling and covered most of the walls, making the room feel more like a library than a bedroom. And like in his living room, the shelves were crammed with books stacked horizontally over vertically lined volumes sharing space with loose papers, sculptures, ceramics, and picture frames. These were not ornamental bookshelves meant for show.

Cesare flipped on the light and took several steps toward me.

I backed away.

His brow lowered as his chin dipped toward his chest, like a bull getting ready to charge.

The only exit was behind him through the door we came in.

Keeping my glare on him, I reached down and took off my heels and tossed them aside.

He raised an eyebrow.

I knew what he was thinking.

He was wrong.

I ran toward the bed to gain momentum. Reaching for the lower bedpost, I grasped it and used it to swing myself over the footboard and onto the mattress. My plan was to run to the top of the mattress and jump down, landing behind Cesare and right in front of the bedroom door.

It was a good plan.

The problem was, I hadn't factored in how years of working in the fields with his father had made Cesare incredibly strong and athletic beyond the typical businessman.

He launched himself onto the bed, tackling me.

We rolled until I was pinned under him.

He stretched my arms over my head as he easily secured my wrists in one hand. "Are you going to stop struggling and be a good girl, or do I need to tie you up?"

"Che due coglioni!"

He pulled on his tie. "Is that a no?"

I stilled. "Fine, but if you think we are having sex again, you are out of your mind."

The corners of his eyes crinkled as he smiled down at me. He leaned in and kissed the tip of my nose. "You are adorable when you're wrong, but that isn't the reason I brought you in here... for now."

He released my wrists and pushed off the bed. He shrugged out of his coat and tossed it over a nearby chair.

I sat up and rested my back against the headboard. "What are you doing?"

He raised up one palm as he loosened his tie before pulling it over his head. "Just getting more comfortable. You know how much I hate these fucking suits."

I hated the familiarity of that statement, even more so because I knew it was true. Despite running the family's property management interests, Cesare would have preferred to be among the vines and working outside with his hands in the soil all day. He had been that way when we were younger, too. Always hating being cooped up inside during school hours.

I narrowed my eyes. "I guess that's the curse of having gobs and gobs of family money. Sometimes you have to make *great sacrifices* for the common good."

He had undone the first few buttons of his dress shirt and pulled it over his head. He now reached for his belt. My cheeks warmed as I held my breath. Noticing my reaction, he issued a warning in a dark, seductively teasing voice as he pulled his belt through the loops and folded it between his hands. "Behave."

I didn't breathe again until he set it aside. As he did so, he walked over to the first bookshelf to the right of the bed. He picked up a picture frame and handed it to me.

I stared down at the image.

The mattress dipped as Cesare sat on the edge near me, but I didn't look up. I just kept staring at the framed photograph.

My fingertips reached out to trace the simple black frame as if to reassure myself it was real.

I hadn't known he had this photograph, let alone had it framed and displayed in a place of honor by his bed.

I continued to stare at the image, not sure what to think.

Cesare's voice broke into my thoughts. "Do you remember when it was taken?"

I nodded before clearing my throat. "The Feast of the Epiphany at the *La Befana* festival."

It had always been one of my favorite times of the year. When the entire village was strung with holiday lights and filled with music and festivities. On the night of the festival, the children of the village would hang stockings around the piazza in the hopes *La Befana*, The Witch, would bring them sweets or a toy. In our village, *La Befana* was actually the Cavalieri family, who paid for the local shops to provide candies and toys for the children as well as all the entertainment and food for the villagers on the night of the festival.

The night this photograph had been taken, we were seventeen. Cesare, Enzo, and a few of their friends had escorted Amara, me, and some of our friends to the festival. I remembered getting Cesare a piece of *carbone* candy, teasing him that *La Befana* was leaving him only coal because she knew he had cheated off one of my exams.

He had retaliated by pulling me onto his lap and pushing a piece of traditional *panettone* cake he had been eating into my mouth, like grooms do to brides after cutting the wedding cake. I had grabbed another of the powdered sugar-sprinkled pieces and done the same to him. We had both broken out into hysterics.

Amara had snapped a photo of us at that precise moment. I hadn't seen it in years.

In the photo, my head was tipped back and my mouth was open on a laugh, a piece of cake on my tongue. My lips and the tip of my nose were covered in white powdered sugar. Cesare's head was dipped near mine. His right cheek was smeared with powdered sugar from where I'd missed his mouth. He too was laughing as he gazed at me with what could only be....

I looked up.

Cesare was watching me intently.

I looked back down at the photograph as my heart raced and my hands trembled.

Love.

It was love.

He was looking at me with love.

Unmistakable love.

Something was wrong. This didn't make sense. Only a few months later, he'd orchestrated the attack that would send a very clear message about just how little I truly meant to him. Fuck. Fuck. Fuck. This wasn't the first sign in the last few days that I might have gotten this entire thing wrong.

I looked back at Cesare. "How did you get this photo?"

"I asked Amara for a copy the night she took it."

"And you've kept it all this time?"

His gaze remained on me as he nodded slowly, as if he were studying my every movement, my every reaction.

"Why? Why are you showing me this?"

Cesare took the frame from my hands and looked down at the picture. "There is no denying that you are a stunningly beautiful woman, Milana, and I am personally looking forward to spoiling you rotten with more dresses, purses, and shoes than you could possibly wear in a lifetime, but...."

He handed the frame back to me and gestured toward it. "This is how I see you. This is how I will always remember you. *This is my favorite version of you.* You, in my arms, laughing with abandon. In this moment, your makeup isn't perfect. Your hair was still super long back then and you have it up in a messy thing on the top of your head. You have powdered sugar all over your face and half-chewed food in your mouth. And to me, in that moment, you couldn't have looked more beautiful."

He reached out and cupped my cheek. "I fucked up. Again. I can't seem to get things right with you. I will not deny that you deserve better than a half-assed engagement announcement, but I will deny to my dying breath all that bullshit that horrible woman fed you growing up. Milana, you are not trash, far from it. You are the most amazingly unique, exquisite, treasure of a woman I've ever known. And you don't need makeup or designer clothes for that. Just you... and the most beautiful laugh I've ever heard. One that I hope to hear again one day."

I swallowed past the lump in my throat as I averted my gaze, breaking the distracting contact of his hand.

Cesare sighed.

He rose off the bed and left the room without another word.

I barely noticed.

I just kept staring at the photo through blurry eyes. I was so tired and confused. I just wanted to curl up in a ball and cry as I stared at the girl I used to be... the *before* me... wondering what could have been... if there hadn't been an *after* me.

Cesare returned several minutes later. He gently took the frame from my loose grip.

Cupping my shoulders, he lifted me off the bed to stand before him. My eyes half closed with exhaustion. Despite it only being late afternoon, I swayed on my feet. He pulled the wrinkled and ruined Valentino dress over my head.

I whimpered and crossed my arms over my breasts.

"Shhh, babygirl. Let me take care of you." He reached around and unhooked my bra. After pulling it off me, he gently took my wrists and raised my arms. My eyes closed as I was engulfed in soft, cozy fabric.

I looked down to see I was wearing one of his old football jerseys. It was so worn, the lettering on the front was hard to read. "I have my own clothes, you know."

His voice sounded far away as he leaned in to whisper against my ear, "Yes, but I prefer you in mine."

He wrapped a steadying arm around my waist as he leaned to the side and pulled his bedcover back. He then lifted me in his arms and placed me between the duvet and the sheet. It felt so safe and warm, I didn't have the strength to object. I nestled my head down on his pillow. I could smell the scent of fresh laundry mixed with that of his cologne.

The last thing I was aware of before falling into an exhausted sleep was Cesare turning on a nearby floor lamp and opening the window across from the bed.

CHAPTER 20

CESARE

I leaned against the headboard and read while Milana slept. I didn't want her to awaken in the middle of one of her night terrors alone in a strange bed. Through my research on the subject, I had learned it could make the situation worse.

I had to resist the urge to touch her.

She looked so small and vulnerable curled up next to me. I just wanted to surround her with my body and protect her from everything. The problem was, I couldn't protect her from the past.

It was clear from the things she let slip earlier today that someone, whether it was an asshole from school or perhaps her own grandmother, had gotten it into her head back when we were in school that she wasn't good enough to date a Cavalieri. If I ever found out it was one of our old classmates, I didn't give a damn that it was seven years ago, I would ruin their life just for the pain they had caused my girl.

I was close, though.

I could feel it.

She was second-guessing her conclusions about the past. Slowly, she was beginning to trust me again. I just needed more time with her. Time—it was my ally and my enemy.

Milana stirred.

She let out a sweet little moan as she lifted her head and blinked up at me like a little puppy waking from a nap.

Unable to hold back any longer, I caressed her silky, tousled locks back from her face. "Did you have a nice nap, little one?"

She frowned as she looked at the darkened sky outside. "How long have I been asleep?"

I closed my book and rested it on my lap. "A few hours."

She sat up and pulled the duvet protectively over her chest, despite wearing one of my jerseys which, regrettably, completely covered her luscious breasts. "And have you been here the whole time?"

"Yes."

She bit her lip as her fingers curled into the edge of the duvet.

I knew what she was thinking. "You didn't have one," I reassured her.

From my reading, I had learned that times of high stress could particularly bring on night terrors. I also learned that it wasn't uncommon for the person to have one and not recall it, hence Milana's anxious demeanor. She was worried she had lost control of the situation and had no memory of it.

The tension in her shoulders visibly relaxed. Knowing she'd rather walk over hot coals than talk to me about her night terrors, since that could lead to questions regarding their source and I knew she wasn't ready to talk to me about that yet, I stood and said, "Are you hungry? How about something to eat?"

She hesitated.

"It's just food, babygirl." I threw the bedcover aside. "Come on. You haven't eaten all day."

She let out a long, dramatic sigh. "I guess so."

I resisted the urge to roll my eyes. Damn, nothing was easy with this woman. She really was making me work for every inch of battleground I won. The stubborn little minx.

She got out of bed and followed me into the kitchen, where we surveyed the contents of the refrigerator and pantry together.

"How about *pizza senza crosta?*" I offered. "We could make it over the fire pit outside."

She nodded.

She gathered up the ingredients, dropping them into a woven basket as I searched for the flat, cast-iron pan and metal grill basket in the cabinets. I took the ingredients from her and called over my shoulder as I headed for the veranda, "Get the glasses and the bottle of *Franciacorta Bellavista* out of the wine cooler."

The moment I saw her heading outside with the bottle and glasses, my mouth dropped open. "*Madonna santa!* What are you doing out here half naked?"

"You said to bring the bottle and glasses!"

"I said to get them out of the cooler, not to come out here practically in the middle of winter in a jersey and bare feet!" I picked her up and carried her back into the house, muttering under my breath about how she was going to catch her death and how she couldn't be relied upon to take decent care of herself. After tossing her into the center of my bed, I stormed into the dressing room and returned with a pair of her yoga pants. "Put these on."

I left and returned again, holding a pair of my white athletic socks. I went down on my knees before her and grabbed one of her ankles.

"Wait! I have my own socks!"

I looked up at her. "Yes, but I like you wearing my socks."

It was silly, of course. My socks stretched all the way up her calves under her yoga pants, but I didn't care.

I then left a third time and returned with one of my large hoodies.

"What's that?"

"Arms up. No arguments."

With a sigh, she raised her arms. I pulled the hoodie over her head. It might as well have been a blanket on her, it was so big.

She pulled out the front and looked down. It said *Cavalieri Wines*. She smirked. "You did this on purpose."

I winked. "My name looks good on you."

"Don't start. I'm hungry."

I lifted her back into my arms and carried her through the house.

"I can walk, you know."

"Stop arguing."

I carried her outside to the fire pit, which was placed just to the side of the cabana in front of the grotto pool. I lit the fire with ease, placed the cast-iron skillet on the flames, and poured a mason jar of *salsa di pomodoro* into it. While she used the peppermill to crack Tellicherry black peppercorns over the mixture, I sprinkled some sea salt over it then added several sprigs of basil. As we waited for the sauce to bubble, I brushed several slices of ciabatta with garlic and arranged them in the grill basket, setting it over the open flame to make crostini.

I popped open the chilled bottle of *Franciacorta Bellavista* and poured two glasses as she snuggled into the faux fur blankets on the cabana mattress. I handed her a glass before turning my attention back to the simmering sauce. I added the *mozzarella di bufala* and covered the pan to let it melt. I then flipped the ciabatta grilling basket to char the other side of the bread slices before leaning back into the cabana with my glass of sparkling wine.

We clinked glasses and sipped as we stared out over the neat rows of twisted, naked vines and trampled soil that was the Cavalieri vineyard after the harvest.

I took another sip and savored the crisp, floral pear notes as I listened to the crack and pop of the fire and the gentle buzz of the nearby insects.

I pulled the cast-iron skillet from the flame and opened the grilling basket, transferring the warmed slices of ciabatta bread to the edges of the skillet. Using the edge of one slice of bread, I pushed some gooey mozzarella, tomato sauce, and basil onto a crostini and handed it to her.

She took a bite and moaned.

I gave her a knowing look. "Don't start. *I'm hungry.*" Giving her own words back to her as a double entendre.

Just to tease me, she took another bite and let out another exaggerated, porn star-worthy moan.

I pounced, knocking her backward, deeper into the cabana.

She laughed as she spilled her wine. "Stop! I'm getting wine everywhere!"

I leaned up, caging her in with my forearms, and stared down at her in awe.

She laughed again. "What?"

I smiled. "There it is."

Her brow wrinkled. "There what is?"

I leaned my forehead against hers. "Your laugh. I missed it."

* * *

"No."

"This is not up for debate, Milana."

"This was not part of our deal."

"Fuck the deal."

"There is a perfectly fine bedroom down the hall."

I raised my arm above her head and pointed to my bedroom door from where we were standing in the narrow hallway. "You're sleeping in there... with me... and that's final."

"Don't I get a say in this?"

"No."

"I'm not having sex with you!"

"Fine."

"What?"

"Fine."

She threw her arms up in frustration. "Then why are we arguing? Just let me sleep in the spare bedroom, like you agreed in our deal."

I placed my hand against her lower back, pulled her flush against my front, and then lifted her chin up so I had her full attention. "I am capable of sleeping next to a woman and not fucking her. I know you'll probably find that hard to believe given my reputation with other women in the village...."

"And Rome... Milan... probably Paris, London, Brussels...."

I gave her ass a quick spank. "In my defense," I said over the droning cadence of her voice listing all the major cities in Europe, "none of those women were you."

Her mouth dropped open as her brow furrowed. She placed her hands on her hips. "So you're saying you don't want to fuck me? Wait. You'll fuck anything that moves, but suddenly I'm not good enough for you? *Not fuckable enough for you?* Because I have news for you, Cesare Cavalieri. Just because I was a virgin doesn't mean that I didn't have *plenty of offers* from men who wanted to fu—"

I wrapped my hands around her middle, lifted her off the floor, and took two steps forward to slam her back against the wall. Pressing my cock into her hips, I wrapped my hand around her throat and ground out through clenched teeth, "Don't say another fucking word," before claiming her mouth.

I shoved my tongue between her lips. Tasting the sweet, sparkling wine from earlier only slightly cooled my anger at her daring to mention other men in my presence. I had to remind myself that she was mine. That I had claimed her, not them. It was the only thing saving me from flipping her around, shoving her pants down, and fucking her hard against the wall to remind her who owned her now.

When I released her mouth, her lips were bruised and swollen. The delicate skin on her cheeks and chin was chafed from my beard, and she was breathless, with a glazed, unfocused gaze. She looked beautiful.

I propped my forearm over her head and leaned in. "I want you to listen very carefully, *carissima*. If you ever make the mistake of taunting me with the idea of the other men who wanted you before me, I will make you write their names down and then watch as I take great pleasure in ruining their lives, one by one."

She stared at me wide-eyed and slowly nodded.

Knowing she understood my words were not an idle threat, I continued. "I never said you were not fuckable. I consider it a matter of great self-restraint that I permit you to wear clothes and leave this house. If it were truly up to me, you would do nothing all day but stay in bed naked, waiting for me."

She opened her mouth to object.

I placed a finger over her full lips. "Don't."

She subsided.

I moved my hand to cup her jaw. "What makes you the rarest, most unparalleled, exquisite creature I have ever met is there is more than just the fleeting pleasure to be found between your pretty thighs in bed. There is the pleasure of holding your warm body close to mine, knowing that while in my arms, you will be protected and safe throughout the night. There is the soft feel of your breath on my skin as you nestle against my shoulder. There is being there when you open these gorgeous dark eyes of yours in the morning. So, while I am looking forward to the moment your sweet lips moan as I sink my cock deep inside your pussy again, it is definitely not the only reason I want you in my bed, close to me, tonight."

She averted her gaze. "What if I...."

Knowing she was weakening, I pressed my advantage. I lifted her into my arms and carried her into my bedroom. "If you have a nightmare, then I will be there to hold you and make you feel safe again. And maybe this time, things will be different. Maybe this time, I won't be the monster in them."

CHAPTER 21

MILANA

I awoke alone.

I ran my hand over the indentation in the pillow next to mine. It was cold. I leaned back and sighed.

This shouldn't be happening.

None of this should be happening.

I shouldn't have been able to fall asleep in Cesare's arms last night.

I shouldn't be waking up with a sinking disappointment that he's not here.

I shouldn't be having doubts about his involvement seven years ago.

Yesterday morning I'd been certain of two things: that I hated Cesare Cavalieri and that I was leaving at the end of the week.

This morning?

I was certain of nothing.

I turned my head to check the clock. A cup was waiting on

the nightstand with a note propped up next to it. The cup was still warm as I wrapped my hand around it. It was a latte macchiato. I picked up the note.

FROM NOW ON, you get these from me.
    Alfonso will drive you in when you are ready.
    Don't worry about yesterday's announcement. I will fix it.
    See you soon.
    - C
    P.S. Don't try not coming in. I'll find you.

I CRUMPLED the note up in my hand and tossed it onto the nightstand. Because I didn't know what else to do, I headed into the dressing room and got ready for work. I put Tori Amos's *Little Earthquakes* on my phone as I dressed.

Not wanting to take any chances, I chose a secondhand Gucci black and ivory A-line tweed skirt with the GG jacquard pattern that reached just above my knees, paired with black knee-high boots and a simple black V-neck sweater. Just in case, I bent over in front of the mirror to make sure not even a hint of my bra or cleavage showed. After looking for my knockoff black alligator Gucci purse then remembering it was already at the office, I headed out toward the stables to find Alfonso.

Taking a deep breath, I schooled my features into my best resting bitch face as I approached the receptionist's desk. Not that I had anything against Liliana, I just didn't know what to expect after Cesare's announcement yesterday and his note today.

Liliana smiled. *"Buongiorno,* Milana. Here are your messages. There are a few memos from Luigi on your desk for your review. Mr. Cavalieri is in his office, but he told me to tell you he has a meeting this afternoon with a Mr. Romolo Castiglione and would like you to join them in the conference room when he arrives, to discuss that report you did on his project."

Romolo Castiglione. The name sounded vaguely familiar, but then again, every name in this village was vaguely familiar.

I took the messages from Liliana. "Thank you." I paused, trying to read her expression for any sign of a hidden meaning, but there was none.

She raised both her eyebrows. "Is there something else I can do for you? Do you need something copied? I'm happy to help! I want to be as useful as possible."

I held up a hand. "No, thank you. Nothing right now."

I stared past her into the open area of the office where people sat at their desks. Everything seemed strangely normal. There was the occasional ring of a phone, the tap of a keyboard, the squeak of a rubber sole on the ancient marble floor. Inhaling a deep breath to ease the lightheaded, queasy feeling in my head and limbs, I took several faltering steps forward. I half expected to hear a record scratch and for everything to stop as everyone suddenly looked up and stared

189

like they did in the movies, but nothing happened. Nothing. Not only did no one approach me, no one seemed to even be weirdly avoiding eye contact with me.

What the hell had Cesare said to them this morning?

Part of me wanted to ask, and part of me would rather be forced to wear polyester neon jumpsuits from the seventies for the rest of my life than ask.

Pasting a smile on my face, I headed to my desk. Locating the memos, I sat down and got to work. This would be my saving grace. My solace. No matter what anyone said, I knew I was good at this job. Damn good. It took a special skill to navigate all the red tape of Italy's bureaucratic and more than a little corrupt property and building permitting system, and I seemed to have a knack for it.

It wasn't glamorous work, but it was satisfying. It was like playing monopoly with someone else's money. I liked to imagine all the properties like a big game board that I was circling around as I helped drop hotels, high-rises, and housing developments on it. It was exciting to think about one day visiting one of these projects and seeing all the businesses and families and knowing that I helped make it happen.

I had lost myself in my work, so it was hours later when I heard some movement up at the front desk. Mr. Romolo Castiglione must have arrived. Cesare would come down from his office any second now. I tightened my stomach muscles to kill the butterflies and reached for the Tuscany files to make sure that everything was precisely in order.

As I stood and smoothed my skirt, Cesare appeared on the

partially hidden staircase at the side of the room. His gaze zeroed in on me.

Time slowed.

Gone was the easy-going, denim and T-shirt Cesare. He was back to being the Cavalieri tycoon billionaire with slicked-back hair and a bespoke suit that probably cost more than my entire wardrobe.

He crossed the room in long, slow strides as he buttoned his suit coat, all the while keeping his intense, dark gaze on me as a warning. I was afraid to open my mouth to breathe for fear he would suck the oxygen straight from my lungs. I could practically hear his voice growling, "behave, babygirl," in my ear. Extremely graphic visions of what he was capable of doing if I didn't behave flashed across my mind, warming my cheeks. The corners of his eyes crinkled as his mouth lifted in the barest hint of a smirk, like he had read my mind, damn him, and knew precisely what I was remembering.

It was only after he broke eye contact that I felt the blood moving in my veins again.

Che diavolo!

I grabbed the files with shaking hands and snapped them together against the desktop with more force than was necessary. I could do this. I could definitely do this. I could sit in a conference room across from Cesare like a professional and not imagine his face between my thighs.

Oh God, I was screwed.

I pounded the already neat stack of files into order again. It was fine. Everything was going to be fine.

Out of the corner of my eye, I saw Cesare reach the reception area. "Romolo, how have you been, my friend?" He grabbed Romolo by the hand and shook it, slapping him affectionately on the back.

"I have been good. It has been too long since we have seen one another. I'm looking forward to doing business together," answered Romolo.

And my entire world shattered.

I shook so violently I had to grab onto the edge of my desk to remain standing.

That voice.

I knew that voice.

I never knew their names.

Never saw their faces.

But I would never forget their voices.

And this was one of them.

One of the boys who'd attacked me seven years ago.

One of the boys who'd attacked me at Cesare's bidding.

To teach me a lesson.

I couldn't look up.

I froze.

Bitter bile burned the back of my throat.

"The cap rate appraisal regarding the potential of the property in question is troubling. I'm not sure if it's an investment worth the Cavalieri name. Follow me into the conference room so we can discuss it in private," said Cesare.

Romolo laughed. "Same old Cesare. Just like back in school. Always worried about the Cavalieri name."

Cesare slapped him on the back again as he threw his head back and laughed. "Of course. I have to protect the Cavalieri name at all costs. You know that."

As they crossed into the glass-walled conference room, I

fell into my desk chair and bent below my desk to dry heave into my wastebasket. I opened my desk drawer and grabbed my purse, heading straight for the door.

Luigi stepped in front of me.

I tried to move around him.

He held up his hand. "Where are you going? Cesare wants us in the conference room. Do you have the files?"

I tried again to step around him. "I have to go."

"What? You can't. We have the meeting. Are you okay?"

Fuck. He was drawing attention to us. I looked in the direction of the conference room, where Cesare was staring at us with a frown on his face. The walls wobbled and swayed. I needed to get out of here.

I licked my lips. "The files are on my desk. I just need to go to the powder room. I'll be right in."

Luigi laughed. "Milana, your lipstick looks perfect. Come on, Cesare's waiting." He tried to take my elbow to escort me into the conference room.

I pulled away and shouted louder than I intended. "Get off me!" This time the entire office stopped as if there actually was a record-scratch moment. I laughed, the sound high-pitched and hollow. "Sorry, I just really need to pee."

Without waiting to see his reaction, or checking to see if Cesare noticed the drama, I practically ran out of the office and down the building stairs. I didn't take a full breath until I reached the piazza.

In a panic, I looked from left to right, uncertain of what to do next or where to go.

As if drawn by a hidden thread, I looked up in time to see Cesare at the window of the conference room, staring down at me. Even from that great height, I could feel his anger.

Fuck him.

He lied to me.

It was all just a big con.

And I had almost fallen for it.

Loud blasts of a train whistle filled the air.

The late afternoon train.

Without giving it a second thought, I raced across the piazza to the *Cavalieri Porta Nuova* train station.

I bolted up to the *biglietteria* counter and breathlessly asked for a ticket. I didn't care where the train was going as long as it was leaving the village, and one particular Cavalieri, behind. The moment the man handed me the paper ticket through the window, I ran straight onto the train.

Navigating down the narrow aisles, I crossed over several cars until I got to the front carriages where the private compartments were. I slid open the last compartment door, grateful to see it was empty as I let the door close behind me. I fell onto the padded bench just as the train churned into motion.

I tossed my purse onto the seat beside me and bent in half, cupping my face in my hands. Before I could give in to tears, the train slowed.

Oh God.

It can't be.

I sprang up from my seat and cautiously looked through the window, not daring to lower it and poke my head out. I could see only partially down the platform, but everything looked quiet and still. The train station had been mostly empty since, with the grape harvest over, most of the tourists had left.

After another minute, the train began moving at full speed.

I sat down and closed my eyes.

I was... broken.

I hugged my arms around my middle. Everything hurt. I just wanted to curl up into a tight ball and make all the pain go away. It wasn't fair. I hated people who said that, but it was true. It wasn't fucking fair. I didn't ask for any of this. Why did he have to come after me? Why hurt me? What pleasure did he get from being so cruel?

Just when I was starting to believe...

My thoughts were interrupted by a shout inside the carriage and the slamming of a door.

Then the slamming of another door.

Then another.

And another.

Oh God.

I stood and spun in a circle.

Of course, there was no place to run. I was trapped inside of the small train compartment.

Another shout.

Another slamming door.

It was him.

It had to be.

Cesare was on the train.

Fuck. Fuck. Fuck!

The compartment door next to mine slid open, then slammed shut with a deafening bang.

There was a long pause.

Like a rabbit caught in a snare, I stood frozen in the center of the compartment, staring at the closed door... willing it not to open.

The metal door latch rattled....

CHAPTER 22

CESARE

*M*y hand shook as I reached for the door of the final compartment. If she wasn't behind this door, I was going to lose my fucking mind.

I knew something was off when I saw her body language as she interacted with Luigi, but I had stupidly assumed the damn fool had ignored my order to not mention our engagement and upset her.

It wasn't until a visibly nervous Liliana had interrupted my meeting with Romolo that I knew something was truly wrong. It was obvious I intimidated Liliana, especially with her being a new employee. She could barely get the words out. Her teeth were chattering badly, but she was too concerned for Milana to not approach me. Brave girl.

I had raced over to the conference room window in time to see Milana standing in the middle of the piazza, looking pale and terrified. It was only the sound of the train whistle and the sharp turn of her head that had clued me in to her probable destination.

She was running.

By the time I reached the platform, the train was accelerating to reach full speed as it pulled out. Thankfully, being an arrogant Cavalieri heir with the power to have a man killed with no questions asked had its privileges. The train was slowed down enough for me to run alongside and jump on.

I had now searched every fucking compartment on the train except this one.

If she wasn't in this one, I had guessed wrong and wasted precious time in stopping her escape from me.

I forced the door open.

I threw my head back and sucked air into my lungs before blowing it out in a fierce growl as I viewed Milana standing frozen in the center of the compartment.

Rage and relief raced in equal measure through the adrenaline-elevated blood pumping through my veins.

I slammed the door shut behind me.

Neither of us said a word.

The only sound was our mingled, harsh breathing.

Mine from anger.

Hers from fear and panic.

I had ripped off my suit jacket in my pursuit of her. Now I pulled at my tie, which was like a noose around my neck. I yanked the silk length free, holding it between my hands and wrapping the narrow end slowly around my right fist. "Start talking."

Milana's gaze fixated on my silk tie. "I don't owe you an explanation."

"The fuck you don't, Milana. I thought we had finally gotten past this bullshit."

She swiped at her cheeks. "You mean you thought you finally had me fooled? Again."

I realized with a start she had been crying. Alarmed, I stepped forward, reaching for her.

She stumbled backward, one fist raised in defense. Her eyes were wide and wary.

My chest tightened. Every nerve in my body seemed to go on high alert as the thump of my heart beating a manic cadence in my ears matched the whir and spin of the metal train wheels on the track. This wasn't one of our usual fights, where the give and take was rife with a sexual tension that I knew secretly thrilled and challenged us both.

This is different.

Dangerous.

I switched tactics.

Lowering and softening my voice, as if calming a startled bird, I said, "Babygirl, you need to tell me what happened—right now."

She sniffed as she jutted out her chin. "Why don't you ask your *good friend Romolo* what happened?"

My brow furrowed. Romolo? What the fuck did that asshole have to do with anything? "Baby, I don't understand. Did that asshole insult you in some way today? Because we'll go straight back to the office and tell him to fuck off. I won't do business with anyone who insults you or makes you uncomfortable. You have to know that. You didn't have to run off like this. You could have just come to me."

She shook her head as she crossed her arms over her

middle. "I'm not falling for it, Cesare. You know damn well I'm not talking about today." Her voice rose as she flung her arm out and pointed back in the village's direction. "Don't act like you don't know he's one of the *pieces of shit* who attacked me seven years ago."

The incandescent rage I felt in that moment was so overwhelming, my vision blurred for a moment. There was a sharp pain between my shoulder blades as I jerked forward, intending to pull her into my arms, but I drew back at the last second at seeing the disgusted horror in her eyes. Feeling like a caged animal, I spun in a circle, flinging my head back and howling before I threw my right arm back and punched the train compartment door three times in succession. But the splintering of the wood and the pain in my hand did nothing to ease the crushing despair and fury I felt at her accusation.

Yesterday I had convinced myself that her trauma had only been caused by hateful words. I hadn't allowed myself to imagine it could have been something so horrific as a physical attack... one she thought I had played a part in.

Through a distant fog of wrath, I could hear Milana's screams.

The door slid open, and a terrified rail worker faced me.

"Get out," I raged.

The man ran off.

I slammed the broken door shut again and turned to Milana.

Tears were streaming down her cheeks. "Oh God, you really didn't know?"

I fell to my knees before her and wrapped my arms

around her hips. Overcome with relief that she was now realizing that I wasn't capable of treating her with such sadistic cruelty, I was simultaneously almost paralyzed with guilt that I hadn't been there to protect her when she'd needed me most. Never again.

Her body collapsed, folding on top of me. I grabbed her tightly and, lifting her into my arms, sat on the bench and held her close. For several minutes, I just held her, rocking back and forth. I had to school myself not to squeeze her too tightly because, in that moment, I wanted to press her inside my chest, where she would forever be safe and protected.

I pressed my lips to the top of her head. My voice was hoarse as I spoke. "You need to tell me everything, baby."

She whimpered and shook her head.

I stroked my palm against her temple and soothed her. "Shhh… I promise with every drop of blood in my body that I had absolutely nothing—nothing—to do with any attack on you. I know it's hard. And I know this hurts, but I need to know what happened…."

She looked up at me.

Her beautiful eyes were filled with such pain, I wanted to howl with rage all over again.

"I should have come to you when it first happened, but I let my stupid pride get in the way, and I allowed them to convince me you were involved."

I cupped her cheek. "You believe me now when I say I wasn't involved?"

She nodded.

I let out the breath I'd been holding and leaned forward to

kiss her forehead. "Thank you for that. Now I need you to tell me everything you remember about who was involved."

She pulled away and got off my lap. "You once told me that the past was the past and I should move on. I realize now that you were right. Nothing good can come of dredging all of this up now. So let's just let it go and move on."

I wanted to pull her back into my embrace but resisted. I stood and faced her as I rubbed my hand over my face. Apparently, she didn't understand how this was going to work moving forward. I lowered my brow and chose my next words carefully. "Milana, you can't think that I'm going to allow these men to live?"

She blinked up at me. "You mean... not allow them to live in the village like how Barone chased away Amara's stepfather and stepbrother, right?"

It would make things so much easier on multiple fronts to let her believe that lie, but there had already been enough doubt and miscommunication between us. I crossed my arms over my chest and stared down at her. "No. That's not what I mean."

She sucked in a shocked breath. "Cesare, look, they... hurt me... but they didn't *hurt me*. You're talking about cold-blooded murder."

I placed a hand under her chin and lifted her head. "If I know *la mia piccola gattina selvaggia*, it is because you fought back, not for lack of trying on their part. The moment they laid a hand on you, they sealed their fate. And while they can thank God for a few extra years on this earth, the devil's justice is coming. This is not up for discussion, babygirl. It's very simple. They hurt you. And now they're going to pay for it."

She paced the small confines of the compartment. "You're doing it again. Just taking control and coming up with a solution without bothering to ask my opinion."

I ran a hand through my hair as I turned my back on her to quell my anger. I watched the bare hills and valleys of the Italian countryside race by through the narrow train window, devoid of its usual flares of emerald greens and warm golds as winter approached. The bleak vista reminded me of how my girl was forced to sleep with a window open, no matter the temperature outside, because she was too afraid of enclosed spaces, because of whatever those bastards had done.

No, non ci sarebbe pietà.

I turned back to Milana. "This is no longer your concern. We will head back to Cavalieri, and you will stay on the vineyard grounds, where it is guarded and safe, until the matter is resolved. End of discussion."

Her eyebrows rose. "End of discussion? End of discussion! There would have to have been a beginning of a discussion for there to be an end." She placed her hands on her hips as her gaze hardened. "You know what, Cesare? You may not have been involved, but all of this is still *your* fault."

The space between my shoulder blades tightened as my body stilled. My gaze swept over her. "Careful, *carissima.*"

"What's the matter, Cesare? I thought you wanted the truth?"

She moved until her back hit the furthest wall in the small compartment, shifting as far as possible away from me, both physically and emotionally. It was like I could actually feel the wall of ice crystalizing between us, shard by icy shard.

Her dark eyes became sightless as she stared over my shoulder into the past. "They lured me to the school music room with a cheap Valentine's card...."

CHAPTER 23

MILANA

 even years earlier

I CLUTCHED THE CHEESY, American-style Valentine's Day card in my hand as I peeked around the corner to make sure the school hallway was empty before hurrying down the darkened corridor. If I got caught there would be hell to pay. Cesare, Amara, and I were already in trouble for sneaking out early three weeks ago for a football game. My nonna had locked me in my bedroom and berated me for being a whore who only cut school to have sex with boys, just like my mother, for an entire week after that stunt. I was still buried in schoolwork because of it.

I looked down at the silly Valentine's card he had given me for *La Festa Degli Innamorati.*

Bee mine.

There was a cartoon bee with a goofy grin holding a heart and a bunch of flowers. I rolled my eyes but couldn't suppress a smile as butterflies fluttered in my stomach. If this had been a few months ago, I would have known it was just a stupid prank. We were always playing them on one another.

But something changed back in January at the *La Befana* festival.

Something had shifted between us.

It was nothing I could put into words.

It was more like a feeling, a sense.

It was in the way I caught him looking at me when he thought my attention was elsewhere. Or in the protective way he now always put his hand on my lower back when we were in the crowded school hallways. He never used to do that before.

Then yesterday, we were walking through town and I turned down the wrong lane. We found ourselves in a narrow, secluded alleyway. I had turned around so abruptly I had slammed into his chest.

All the breath left my body.

How had I never noticed before how... big and strong he was? His chest was like a freaking wall of muscle.

His arms wrapped around my waist, and time seemed to stop.

He then said my name... but not in the usual way. Not in the casual way he had said it a thousand times over the years and years of our friendship. No, this time my name was like dark honey slowly dripping off his tongue.

When I froze and didn't respond, he had wrapped his fist around my long ponytail.

I could still feel the gentle tug on the back of my skull.

He forced my face to tilt up to his, our lips a breath apart...
when a woman above opened her shutters and shouted at us.

The spell was broken.

Coming back to the present, I stared down at the silly
Valentine's card.

He was going to kiss me.

Cesare Cavalieri had planned to kiss me at that moment. I
was sure of it.

I hadn't slept a wink all last night thinking about it.
Tossing and turning, worrying about what dating would do to
our friendship. Amara was firmly on Team Cesare. She
thought we were perfect for one another, and I should go for
it. I still hadn't decided when I got to school and found this
card tucked into my desk.

On the back was a simple message.

MEET *me in the music room after school.*
   -C.

I HADN'T SEEN him all day. He wasn't at school. Until I found
the note, I thought he was avoiding me because he was
embarrassed and didn't want me to get the wrong idea about
what almost happened. Maybe he had really been giving me
space.

I got to the music room and frowned. Through the frosted
glass window in the door, I could see the lights were turned
off. I guessed it would make sense. We couldn't really turn on

all the lights. Then a teacher would know someone was inside.

My hand shook as I reached for the doorknob.

I hesitated.

The moment I entered this room, everything in my life was going to change.

Dating Cesare Cavalieri was a big deal.

There would be a ton of scrutiny and gossip not only from the mean girls at school, but from the horrible gossips in the village who hated my mother and blamed me for her sins. Then there were those who'd feel I was unworthy of dating an heir to the rich and powerful Cavalieri legacy.

I reached for my Gemini charm. I had gotten it at a bazaar a year ago and rarely took it off, ever since learning I was a Gemini down to my core, easily flipping between having fun, trusting and loving, to being stubborn, argumentative, and standoffish. At times, I was my own worst enemy.

I took a deep breath. Not this time. I controlled my fate, not the stars.

I would trust Cesare.

I reached down and opened the door. "Cesare? Hello?" I whispered, keeping my voice low.

"Over here," came the muffled reply.

I headed toward the practice room in the back of the music room. It was a small, padded room with no windows that blocked out all sound so musicians could practice without outside noise interruptions. It also blocked out the musician's music so class could be held while someone practiced.

"Cesare?"

A hand grabbed me and pulled me inside so roughly, my face smashed against the wall, splitting my lip. I jerked my head back as a pounding pain exploded behind my eyes, a warm gush of blood pouring from my nose. My hand flew to my face. The hard bridge bone was still intact, so as far as I could tell, it wasn't broken.

The door had slammed shut the moment I was yanked inside. It was pitch black. All I could hear was the shuffling of more than one body and some heavy breathing. "Let me out of here!"

There was a metallic click, then a bright flame was held so close to my face, the acrid scent of my own singed hair filled the small space.

"Fuck, you broke her fucking nose. How's she supposed to suck cock now?"

Cold, crippling fear squeezed my chest like a fist.

"So we fuck her instead," said a different boy.

I didn't recognize either of their voices.

"The plan was for her to suck our cocks and we take photos, to teach her a lesson about learning her place as the village whore. We weren't supposed to fuck her. You want to tell Cesare you fucked her instead, that's on you," said the first boy.

Cesare?

I struggled to breathe through the sickening, metallic taste of blood as it oozed over my upper lip into my mouth.

Had they said Cesare?

No. No. No.

This isn't happening.

He couldn't be so cruel.

209

We are friends.

Why would he do this to me?

I had to get out of here.

I launched myself in the door's direction. Two pairs of hands grabbed at me as I screamed and kicked. "Help! Help! Let me go! Help!"

I was thrown to the floor. My head bounced against the hard surface. Sparks burst before my eyes.

"Fuck! I didn't sign up for this shit."

I blinked as bile rose in the back of my throat. I struggled to remain conscious, their voices becoming muddled and indistinct.

The door opened.

My heart surged. Someone had heard me. I was saved.

There was a burst of bright light. I couldn't see who it was but could tell from the voice it was a female. I didn't quite recognize it, but it sounded familiar, like a song you couldn't quite remember the name of or the words to but knew you had heard before.

The female yelled at the boys. "Where is the other one? You were supposed to get them both."

The other one?

I panicked. Please don't let them mean Amara.

The first boy spoke up defensively. "We left the note with her art supplies like you told us."

Art supplies.

Amara didn't take art. They weren't talking about her.

I fought nausea and darkness as my vision blurred. I couldn't hold on for much longer.

I could hear them arguing, but it was like they were down a long tunnel.

Finally, the female said, "Just leave the trash. Maybe she'll die and solve the problem for us."

With that, the door slammed shut.

Trapping me alone in the stifling darkness.

* * *

I HAD BEEN BANGING on the padded walls and yelling for hours until I was hoarse, but no one heard.

It was late Friday afternoon.

No one would be in the school until Monday.

I slid down the wall to the floor.

My breathing was shallow. Sweat poured between my shoulder blades.

There were no windows or vents in the room. It was pitch black since the light switch was on the outside of the room. The air was hot and stale. The padding seemed to suck up what little oxygen there was in the space. I lay down, pressing my ear to the floor, pushing my mouth as close to the bottom of the door as possible, to catch the barest hint of air that was coming into the room.

I was going to die in the dark, alone.

I might as well die.

I had been betrayed by one of my closest friends.

Cesare Cavalieri betrayed me.

Worse.

He had set me up to be attacked, humiliated, and left for dead.

211

*   *   *

I DIDN'T KNOW if it was hours or days later, but when I heard the doorknob lock rattle, I panicked.

I couldn't know for certain if it was help... or the boys returning to finish what they'd started.

As a blinding white light made me cringe and hide my eyes, I heard horrified exclamations.

I was lifted into the arms of an older man. "What has happened to you, sweet girl?"

Through swollen eyes, I watched as a matronly woman came rushing over. "Holy Madonna! Sal, put her over here. Lay her down gently. Gently. Get some help, Sal."

I reached for her wrist as I shook my head. "No, please. Don't. *Cavalieri,*" I choked out past my dry, chapped lips.

The woman and the man named Sal exchanged concerned looks.

That one word... Cavalieri.

It spoke volumes in our mountain village.

Wealth. Power. Privilege. Legacy. Authority.

And one phrase especially... *above the law.*

CHAPTER 24

CESARE

resent.

MILANA SWALLOWED as she swiped at the fresh tears on her cheeks. "I learned later that Sal, who worked as a janitor at the school at the time for extra money, hadn't found me until late Saturday afternoon."

Sal. It explained the man's almost fatherly devotion to Milana. He had been the one to rescue her. Not me.

I reached for her.

She flinched.

In a rage, I turned and punched the compartment wall, leaving a rusty crimson smear of blood and further damaging my already split-open knuckles. "Fuck! God fucking dammit, Milana. Jesus. Why didn't you tell me? How could you, for a fucking second, think I would be part of something so disgusting?"

"Are you forgetting the rumors about how your father got away with murdering your mother? And those are just the tip of the iceberg. Your family's hands aren't exactly clean, Cesare."

I pounded my palm against my chest, not caring I was getting blood on my white shirt. "That is my family. This was us. Us! You and me. You could have told me what happened. You didn't have to believe that bullshit. You should have trusted in us. Trusted in me."

She threw her arms into the air. "Us? There was no us! Don't you get it yet?" She slammed her pointed finger into the center of my chest. "There are the Cavalieris and then there is the rest of the world."

Her eyes flared to life with righteous anger, and I welcomed it. Anything was better than her pain.

She curled her fingers into a fist and hit my heart. "I was a pawn. *A fucking pawn.* A nobody. Don't you see?"

She hit my chest with both her fists as her tormented voice rose in volume. "I didn't matter. My life didn't matter. Even if you weren't involved, they obviously did this to me *to strike at you.* I was just the minor character to be killed off in the revenge plot against the great Cavalieri hero."

My entire life, I had taken great pride in being a Cavalieri. It was integral to my identity.

And it wasn't just the money. It was the land, the soil, the vines, the heritage.

Our guardianship of the valley and the village and its people.

I had always known I was part of a powerful and noble lineage that had molded the history of Italy itself.

Yet, in this moment, I had never been more ashamed of my legacy.

They had hurt her to get to me.

She was right.

I didn't swing the fist, but I might as well have been the one who hit her.

This was all my fault.

Not only had I not been there to protect her before or after, the whole attack had been because of me. If I had a life-time with her, I could never clean that stain from my soul.

In a rage as all the trauma, fear, and anger from the past came spewing into the present like molten poison, she drew back her hand and slapped me hard across the face. "I matter!" she screamed. "Do you hear me, Cavalieri? *I fucking matter!*"

I stepped into her storm, caging her in. "Hit me again," I snarled.

She blinked as she tried to move back. "Don't you dare taunt me."

I placed the tips of my fingers under her chin as I hissed between clenched teeth against her lips, "Hit me again, Milana. Go ahead. Bring it on."

She needed this.

I needed this.

She rose to the challenge, slapping me even harder this time. "Fuck you!" She pounded her fists against my chest. "I'm not a nobody! I'm not a fucking pawn. I matter! I matter!" she sobbed as she tried to turn away and escape through the train compartment door.

I grabbed her wrist and snatched her to me, lifting her off the floor and spinning her around until her back hit the train windows.

She pummeled my shoulders with her fists as I claimed her mouth.

She sunk the sharp edges of her teeth into my lower lip and then wrenched her face to the side.

I wrapped my hand around her jaw and forced her head forward and claimed her mouth again. Mixing the taste of our kiss with our blood.

Her tongue wrapped around mine at the same time as her fingernails clawed at the side of my neck.

I deepened the kiss as the hiss of pain stung my skin. "That's it, babygirl. Hit me. Hurt me. Make me bleed."

I shoved my hips against her core, rubbing my hard cock between her legs.

Milana cried out.

I turned again and kicked at the nearby bench. It folded up against the wall with a bang. I pushed Milana's back to the surface as I wrapped her legs around my middle. "Hold on to the luggage bars, babygirl."

Breathless, Milana reached up and grasped the metal bars that ran overhead.

I laved at her neck, tasting her elevated pulse, feeling the vibrations of her blood pumping against the tip of my tongue. I was like a beast, needing to feel the heartbeat of my prey before I devoured it.

Reaching between us, I lowered the zipper to my pants and shoved her panties aside. Her slick arousal coated my fingers. I grasped my cock and placed the head at her entrance, then leaned down and nipped at the edge of her mouth to capture her attention. "Listen to me, *carissima.* Nothing—absolutely *nothing*—in this entire fucking world matters more to me than you. Do you understand me?"

Her head fell against her arm as she avoided eye contact with me.

Wrapping my arm tightly around her middle, I grabbed her jaw with my free hand and turned her head to face me as I stared into her eyes. *"You matter to me, Milana."* I thrust deep inside her wet warmth in one stroke.

She cried out at the violence of the claiming.

I growled into her mouth as we shared the same heated breath. "You matter to me. *You matter to me,"* I repeated over and over again with each thrust. "Do you hear me, Milana? You are all that matters to me. I would die for you. *I will kill for you.* I will anger God himself and risk damnation for you."

I thrust harder and faster. The pounding of the train wheels on the track spurring me on.

All my rage, horror, fear, and despair coalesced into a twisting, churning need to fuck her so deeply and completely that she would never again doubt my devotion to her. I wanted her to feel me inside of her to her very soul. I needed her to understand that after this moment, it was no longer possible for us to have separate identities, separate lives. She was no longer just mine; she was a part of me. My heart wouldn't beat without her. Her air was my air. I wanted her blood to beat in my veins.

I was barely holding onto my sanity.

This wasn't fucking.

This was salvation.

As her sweet pussy clenched around my flesh, I clung to her, inhaling the exotic scent of her perfume on her skin, tasting the salt of her tears on her cheeks as I continued to murmur into her ear how she was mine and I would never let anyone hurt her again. Ever.

I wrenched the collar of her sweater down, exposing her lace-covered breast and pulling her nipple between my lips, suckling, wishing I tasted the milk that would nourish our children, hoping and praying one day soon I would.

I sucked on her nipple as I pounded my cock into her tight pussy, slamming her hard against the wall with each frenzied thrust.

Everything about this was crazy, violent, intense, and passionate.

Just like us.

Milana dropped her hand to my front, wrenching the top buttons off my shirt as she twisted the fabric in her fist, holding on to me with one hand as she kept her other arm stretched high, clinging to the luggage bar for purchase. "Oh God! Fuck. It hurts. You're so deep."

I knew the weight of her body pressing down was pushing me deeper inside of her than I had ever been. Stretching her with the thick girth of my shaft. "Come for me, baby. Come on my cock. Let me feel your body clench around me."

Milana's back arched as her body bucked. She lost her grip on the luggage bar and her body fell forward into my arms. I held her close as she trembled with her release. Pressing her head onto my shoulder, I held her with my other arm under her ass and thrust several more times before finding my release, filling her with my hot seed.

I stood there in the center of the small, now trashed, train compartment.

The calm after the storm.

I held her close, not wanting to let her go.

My semi-hard cock still buried deep inside of her.

A tremor wracked her body. I knew this wasn't a remnant of her climax… this was shock.

I tightened my grip. "Don't worry, baby. I've got you."

I looked out the window up at the sky. Where was it?

Just as I was thinking it, the helicopter came into view. It dropped dangerously low until it was flying alongside the train cars. I pulled on the emergency cord, stopping the train.

I absorbed the shock of the sudden stop in motion with my body.

Milana raised her head. She sniffed as she stared at me with unfocused eyes. "What's happening?"

"I'm taking you home."

CHAPTER 25

MILANA

I grasped the lapels of the conductor's borrowed wool jacket closer as I stared at the helicopter landing in a nearby field. The sterling silver Cavalieri crest of two rearing stallions and a cluster of grapes emblazoned on the side glowed in the last rays of the setting sun.

Of course.

Only a Cavalieri could get an entire train to stop so that a motherfucking helicopter could pick them up in the middle of nowhere. I glanced over my shoulder at the passengers who had lowered their windows to stare at the spectacle. They were all calling out and waving their arms, but I couldn't hear what they were saying over the helicopter's rotor blades. With Italians, it was anyone's guess if they were annoyed or amused. Probably both.

The co-pilot door opened, and a man jumped out. It was Alfonso. He bent his body low as he ran toward us carrying a leather satchel.

He nodded toward Cesare and me, and then held out his hand to the conductor. After shaking hands, he passed him the leather satchel. "Barone Cavalieri sends his apologies for the delay in your schedule. This is for you and your passengers for the inconvenience. Please see they get it."

The conductor opened the satchel. It was filled with crisp euro bills in neat piles.

I didn't even want to think about how many thousands of euro had casually been tossed into a leather bag to bribe a train full of people as I was being escorted across the field toward the waiting family helicopter.

This couldn't possibly be my life right now.

At any moment, I was going to wake up from this twisted night terror.

Cesare got into the back of the helicopter first. Then Alfonso gently took my arm and helped me inside.

I was so numb and overwrought from everything that had happened that I was like a doll, allowing myself to be handled and moved about. Cesare reached over and buckled my seat belt for me. He then fitted the headphones over my ears for protection. I watched with only half interest as Alfonso climbed into the front co-pilot seat and gave the pilot a thumbs-up. The helicopter lifted smoothly off the ground.

I looked out the window as we climbed higher and higher. Soon, the train looked like a toy model as it continued on its path through the countryside. The passengers allowed to continue on with their lives, a little richer for having crossed paths with a Cavalieri.

The little people inside were no more than the size of ants.

Was this what it was like to be a Cavalieri?

To feel like a god, looking down at all the little people?

Knowing you could stop and start someone else's life to suit your own purposes, as if you were just stopping a toy train on a track?

* * *

IT WAS dusk by the time we arrived at the vineyard.

I had expected Cesare to take me to his home, but instead, he bundled me off the helicopter and across the yard to the villa.

Barone opened the massive, arched double doors as we neared. It was obvious I had interrupted his work at the winery. He was still wearing a pair of roughed-up denim pants with ground-in dirt and grape-skin stains, heavy work boots, and an oatmeal-colored thermal shirt with the sleeves pushed up.

Before I could say a word, he enfolded me in his arms. It was like being hugged by a muscular, super scary, yet sexy Santa Claus. It was oddly comforting. I couldn't help but feel protected and safe... I was starting to understand why Amara had fallen under this man's spell.

Barone leaned back. "I don't know all the details, but I know enough. I'm sure my son has already told you this, but I want you to hear it from me as well. We consider you family now. A Cavalieri. No one hurts one of our own and gets away with it."

We consider you family now. A Cavalieri.

Why did that sound like a warning? Almost like a threat?

Amara saved me from responding. She and Rosa appeared together.

Amara took charge of me while Rosa clucked and cooed over Cesare's busted-up hand.

Before Amara could take me upstairs, Cesare pulled me aside. He placed both hands on the sides of my face and looked down at me. "You matter, babygirl. Above all else, please never forget, you matter to me. I'm going to make damn sure I spend the rest of my life showing you just how much." He kissed me on the forehead, and then turned and followed Barone and Rosa down the hall.

I watched as Barone placed an arm over his shoulders and Cesare's head bowed.

My fingers flexed as I half raised my arm.

It was strange wanting to comfort him, wanting him to comfort me.

I had spent so many years hating him.

Amara slipped her arm around my waist. "Come on, sweetie. Let's go upstairs. You look like you could use a bubble bath."

I rested my head on her shoulder as we climbed the central staircase. "Does that bath come with an obnoxiously big bottle of wine?"

Amara laughed. "Duh."

I was ushered into a ridiculously enormous bathroom with a massive tub surrounded by windows with a view of the mountains. Amara turned on the faucet. As the tub filled, she squeezed a generous amount of pale pink liquid under the water stream, which produced mounds of fragrant bubbles.

As I stripped out of my clothes, my hand went to my neck.

My Gemini charm was gone. It had always been on a cheap chain. It must have gotten torn off during our insane hate fuck on the train. I brushed off my sadness at the loss. I had enough on my plate without fretting over a cheap, gold-plated charm right now. Although I would miss it. I loved that charm.

Amara sat on the edge of the tub and tested the water with her fingertips before adjusting the tap. "Almost ready."

I slipped into one of her silk robes and padded over to the tray someone had set before the glass-fronted fireplace. On it was displayed a bottle of wine, two glasses, and a small crystal plate of *ciambelline al vino rosso*. I picked up one of the sugar-coated, ring-shaped cookies and took a bite. As I poured us both a glass of wine, I took another bite, pleased that Rosa's recipe for red wine cookies included cinnamon. I preferred those to the anise ones.

I handed a glass to Amara. As I stood over the bath, I frowned. "Wait, this isn't the bathtub where Barone...." I looked down at her and raised an eyebrow.

She looked to the side, her cheeks bright red, as she raised her wineglass to her lips. "Where Barone what?" she asked, feigning innocence before taking a large gulp.

My mouth dropped open. "Oh. My. God. Ewwwwww. I'm about to take a bath where you and Barone fucked?"

Amara had told me about the night Barone had kidnapped her from the tub in my apartment, only to bring her back to his home to fuck her in his tub.

Amara waved me off. "Don't be such a baby. It's been cleaned since then. Get in before it gets cold."

I shrugged out of her robe and slipped into the tub. After

leaning back, I picked up the wineglass I had propped up on the edge. I took a long swallow before closing my eyes and resting my head back. "As long as you didn't do something freaky, like take it up the ass while calling him daddy."

Silence.

I opened one eye. "Amara?"

Amara shrugged as her blush deepened.

I splashed some watery bubbles at her. "You're such a dirty girl!"

Amara shrieked with laughter as she backed up out of range. "That's what *he* said."

"Oh, God!"

Amara bent over, laughing so hard, she could barely get the words out. "That's what *I* said. Several times, in fact!"

I waved my palms in the air. "Stop! Stop! No more. I'll never be able to look *Daddy Barone* in the face again."

After a few moments, our laughter died out.

Amara sat on the edge of the tub and popped a few of the bubbles, keeping her gaze averted. "So, are we going to keep making jokes or are you going to tell me what's going on?"

I sighed. "You know the thing that we never talk about?"

She nodded.

"It's time to talk about it."

* * *

AFTER A BOTTLE OF WINE, lots of hugs, and countless tears, Amara and I were laying on her bed, mentally and emotionally exhausted.

"So what happens now?" she asked.

I puffed out my cheeks as I let out a frustrated sigh. "The fuck if I know. Cesare doesn't even want to discuss it. He seems intent on murdering the men responsible." I rolled onto my stomach and looked at her. "You don't think he was serious, do you? I mean, I know the Cavalieris have a mafia-like reputation in Italy... but that's all talk, right? It's not like Cesare would *actually* go out and murder someone."

Amara rolled onto her stomach as well and leaned up on her forearms. "Do you want the truth or a beautiful lie?"

My eyes widened. "Fuck."

"I've been thinking about what you said, about my stepfather and stepbrother just disappearing."

"I meant what I said. Your pieces of shit stepfather and stepbrother deserved whatever they got... but the guys that attacked me back at school?"

"Stop that."

"What?"

"You know what. Downplaying the trauma. I know you're embarrassed. It's why it took you so long to tell me what happened. I know you hate how it affected you and still affects you with the night terrors and all. I know the lack of control drives you crazy, but just stop. Because if the next words out of your mouth are, 'it was just a bloody nose,' I'll scream."

"Yeah, but...."

"It wasn't just a fucking bloody nose, Milana. I may not agree with whatever the men have planned, but between the two of us, let's agree on one thing... it wasn't just a fucking bloody nose."

I swallowed past the lump in my throat. I nodded. "Okay."

Amara sat up and smiled. "Damn, how did I do? Usually it's you giving me the boss bitch speech."

I sat up next to her and leaned against the headboard. "Not bad for your first time. Now that we have that settled, we really should find out what they have planned."

Amara looked at the closed bedroom door and then back at me. "You know we are literally the very last people on the face of the earth they are going to tell." She held up her hands and curled her fingers into air quotes. "For our own protection."

I slid off the bed. "Then I guess we'll just have to find out for ourselves." I walked over to her closet. "Where do you keep your black yoga pants and T-shirts?"

Moments later, we were creeping down the back servants' staircase toward Barone's study, where he and Cesare were drinking and talking.

CHAPTER 26

CESARE

J followed my father into his study and sank into an oxblood leather chair by the fire as he moved to the sideboard to pour us a drink.

Rosa entered with a basket of first aid supplies. She shook her head when she saw my hand. Pulling up an upholstered stool next to the chair, she placed my hand on her lap. "*Come hai potuto farlo alla tua bellissima mano? Che vergogna! Una violenza cos! Hai fortuna che non l'hai rotta. Che ragazzo sciocco. Proprio come tuo padre. Che temperamento!*"

She rummaged in her basket and pulled out a familiar brown glass jar. Unscrewing the cap, the nostalgic scent of yarrow, basil, and olive oil she released mixed with the burning scent of charred embers coming from the fire. She scooped a generous amount onto her fingertips and smeared it onto my torn and cut knuckles.

I hissed.

She looked up and scowled. *"Te lo sei meritato. Un uomo adulto che colpisce i muri. Dovresti vergognarti di te stesso. Quel dolore è come la coda del diavolo che ti flagella la pelle. Dirò una novena extra per te alla Messa di questa domenica."*

My father tried to hide his smile behind his glass as he raised it to his lips.

He failed.

Rosa's sharp eyes caught him. "And don't you stand there smirking, Don Cavalieri. You are no better. Don't think I don't know about all the devilish things you have been doing to that poor innocent girl up there in your bedchamber," she admonished as she wagged her finger at him.

I was taking a sip of Scotch when she blurted out that gem. The liquid went down the wrong pipe. I choked as I tried to regain my composure. Lord, help us all. I certainly hoped our sweet, matronly Rosa didn't know all the details of what Papà got up to in his bedroom.

Unable to resist, I gave Rosa a wink as she wrapped my hand in gauze. "If that were true, dear Rosa, I don't think a few extra novenas will cut it."

There were only two women on earth who could scold my Papà like he was an errant schoolboy and get away with it, my Aunt Gabriella and Rosa, who had been with us since before I was born.

Papà raised his hand in submission. "Don't blame me, Rosa. If it were up to me, I'd rouse Father Luca out of his bed and demand he marry us this very night. It's Amara who refuses to consider it. She says it's too soon."

Rosa puffed out her chest like a flustered chicken. She

tossed her supplies into her basket one by one with an angry huff. "I shall give a good talking to that girl in the morning. She cannot continue to live in sin with you. A girl should be married and settled."

As she stood and tucked the basket handle in the crook of her arm, my father stoked the flames further. "And just think, the sooner she marries me, the sooner we give you babies to help raise."

Her eyes lit up as she clasped her hands to her chest. "*Oh, i bambini. S, abbiamo bisogno di bambini in questa casa di nuovo. Parlerò con lei per prima cosa domani per farle ragionare. Forse cercherò la guida del Padre Luca su come persuaderla al meglio. Pensa solo. Una casa piena di bambini di nuovo!*"

She was still chattering animatedly as she left the room.

I shook my head. "Amara is going to be mad as hell when she finds out what you just did."

Papà smirked. "All's fair in love and war, my son. I need Amara to agree to marry me soon or Father Luca is going to get that damn new roof for the church he's been hinting at, because I'm going to need him to look the other way when I show up at his altar with a hogtied and gagged bride."

I lifted my glass. "Care to make that a double wedding?"

"That bad?"

I leaned forward and rested my forearms on the tops of my thighs as I stared down at my drink. "It's all my fault. All of it." I took a deep breath. "I thought I understood when you talked about Mom and the guilt you felt... I didn't, not really... but I do now." I gestured with my injured hand. "It's like this weight crushing down on my chest."

He rested a hand on my shoulder.

"What they did to her... *what they had planned to do to her...* because of me. All that pain and terror she must have suffered. I can't get the image out of my mind of her curled up on that fucking floor, alone in the dark, beaten and broken... and all the time thinking I had betrayed her." I wiped the heel of my palm over my eyes as my vision blurred.

I stood up and paced the room. I drained my glass and stormed over to the sideboard to pour another. Tossing my next words over my shoulder, I snarled, "I just want to go over there right now and burn that entire fucking school to the ground."

"Do you want to use C4 explosive charges or just good old-fashioned gasoline?"

We both turned to see Enzo strolling into the room. He crossed to me and clasped me to his chest, hugging me close as he patted me on the back.

When we pulled apart, he laid the flat of his hand against my face. "I'm serious. I have the explosive charges back at home from that side project I'm working on. Just say the word, brother."

The family business was wine and land management. Enzo had expanded that to development, but only to an extent. I organized certain projects and Enzo cherry-picked the ones which interested him from an architectural point of view. Usually it was limited to historical renovations. He had no interest in my "from the ground up" projects, only the preservation ones.

Papà slapped Enzo on the back in greeting as he moved behind us to pour him a drink. "Don't encourage your brother. I'm not paying for a fucking new school in the village."

Enzo accepted the glass from our father as he cast a worried glance between the two of us. "We're still going to kill the bastards responsible, though, right?"

Papà and I answered in unison. "Hell, yes."

We all returned to take seats before the fire.

Papà asked, "So, what do we know?"

I told them as much as was necessary. I hated I had to betray Milana a second time to resolve this. She had kept this secret for years and now that she had finally unburdened herself, the first thing I was doing within hours of hearing it was telling my family, but it had to be done.

Milana had never benefited from the support and love of a family in her life. She didn't understand what it would feel like to face a problem with a small army who had your back as opposed to facing it alone.

She would now.

She was no longer alone in this, and never would be again.

But family loyalty stretched in multiple directions.

I studied my father's profile before speaking. "If we do this, it could cause problems for you and Amara. She's smart, both of them are. They are going to put two and two together."

Papà lifted his glass and stared down at the amber contents for a moment before taking a sip. He then leaned his head back and closed his eyes before responding. "You mean, am I worried Amara will find out her stepfather and step-brother are currently pig shit fertilizing my northern field, instead of enjoying life somewhere else other than Cavalieri village?"

I smirked. "Something like that."

He opened his eyes and rolled his head to the side to observe my brother and me. "I can't say it was a conversation I was ever planning on having with her, but I will deal with any consequences."

There was silence in the room for several moments. Then, an ice cube rattled as it settled in my drink. "I'm sorry, Papà. Milana has serious trust issues and knowing what I know now, I can't fucking blame her. I couldn't lie to her, not even by omission."

"And how does she feel about your plans?"

I leaned my elbow on the leather sofa arm and rubbed my forehead. "She hates them. In hindsight, it might not have been the best course of action, telling her the full truth. She thinks I'm taking over her problem and handling it myself while being an overprotective bully."

Enzo raised his eyebrows. "Well… yeah. You're a Cavalieri man. It's kind of our thing."

I gestured toward him. "Thank you. Mind telling her that?"

He shook his head. "Fuck no. The way I see it, after tonight, I'll be the last male in this household the women actually *like*. I'm not going to ruin that."

"Traitor," I grumbled.

Right at that moment, we heard a noise beyond the closed study door.

We exchanged looks.

Since he was seated closest to the door, Enzo quietly stood

and moved silently toward the portal. He listened before quickly opening the door and stepping out into the hallway.

After a moment he returned, shaking his head. "I didn't see anyone."

I stood. "We should get going. Romolo lives in Palombaro."

Enzo drained his glass. "Let's go wreck his evening, shall we?"

CHAPTER 27

CESARE

*A*lthough my father and Alfonso would have liked to have joined in on the fun, it didn't seem sporting to have four against one, so only Enzo and I made the trip to Romolo Castiglione's house.

By the time we arrived, it was close to midnight.

We got out of the car and surveyed the modest villa.

Enzo leaned against the driver's side door and lit a cigarette. "How do you want to play this? Want me to hang back and only come in if the screams get annoyingly loud enough to attract attention?"

I nodded as I cupped my right fist in my left palm.

Enzo placed his hand on my shoulder. "Try not to beat him to death until we get the name of the other male and the female."

I nodded again. Too angry to speak.

We had already done some preliminary reconnaissance. Romolo was twice divorced and lived alone in the villa he'd inherited from his mother. The villa was too small for live-in staff, so there was a high likelihood he was alone.

I walked up to the door and knocked.

After several minutes, Romolo answered, wearing only a pair of boxers and a white T-shirt. "Cesare?"

He leaned out and looked up and down the street. "What are you doing here at this hour?"

I smiled. "I thought we would continue our meeting that was unfortunately interrupted today."

He shifted to look over my shoulder. "Is that Enzo with you?"

Without taking my eyes off Romolo, I answered, "He's just finishing his cigarette and a quick phone call."

"It's late. Shouldn't we just schedule this for tomorrow at your office?"

I laughed, hoping he wouldn't notice the lack of humor in it. "What are you, an old man, Romolo? In bed before midnight? Or do you have a nice piece of ass in there keeping you warm?"

Romolo puffed out his chest. "Well, I did, of course. That's the only reason I was in bed, but she just left."

Fucking liar. At least now I had confirmation he was alone.

I muscled my way inside. "Good. Then you're free to talk business now."

Romolo closed the door. "Let me put on some clothes. My study is through there. Help yourself to the bar."

I walked down the hall into his study. I moved straight to the bookshelves. They were filled with leather volumes with pristine spines of all the supposed right titles. All for show. Taking out my mobile, I snapped photos of all the displayed frames that showed any photo of Romolo with a group of people, especially if it looked like it was from our school days. I texted them to Enzo.

Romolo entered and went straight to the bar. He poured himself an Amaro and hit it with a splash of soda water. He lifted his glass and raised an eyebrow.

I held up a hand. "None for me, thank you."

Romolo sat behind his desk.

I took the seat opposite.

He shuffled a few files. "Earlier you mentioned you wanted to go over the cap rate appraisals?"

I nodded as I leaned to the side and pulled out a pair of black leather gloves from my back pocket. "I wanted to chat about that... earlier. Now I have a different topic in mind," I said as I dragged the gloves over my hands, keeping my hard gaze trained on him.

Romolo's hands stilled on the open file he was holding. His gaze shifted from the gloves to my face and back. "Look, Cesare... I don't know how I may have offended you... but... I assure... you...."

"Don Cavalieri."

"What?"

"Only my friends call me Cesare. You will call me Don Cavalieri."

Romolo blinked several times as a bead of sweat trickled between his bushy eyebrows and down the bridge of his nose. "Of... of course. Don Cavalieri."

I adjusted the gloves. "I must say, it does take balls to cross a Cavalieri like you have. One would almost say you had a death wish."

"Cesa—Don Cavalieri, I swear on my mother's grave, whatever you think I may have done, you are wrong. I would never cross the Cavalieri family. You have my word."

I cocked my head to the side. "Your word? I have your word? Now that is something."

"Someone has been spreading slanderous lies about me." He swiped at his brow with his hand. "It's probably my competitors! They are jealous of the project I am pitching to you."

I nodded, seeming to consider it. "That's a possibility."

Romolo seemed to breathe a sigh of relief.

"Then again...."

You could practically feel the man's butthole tighten.

I narrowed my eyes. "The betrayal I'm referring to took place seven years ago when we were still in school."

Romolo frowned. "In school?"

I observed him. "Do you remember a girl named Milana Carbone?"

Romolo grabbed his glass and slurped down the bitter contents. Not that the digestif would do him much good. He wiped his sweating brow again. "You have to understand. We thought we were doing *you* a favor. We didn't find out until afterward... until later... who was really involved."

I kept silent.

"It's not my fault! I was just there to get a fucking blow job. Then the bitch freaked out. Acted like she was some innocent virgin or something. Like we all didn't know what a fucking whore her mother was. Listen, we didn't hurt her! It's her fault she hit the stupid wall. And it was just a stupid bloody nose. It's not like we cut off her tits or something."

In a flash, I rose and wrapped my hand around the back of his head and slammed his face against the surface of the desk, breaking his nose. Blood gushed, spilling over his files and down his front. Romolo cried out and tried to stand.

I retook my seat and growled, "Stay right fucking there." After he obeyed, I asked calmly, "So how does it feel, Romolo? After all, it's *just a stupid bloody nose.*"

Romolo took off his T-shirt and held it up to his bleeding nose. "You've got to listen to me. I thought I was doing a favor for you! A favor for the Cavalieris! This isn't my fault!"

"So you thought I wanted you to viciously attack a close female friend of mine as a fucking favor to me? What kind of motherfucking moron are you?"

"Listen. Listen. I know! All right? I know that now. It was stupid. I didn't know who I was really dealing with."

"I'm going to need the name of the other male and the female who were with you that day, as well as who the other female target was."

His eyes widened over the bunched-up, bloodied shirt. "No. I can't. You don't understand. I can't. Listen. That was years ago. Why do you care? It's ancient history. It's in the past. Let it go."

Fuck, that was precisely what I had been guilty of telling Milana. It was in the past. Just let it go.

A lifetime would not be enough time to make up for my sins against her, but I sure as hell was going to try.

"It's not ancient history for Milana. You kept her caged up in that room, injured and alone, for over twenty-four hours."

He flew from his chair and ran over to the bookshelves. He pulled back a false row of books, exposing a wall safe, and punched in a four-digit code. "Does she want money? How much to keep her quiet? It probably won't take much. I'll pay." He opened the safe and exposed a handgun and several stacks of euro.

Bile rose in the back of my throat. I had to restrain myself from rising from my seat and just snapping this man's neck. I needed information first.

"She doesn't need or want your money. The names, Romolo."

He stopped, keeping his back turned to me. He lowered his head. "I can't. Please, just let me pay her off."

"No."

He turned. "You're right. Her kind will always want more. If we pay her off once, she'll just keep coming back for more. Thank you for coming to me with this, Cesare. You're a true friend. The other man involved will have a more permanent solution. That is the better way."

I watched him carefully. His eyes were unfocused. He had dropped the shirt and was just letting the blood flow freely down over his mouth and front. He was becoming desperate, unhinged.

I stood and spoke slowly, as if to a child. "I don't think you understand, Romolo. Milana is under my protection. She's mine. Always has been. You hurt someone who belongs to me. I'm not your friend in this situation.... *I'm your executioner...* unless you give me the names of the other male and female involved."

Romolo's body shook. "He'll kill me."

I fired back, "So will I."

"Yeah, but he'll take sick pleasure in it. You don't know him, Cesare. You don't know what he's capable of. And she's just as bad. I'm warning you. Leave this alone. You do not know how close to home this is going to strike."

I raised my leather-covered fists. "The names, Romolo."

His shoulders sagged. He nodded. Lifting his arm to the side, he reached inside his safe and pulled out his gun. Before I could react, he put it to his temple and pulled the trigger.

* * *

ENZO JOINED me in the study after hearing the gunshot.

We stared down at the dead body.

"Did you get the names?"

"No."

"What did you learn?"

I turned to look at him. "That this goes way beyond some school prank that got out of hand."

CHAPTER 28

CESARE

*I*t took forever getting rid of the body.

Even though it was suicide, it would lead to questions and an inquiry, scrutiny we didn't want. So we decided it was best to just get rid of it. Usually these things were planned in advance so you didn't have to deal with all the bullshit in the same evening because it was so fucking time-consuming.

Instead of heading to the villa, I went home first to wash off all the blood, grime, and dirt.

It wasn't until early in the morning that I finally could check on Milana.

I found Papà and Amara outside on the veranda, despite the slight morning chill. Amara was wrapped in a blanket and sitting on his lap. On the round marble-topped table in front of them were the remnants of their breakfast, a platter of fruit, some fresh brioche, and a pot of plum jam. As well as various illustrations. Amara was updating the look of our wine labels and obviously had been reviewing artist submissions with my father.

I exchanged a look with him and nodded, letting him know without saying a word that the body had been taken care of in the usual way.

I gave Amara a kiss on the cheek in greeting. "I didn't mean to interrupt. I'm going to grab an espresso and go see Milana. Is she still in bed? Which bedroom did you put her in?"

Amara leaned up and adjusted the blanket over her shoulders as she looked first at Barone and then at me. She cleared her throat. "Milana isn't here."

I had already turned to head into the kitchen, only half listening to her response. When I processed what she'd said, I pivoted on my heel and faced her, frowning. "I'm sorry. I don't think I heard you correctly. Did you just say she isn't here?"

Amara looked at my father, who remained strangely silent, and responded, "No. She isn't."

Trying to keep a rein on my fast-rising temper, I asked, "Do you mind telling me where the hell she is?"

I had already been to my home, so I knew she wasn't there. She hated the cottage, so it was unlikely she was there either.

Amara rolled her lips between her teeth and shook her head.

I raised my eyebrows. "You can't be serious."

She shrugged.

"Papà?"

My father at least had the decency to look slightly chagrined. "Amara felt…."

Amara interrupted. "*We* felt...."

My father began again. "*We* felt that given Milana's current state of mind, it would be cruel not to give in to her request to return to a place where she felt safe and at home rather than stay at the villa."

"Given what is going on, you just let her leave here?"

"I put a guard on her."

Amara gave him a shocked look. "You didn't tell me that!"

He stared back at her askance. "You can't honestly think I was going to let her just stroll off the vineyard grounds without at least a security detail?"

Her brow furrowed. "Actually, yes, I did."

He tapped the tip of her nose. "You are so adorably naïve."

I ran my hand through my hair. "I've had a *very* long night and I'm fast losing patience. Tell me where my girl is."

"No," they said in unison.

Turning on my heel, I stormed out of the villa and hopped into my Alfa Romeo Giulia Quadrifoglio. There was only one place she felt safe.

Barone

I WATCHED Cesare's retreating back. "There is going to be hell to pay when he catches up with her."

Amara reached for a raspberry. "Like you told me before. It's between them."

I watched her cute mouth as she crushed the berry

between her teeth. "Okay. I did as you asked. I permitted Milana to leave the villa. Am I now forgiven for not telling you the truth about your stepfather and stepbrother?"

She laid her head on my shoulder and sighed. "I had already suspected the truth."

I rubbed her back. "And how do you feel about it?"

"Honestly? Nothing. There was no love lost between me and them. I guess I'm a little bloodthirsty that way."

I chuckled and hugged her close. She was the most innocently sweet, kindest little thing on the planet, but it was cute she thought she was cold-blooded for wanting those two bastards dead.

She lifted her head and studied me. "Does this mean you're in the mafia or something?"

"*Dolcezza*, I'm a very wealthy Italian. We're all in the mafia *or something*, but no. Not really. I'm just a man who's not afraid to protect what's important to him."

"Am I important to you?"

I pushed a lock of hair behind her ear. "You, babygirl, are the most important thing in my life."

She smiled and snuggled deeper into my embrace.

I whispered suggestively in her ear, "Of course, there is still the matter of how you're going to prove to me how sorry you are for eavesdropping at my study door...."

CHAPTER 29

CESARE

I pulled up to Sal's leather shop.

The man himself emerged to greet me. He held out his hand. "She's upstairs."

I grasped his hand firmly. "I figured."

He cocked his head to the side. "So she finally told you?"

I nodded.

His shoulders slumped as he shook his head. "Terrible sight to see. Terrible. Poor little thing. All curled up on the floor like a puppy who'd been kicked. Terrible. I wanted to say something earlier, but it wasn't my story to tell."

I released his hand and lowered my arm, curling my fingers into a fist. I had been deprived of beating Romolo into a bloody pulp. The pent-up violence was still pounding through my veins. I would not make the same mistake with the next man responsible for Milana's pain.

I studied the man before me. The man who'd come to her aid. The man who had been there for her, cared for her, literally sheltered and protected her. The man who'd done all the things I should have been doing.

Sal met my scrutiny with the frank and open gaze of a man who had lived a long and honest life and who knew the evils and goodness of humanity… and the pride of man.

His tanned skin, as leathered as the goods he sold, crinkled around his eyes as he placed a hand on my shoulder, not unlike my father was fond of doing. "You're here now."

I lowered my head and nodded as I forced my hand to unclench. I didn't need to say a word. He understood.

I walked past him and headed toward the staircase leading to her old apartment above the shop.

I turned as Sal called out, "But make no mistake, Cavalieri or not, if you hurt her again…."

I made a mental note to speak to our family's accountant. I was going to set up a trust fund for each one of this man's children, as well as a bank account for him and his wife. The loyalty he had shown my future wife deserved to be rewarded. I would see to it. If he worked, it would only be because he enjoyed it, not out of want.

I gave him a curt nod. "Noted. Your trust is not misplaced, Sal. I promise I'll take good care of her. You have my word as a Cavalieri and as a man of honor."

He lifted his hand in a sort of wave and returned to his shop.

When I got to the top of the stairs, I opened the apartment door with my key.

The place had changed in the weeks since Milana had left. Everything was neat and orderly, but the life and energy was missing from the small space. I closed the door and walked further inside. I found Milana in the bedroom.

That was another change.

Gone were her racks of clothes and the countless shoes which had lined the floor.

Now there was a simple bed with a nightstand and a refurbished bureau in the corner with an antique, gold-framed mirror propped on top, ready to be hung, and a small cardboard box.

Milana met my gaze in the mirror. "This is it. My entire life. In a single box."

She looked down at the box and pulled out a framed photo of her and Amara from a trip to Rome.

I stepped closer.

Her gaze flashed back to mine in the mirror.

Her dark eyes narrowed in warning.

I stilled. The muscles between my shoulder blades tensed as I forced my arms to my sides and attempted to keep my gaze impassive.

She looked back down at the box. "Sal's turning this into an Airbnb for the tourists. This box is all that was left of mine, of me."

My gaze scanned the bedroom walls, taking in the vibrant and eclectic artwork, both in this room and in the rooms beyond. Each piece reflected Milana's retro-glam, artistic style. "That's not true. What about the artwork?"

Just the barest hint of a smile crossed her lips before a melancholy look took hold, like an ethereal ghost disappearing into the gloom. "I don't own any of it. Sal used to sneak me petty cash during market days so that I could brighten up my apartment with any secondhand bits and pieces I found."

Trying again, I said, "Well, I remember a member of Rosa's staff unpacking at least three suitcases of dresses and purses." Hoping talk of clothes would cheer her up, like it usually did.

She stared at her reflection in the mirror, but her gaze was sightless. "All used pieces. Secondhand. It's funny when you think about it. My own mother threw me away, so it makes sense that all my belongings would be clothes and artwork and things that other people threw away. And why those boys treated me like a piece of trash to be used to get back at you. I can put on all the red lipstick and fake gold jewelry and used designer high heels I want. I can put on glamorous airs and talk a good game, but in the end, people know. They know when something is secondhand. Unwanted. Trash."

I had heard enough.

I stormed across the room and grabbed her by the shoulders, turning her to face me.

Before I could say anything, she looked down at my bandaged hand.

A reminder of yesterday's violence.

"Is he dead? Romolo?"

"Yes, but not by my hand. He killed himself."

She shifted her eyes away, looking around the room before settling her gaze back on me. She raised her eyebrows as she cocked her head. "Sorry to disappoint you."

I frowned as my jaw tightened. I didn't like this mood on her.

It was destructive and dangerous.

My Milana was a fighter.

A fucking little half-pint badass who didn't take shit from anyone and gave as good as she got.

It was one of the things I loved about her.

Her spirit.

Her intelligence.

Her courage.

Her pride.

Her fire.

The challenge of making a strong, independent woman like Milana love me, want me, need me, was invigorating. There was nothing else like it in the world. I knew she would never miss an opportunity to remind me that I was only as good as how I treated her, and that at any moment she could decide she'd be better off without me.

If she submitted to me, it was because it was her *choice.* Fuck! The power and enthrallment of knowing that! It was the greatest high in the universe. Sure, I may have compelled her to stay at my home, but we both knew that if she had *truly* wanted to leave, she would have found a way.

The girl standing before me seemed like a dark shadow. If I wasn't physically touching her shoulders, I could almost imagine my hands passing right through her.

My brow furrowed as I eyed her carefully. "Disappoint me?"

She broke free of my grasp and stepped back as she spun in circles around the room.

"I'm sure you were expecting some kind of Disney-like Cinderella transformation the moment the villain, Romolo, died. Perhaps my small apartment was supposed to have transformed into a large villa in the south of Italy, and suddenly my parents would have appeared, and they'd be respectable, from a rich, well-known family in Rome."

Her voice rose in pitch, her eyes widening as she became more volatile. "And the best part is, I wouldn't be the broken little bastard castoff with her weird, PTSD, night-terror-baggage past. No, now I would be an Italian princess with a heritage worthy of the Cavalieri crown!" she called out, throwing her arm up in the air as she ended with a flourish.

I crossed my arms over my chest. She really was the most glorious creature, even when she was pissing me the hell off. I raised a single eyebrow. "Are you finished?"

There was so much reflected in those beautiful dark eyes that stared defiantly back at me.

I had a ridiculous surge of absolutely obnoxiously arrogant, masculine confidence.

There was only *one man* who could possibly understand the complex mixture of fear, bravado, rebellion, challenge... and love... reflected in the depths of those eyes.

And that man is me.

She matched my stance, crossing her arms over her chest and widening her feet. She lifted her chin and stared down her nose at me. "Yes, as a matter of fact, I am."

I nodded as I allowed my gaze to travel slowly over her. She was wearing a crisp white blouse that was tied off in a knot at her waist, an emerald green ribbed skirt, and a red, gold, and black silk scarf around her neck. Large gold hoop earrings emphasized her short, wavy bob. All borrowed from Amara, no doubt. "Good, because you're right."

Her mouth dropped open as she unfolded her arms. "What?"

I advanced on her.

Milana stumbled back.

My hand whipped out like a striking cobra, capturing the knot of her shirt and yanking her toward me. I ripped open the knot and grasped the ends of the shirt, tearing them in opposite directions, sending the buttons scattering across the floor, exposing her lush breasts. "I'm tired of seeing you in secondhand or knockoff clothes," I growled.

I spun her around and tore at the buttons securing her skirt. It fell to the floor. "I'm tired of seeing you in borrowed clothes bought by another man."

I was fully aware that a decent portion of the clothes currently hanging in my closet at home were technically purchased for Amara by my father.

I turned her back to face me and wrapped my hands around her narrow waist. I lifted her high, so her lips were even with mine. "From now on, the clothes that touch *my wife's* skin will be bought by me. Do you understand me?"

Before she could say anything, I tossed her backward onto the center of the bed. Staring down at her, I kicked off my boots and drew the black thermal I was wearing over my head. As I reached for the zipper of my jeans, I said, "The jewels that grace *my wife's* beautiful neck, ears, and hands will only be of the finest gold and diamonds, befitting a Cavalieri queen."

I unbuckled my leather belt and dragged it from its loops. Palming the buckle, I wound its heavy length around my hand as I kept my gaze on her. "And the next time *my wife* makes the mistake of referring to herself as anything but the most amazing, beautiful, intelligent, strong, capable, and in all honesty, too good for the somewhat tarnished and battered Cavalieri name, woman that she is, she will feel the full weight of my leather belt on her cute little ass."

She leaned up on her forearms. The motion pressed her breasts together, enhancing her curves. My mouth salivated. I couldn't wait to wrap my lips around one of those pert, cherry nipples and suck.

She shook her head. "You don't know what you are saying."

My jaw shifted sideways as I cocked one eyebrow. "Do I fucking look like a man who doesn't know his own mind?"

She closed her lips.

"Answer me," I barked out.

She jumped. "No."

"You're goddamn right. So stop insulting my intelligence and my choice of bride," I said with a wink.

Tossing my belt aside, I lowered the zipper to my jeans and pushed them off my hips with my boxers as I stared down at her lingerie-clad form. We had only fucked a few times and each time was such a frenzied coupling that I had had barely enough time to pull my cock out of my pants. This time, I would savor her skin against mine.

I reached down to grasp my hard shaft and stroked it several times. "Open your legs."

She hesitated.

"Don't make me get my belt," I warned.

She opened her legs.

"Pull your knees up. Show me that sweet pussy." The moment she opened her legs, I could see the delicious evidence of her arousal on the pale, pastel green silk of her panties. "Good girl. Now pull your panties down and show me what I missed that time you touched yourself in the tub."

She pulled her panties down. As she neared her ankles, I commanded, "Leave your heels on."

I licked my lower lip, practically able to taste her. "Now touch yourself."

Her slim fingers, with her glossy red nails, slipped between her legs. Her hand moved up and down as her back arched. The moment her mouth opened on a moan, my resolve broke.

I joined her on the bed, burying my head between her soft thighs.

She tried to move her hand, but I grabbed her wrist and brought her fingers back. Capturing her gaze, I pulled each of her fingers into my mouth and ran my tongue over them, licking them clean. I then placed her index and middle fingers in a "V" over her pussy, using them to hold her lips open as I flicked my tongue over her bud.

Only after tasting the glory of her release twice on my tongue did I finally rise on my knees between her legs and position my cock at her entrance.

Breathless, Milana rested a hand on my flat abdomen. "Wait. A condom. We keep forgetting to use one."

I leaned over her, bracing my forearm over her head. I stroked her cheek with the backs of my knuckles. "My sweet babygirl, I'm not forgetting anything."

I thrust inside of her to the hilt.

Her mouth opened on a gasp. My lips fell on hers, breathing oxygen back into her body. Tasting her passion, her fear, her surprise.

I then lightly wrapped my hand around her throat, just under her jaw. "I told you from the beginning. You're mine now. I never promised to play fair. As far as I'm concerned, you're already my wife. The rest is just paperwork."

I pulled out until just the head was inside of her, then thrust in again.

"Say it," I growled, desperation creeping into my voice. "I want to hear you say you're mine. Say you're my wife. Say you'll have my child."

Her eyes softened. "Saying it doesn't make it true. Saying it doesn't magically erase the past, or the obstacles to a future together."

I threw my head back and let out a primal howl of rage and pain. No human being on earth could wound me like this tiny creature lying beneath me.

I captured her wrists and wrenched them over her head. Securing them with one hand, I grasped her under her knee with my other and lifted her leg high to wrap around my hip. With all the power I possessed, I pounded into her flesh as if I could somehow fuse our bodies, like two metals which became stronger through the pain and molten fire of being forced together.

When I came, I refused to pull out, keeping her bound to me.

Rolling onto my back, I pulled her on top of me, holding her close.

I drew a blanket over the two of us then wrapped an arm around her middle and, cradling the base of her skull with my other hand, pressed her head to my heart.

We stayed like that for hours.

We made love two more times that day. We didn't speak. We didn't eat. We just held one another.

Finally, we fell into an exhausted sleep in each other's arms.

* * *

WHEN I OPENED my eyes to the first rays of sunlight, I realized with a start I hadn't put on a light or opened a window for her before falling asleep.

I then realized she had slept through the night, regardless.

I was emboldened by the minor victory until I reached for her... and felt the cold sheets.

I sat up in bed. Written on the mirror in red lipstick was a note.

SORRY.

-Milana

SHE WAS GONE.

I looked around the empty bedroom.

She was gone... and she had taken my clothes, mobile, and car keys with her.

CHAPTER 30

CESARE

I sighed. "Stop laughing."

Enzo slapped the top of his thigh, howling with laughter.

I rolled my eyes. "Seriously, stop laughing."

Enzo schooled his features and stared at me solemnly for all of two seconds before he burst out laughing again.

My eyes narrowed. "You're fucking lucky I don't have a gun right now."

Enzo wagged his finger at me. "A threat I would take *very* seriously—if you weren't wearing a pink, 'I heart Italy' T-shirt that's about two sizes too small, and a bedsheet."

Not wanting Sal to know how my protection of Milana was going, I had snuck down into his shop and stolen the only attire I could find and made my way through the back alleys to the other side of the piazza to bang on Enzo's door.

Pushing him aside, I sprinted up his stairs and marched down the hallway to his room to raid his closet.

Enzo followed. "I called Papà. Tracking on the car has her heading to Rome."

I pulled on a pair of dark denim designer jeans as I let the bedsheet fall away. I turned to face him as I pulled up the zipper. "Does Amara have any idea who Milana may know in Rome?"

"She says Milana doesn't know anyone that she knows of."

"Can we trust her answer?"

Enzo leaned against the doorframe to his closet as he watched me rummage through his shirts. "Papà says he was *persuasive* when he asked her, so I would say yes. I got the impression Amara was concerned as well, so I tend to agree with him."

I grabbed a dark gray, oval neck sweater from a drawer and shook it out before pulling it over my head.

Enzo held up his mobile and asked, "Papà wants to know if you want the helicopter made ready?"

I thought for a moment, then nodded. "Tell him yeah."

Enzo nodded. "It will take an hour." He motioned with his head. "Come down to the dining room for a coffee, then I'll drive you out to the west field to meet it."

As I followed him down to the main level, I took in the massive mural on the far wall which stretched two stories up over the entrance to the dining room. My eyes widened. "*Buon Dio!*"

Enzo didn't even look up. "After a while, you learn to tune it out."

I grimaced. "How? By gouging your eyes out?"

The subject of the mural was Sandro Botticelli's *Birth of*

Venus, except Renata had had the artist depict her, instead of Venus. A naked Renata. A two-story tall, naked Renata.

We moved into the equally garish dining room. Instead of following the beautiful historic aesthetic of the room, Renata had insisted on filling it with contemporary furniture that looked like it had been purchased from the movie set of *Scarface*. Everything was black leather, clear acrylic, and gold.

Enzo motioned toward a chair. "Grab a seat."

I eyed it speculatively. The plastic abomination didn't look like it would hold the weight of a *bambino*, let alone a tall, muscular, full-grown man. "I'm afraid to."

Enzo smirked. "Shut up and sit down." He motioned to a staff member who brought over espresso and brioche rolls.

I reached for an espresso but couldn't eat a bite. As I looked around at the disgusting display of excess and wealth, I thought of the small box of meager possessions that belonged to Milana. A box of framed personal pictures, some makeup, a figurine or two, and a small bud vase. That was all.

I thought of her lying on the bed beneath me. For the first time, I realized she hadn't been wearing that tarnished old Gemini charm necklace that was always around her neck. In fact, I hadn't seen it since the train. It must have gotten torn off. By me. The thought soured the espresso in my stomach. If this had been a day earlier, I wouldn't have thought twice about it. I would have gone to a jewelry store and ordered her another one, a better one, made of solid gold.

After all, hers was just a cheap, gold-plated charm on a thin, crappy chain. Right?

Fuck, what an arrogant ass I was.

That charm necklace was hers. Hers. She had worn it since we were teenagers. Hell, I was there the day she found it in the market and bought it. I remembered casually digging into my pocket for the crumpled, loose bills to pay for it, completely missing the hurt expression in her eyes as she pulled the carefully folded and cherished bills she had earned and saved out of her purse to be able to afford and pay for such a luxury herself.

She loved that charm.

My stubborn little Gemini.

Enzo brought me back to the present. "So what's the plan?"

I leaned back and rubbed my hand over my eyes. "I'm going after Milana, of course, but hell if I know how to move forward with finding out who's responsible for hurting her. Romolo was our best lead."

Enzo slowly spread jam on a piece of brioche as we sat in silence. Then he looked up and smiled.

My brow furrowed. "What are you thinking?"

"You're heading to Rome... and who's the one man in Italy who could find out everything you'd need to know about Romolo and his associates, past and present?"

I matched his smile. "Sebastian Diamanti."

Enzo raised his espresso cup in a salute. "When in Rome, brother."

I reached into my back pocket before remembering Milana had taken my mobile. I nodded toward Enzo. "Do me a favor and text him that I'm coming and need a meeting."

Enzo nodded as he took out his phone. "Done. I'll also

have an assistant from our offices in Rome meet the heli-copter with a new phone for you." He looked up and winked. "Just in case Milana got *creative* with yours."

The moment he set his phone aside, he had to pick it up again when it pinged. He raised an eyebrow. "Well, this is interesting."

"What?"

He handed his phone to me. I looked at the screen and let out a frustrated sigh.

Enzo chuckled. "Looks like you will have *two* stubborn females to deal with when you get to Rome, not one."

My car tracker had just pinged at my Aunt Gabriella's townhouse in Rome.

Enzo lifted his espresso cup to his lips. "Hope your accounts at all the designer stores are up to date because you know our *dear auntie* is going to be hitting them up with a vengeance, with Milana in tow."

At least I knew she was safe and with family.

Getting my appetite back, I sunk my teeth into a buttery brioche roll.

Renata came sweeping into the room wearing a glaring turquoise robe trimmed with feathers, a matching turban on her head. She leaned over and kissed Enzo on the cheek, leaving a neon pink smear of lipstick.

Enzo reached for a cloth napkin and wiped his face.

My gaze moved to her pregnant belly, or rather, her lack of one.

Renata's sharp eyes narrowed. She placed her hands over her stomach. "I know! I'm just one of those lucky women that doesn't show much. It's quite common among elite models and fitness instructors." Her gaze skittered to Enzo and back to me. "I can show you lots and lots of photos on Instagram, if you want?"

I raised my palm up and shook my head as I studied my brother's reaction to the ridiculous bullshit spewing from this bitch's mouth. Now was not the time to ask how her doctor's appointment, to confirm if she really was, in fact, pregnant, had gone.

A staff member brought over a silver tray with a porcelain pot of tea and a fresh plate of brioche, placing it at Renata's elbow.

She snapped, "Take this away. I've told you before, I can't abide herbal tea. Bring me a double espresso."

Enzo's gaze hardened. "And *I've* told you before that caffeine is not safe for the baby."

"I'm the mother. It's my body. Don't tell me what is and is not safe for my child." She then turned to the staff member and yelled, "Go! Get me my coffee, you stupid cow."

The poor girl jumped, then looked helplessly to Enzo for further instructions.

He nodded. "Go ahead, Marie. Bring Signora Cavalieri what she requests."

As if she hadn't just berated a subordinate, insulted her husband, and endangered her unborn child, Renata turned to me and smiled. "So I hear you and Milana Carbone are getting very cozy lately."

Focusing my attention on spreading jam on a piece of brioche, I answered, "You have heard correctly."

She smoothed her manicured hand over the tablecloth.

The obscenely large diamond wedding ring she'd insisted Enzo purchase for her glimmered in the morning light. "Well, having fun with one of the *village girls* is all well and good, but you really should start thinking about finding a suitable wife and settling down, Cesare."

I tightened my grip on the butter knife I was holding, thinking she should be grateful it was dull-bladed. Refusing to take her bait, I smiled, the mirth not reaching my gaze. "As a matter of fact, I have. Milana and I are to be married as soon as I can arrange it."

Her eyes widened. She looked at Enzo. "You're going to let this happen?"

Enzo barely looked up from his daily edition of the *Corriere della Sera* which he had picked up to read the moment she entered. He folded the newspaper in half and laid it on the table to the side of his plate. "And why, *dear wife*, do you think it should be of any concern of ours who my brother marries?"

She huffed as she pulled her head back, giving her a momentary and rather unflattering double chin. "Am I the *only one* who cares about the Cavalieri name? You do know her family has an unsavory, trashy reputation?"

I drew in an angry breath through clenched teeth before responding. "I'd be very careful what you say about my bride, Renata."

The table fell into an awkward silence as poor Marie brought Renata her espresso.

Renata added a pack of artificial sugar, another harmful thing for the baby, before clanking her spoon loudly against the porcelain edge of the small cup.

The silence was broken by a ping on Enzo's phone. After

checking it, he looked at me. "Sebastian said he will clear his afternoon schedule for you, and he has his best man on Romolo Castiglione."

Renata's spoon clattered onto her espresso saucer. "I'm sorry, did you say Romolo Castiglione?"

I shifted my attention to her, studying her expression. "Yes. Do you know him?"

"I... I think... his name sounds familiar? Didn't we go to school with him?"

Exchanging a glance with Enzo, I leaned forward and rested my forearms on the table. "Yes, we did."

She picked up her spoon and furiously stirred her espresso again. "Why are you looking into him? Are you planning on doing business with him?"

My eyes narrowed. Something was off. "No. Turns out the bastard is responsible for hurting Milana."

Renata laughed. The sound was cold and brittle. "You Cavalieri men and your old grudges. Who cares about something that happened ages ago when we were kids back in school?"

The hairs on the back of my neck stood up. "I never said anything about it happening back in school."

Before she could respond, we received word the helicopter was ready.

As I walked out with Enzo, we exchanged a dark look. His lips thinned as he stared straight ahead. "No need to say anything, brother. I heard it, too."

Before stepping into the helicopter when we got to the west field, I leaned over and said, "I need another favor."

"Name it."

"I need you to contact the train conductor from yesterday."

CHAPTER 31

MILANA

*T*he moment the door swung open, I was enveloped in silk and perfume as Gabriella hugged me close.

"My darling girl! What has my boorish nephew done now?"

I fell into her arms, welcoming the soothing comfort.

She broke our embrace and cupped my shoulders as she stepped back, arms out straight. "Oh, my sweet Madonna! What is this abomination that you are wearing?"

My cheeks burned as she took in the oversized and wrinkled men's shirt I'd tucked into the too-large pair of men's pants that were bunched and cinched around my waist with Cesare's heavy leather belt. That I'd had no choice but to accessorize with my pair of secondhand, nude Gucci heels.

Before I could respond, she waved her hand dismissively. "Never mind. Never mind." She clapped her ring-clad hands. "Upstairs now! Go! Go! Third door on the right. I have had the staff prepare the guest room. Take a long, hot shower. I will lay out some proper clothes and then we will sit down and have a nice, long chat."

Grateful for being spared having to explain that her nephew had torn my own outfit to shreds before fucking me sideways, and in my haste to escape him in the early morning hours I was forced to steal his clothes... and his car... and his phone...I obeyed her and climbed the elegant staircase to the second floor of her Rome townhouse.

When I took Cesare's car and started driving, I'd had absolutely no idea where I was going. I knew I couldn't return to the villa and Amara.

I needed time away to think.

He had broken through.

I hadn't expected it.

Hadn't planned for it.

It was traumatizing and more than a little alarming when the walls I had carefully built and maintained for years with blocks of hate, loathing, and regret had suddenly crumbled like loose sand.

I felt unprotected, weak... vulnerable.

So I ran.

I got onto the main road out of the village, which naturally headed to Rome.

It was then I remembered I had Cesare's phone. It had been in his pants pocket. Easily guessing his passcode since he hadn't changed it from when we were teenagers, I opened it and found Gabriella's number. The moment she realized it was me calling, she insisted I come to her home immediately, no questions asked.

Not even when I asked her not to tell Cesare or any of the other Cavalieri men where I was.

She had laughed. "Darling girl, but of course! We can't make these things too easy for them!"

* * *

WHAT GABRIELLA CALLED the guest bedroom was larger than my old apartment. It had a luxurious, old-world European feel. The walls were painted a beautiful dark blueish-gray with intricate molding highlighting beautiful gold-framed pastel watercolors. A long sideboard displayed a massive gold bowl filled with white hydrangeas and roses, hints of glossy green leaves tucked among them. Almost afraid to touch anything, I moved across the thick, plush white carpet to an open doorway in the far corner.

As I crossed the threshold, my mouth fell open.

The bathroom walls were papered in a gorgeous metallic gold with a stunning peacock and twisted branch design. The shower was a circular glass chamber in the center of the room, with one of those rain shower heads. It was so decadent and slightly wicked looking.

I closed the bathroom door and undressed quickly. Getting into the shower, I sucked in a shocked breath as a blast of cold water rained down on me before it turned hot. Feeling more than a little on display, I quickly washed my hair and body, loving the jasmine scent of the expensive soaps and shampoos Gabriella offered to guests.

After wrapping a wonderfully soft towel around my head and another around my middle, I emerged into the bedroom to see that Gabriella had laid out an outfit while I was in the bathroom.

It was a simple, yet elegant, backless Miu black silk jumpsuit. With my panties ruined and it being backless, I would basically be going commando. I bit my lip, wondering what Cesare would think if he knew.

Cesare.

Even thinking his name caused my heart to physically ache.

What was I going to do?

I had run. Like a fucking coward, I had run from him. It wasn't like I had wanted to hurt him. Deep down, I knew it wasn't fair to blame him for the actions of others. He wasn't responsible for what had happened to me. It wasn't his fault if someone had used me to get to him. It wasn't his fault if I chose not to confide in him afterward. These were all choices we made. Choices that impacted others. Choices that ruined the past and damned the future.

And that was the problem.

I just couldn't see how we could keep the past from bleeding into the future.

I wasn't one of those women who thought a man deserved better. Fuck that. I was a fucking catch. I was intelligent, charming (when I wanted to be), pretty (at least I had always been told so), and hard-working. Any man would be lucky to have me. Even a Cavalieri man. And I had long ago learned to tune out what others thought about me.

The problem was, saying all those things, thinking all those things, believing all those things... and living all those things, were very different realities.

It was easy to think I didn't care what others thought. It wouldn't be as easy to brush off the whispered comments and glares that would surely be leveled at me whenever I entered a room on Cesare's arm.

It was easy to believe I deserved a seat at the table at Cavalieri Property Management because I was damn good at project management. It wouldn't be as easy to deal with the snide comments and backhanded passive-aggressiveness I would surely face from the staff who thought I was an unqualified gold digger.

I placed a hand over my stomach. It would be easy to fall into the fantasy of having children with him. It would bring me to my knees, though, the day my child returned from school hurt and in tears, saying the other kids were teasing them about their mother being low-class trash.

Cesare was prepared to fight those who hurt me, but he couldn't fight the entire world.

Love was hard enough without facing those odds.

I sucked in a breath.

Love.

It was the first time I had allowed myself to even think the word in connection with Cesare since before the attack.

Love.

I was in love with Cesare.

I loved Cesare.

I loved a Cavalieri.

I had always loved Cesare.

I had never stopped loving Cesare.

My eyes filled with tears. It was because I loved him that

I'd left. It would hurt now. It would hurt for a while, probably forever, but I would survive.

He would survive.

We would both move on.

Not all love stories ended with a happily ever after.

Look at Romeo and Juliet. People seemed to forget they both died in the end.

Maybe ours was meant to be one of those nostalgic loves?

That all-consuming first love. The kind of love you never entirely got over. The one you never fully healed from. The one that stayed this small knife wound on your heart, that bled tiny teardrops. Not enough that it killed you, just enough that it stung every once in a while when a memory snuck up on you. The kind that caused a lump in the back of your throat before you returned to your daily routine, a little sadder for what never was. But deep down, you knew it wasn't the kind of love that was meant to be. It was always fated to be a bittersweet memory, never a reality.

Using the corner of the towel, I wiped at my eyes before discarding it and reaching for the silk jumpsuit.

Gabriella breezed into the room.

I cried out as I reached for my towel to cover my nakedness.

Gabriella clucked. "You and Amara, so silly."

She was holding a stunning Sabyasachi necklace. It had a massive gold ram's head pendant and was surrounded by round orange, coral, green, and black onyx stones, as well as gold and diamond embellishments in the shape of bows.

She held it up to my neck and cocked her head to the side. "Yes. *Perfetto!* With your short hair and swan-like neck, of course you must wear a simple outfit with a gorgeous necklace."

I shook my head. "Gabriella, I couldn't possibly borrow that from you. It must cost a fortune."

She waved her hand. "Nonsense. It cost nothing."

"I'm fully aware of how much an authentic Sabyasachi necklace costs."

She winked. "It was a gift from a former lover, darling. And you're not borrowing. It's yours."

My mouth fell open. "Absolutely not!"

"I insist. I never wear it. I don't have the neck for it, but you! Stunning." She clasped her hands under my jaw and lifted my head. "You must allow me these indulgences! I have no daughters of my own. You and Amara are now my precious nieces, and I'm going to spoil you both! Now get dressed!"

I kept the towel wrapped around my middle as I pulled on the jumpsuit. I then reluctantly allowed Gabriella to hustle me over to the vanity, where she fastened the necklace around my neck.

We stared at my reflection in the mirror.

She said, "You know, Sabyasachi necklaces are often worn for Indian weddings and the ram is a symbol of courage and strength in Hindu mythology." She lifted one shoulder. "I'm just saying."

"I'm not marrying your nephew, Gabriella."

She picked up a brush and slicked my hair back. "I know you usually wear it all wavy and windblown, but I think we should straighten it and have it off your face for this outfit."

"Did you hear me?"

She pulled the brush through my damp hair as she lifted one perfectly sculpted eyebrow. "Hearing you and believing you are two very different things."

* * *

AN HOUR LATER, we headed downstairs. After Gabriella's efforts with my hair and makeup, I half expected to see photographers from Vogue waiting for me.

The moment we reached the entrance hall, a staff member with a strained, almost frightened expression came running up to Gabriella. "You have a visitor. He's waiting in the conservatory. He insisted on waiting without us telling you. I'm so sorry."

She frowned. "How odd. Come, Milana."

My lungs seized.

It was Cesare.

I knew it.

I wasn't stupid. I knew he'd find me, or more accurately, his car, eventually. I just thought I'd have more time. I didn't want to face him. I pulled back on Gabriella's grasp of my hand.

She turned and looked at me sagely. "Show passion, anger, disdain, contempt, joy, and—when they serve a purpose and won't ruin your makeup—tears, but never show a man fear, darling."

Taking a deep breath, I nodded, and allowed her to escort me to the conservatory.

Among the fragrant orange and lemon trees, a tall man dressed in a suit stood with his back turned to us.

The moment we entered, he pivoted on his heel to face us.

I let out the breath I had been holding.

It wasn't Cesare.

Sebastian Diamanti crossed the black-and-white marble tile floor. He grasped Gabriella's hand and brought it to his lips. "Gabriella, looking more beautiful than ever."

He then turned his dark gaze on me. He clasped my hand in his and raised it to his lips. "And you must be Milana Carbone. The reports of your beauty precede you."

A frisson of primal fear ran up my spine the moment his lips touched my skin.

I had never met the man in person, but everyone in Italy knew of Sebastian Diamanti. The phrases "infamously dangerous" and "ridiculously wealthy" came to mind. He was at Enzo's wedding a few months ago and even I had had enough sense to stay clear of the man. And now, not only was I standing in a room with him, he was holding my hand... *and knew my name.*

This wasn't good. I inhaled a fortifying breath, pasted on what I hoped was a convincing, charming smile, looked him directly in the eyes, and said, "It is an honor and pleasure to meet you."

The moment he released my hand, I clasped them both behind my back.

Gabriella stepped forward and slightly in front of me.

Sebastian's sharp eyes didn't miss the subtle, protective move.

"To what do we owe the pleasure, Sebastian?"

The corner of his mouth lifted. "I heard you'd returned from the southern coast to brighten our dreary winter days here in Rome and thought I would stop by to pay my respects, as I was on my way to a meeting nearby."

Gabriella tilted her chin up. "That was very kind of you. I would invite you for lunch, but Milana and I were on our way out. Maybe you'd like to return later for dinner?"

He leaned in close and kissed her on the cheek. "Perhaps another time." He captured my gaze over her shoulder. "I have a feeling your evening will be otherwise...*occupied*."

With that, he strolled out of the conservatory.

Neither of us spoke until we heard the front door close.

It was only then that the air seemed to return to the room.

Gabriella looked at me. "We need to go."

"Where?"

"A man like Sebastian Diamanti doesn't just *stop by*. If he knows you are here, then that means Cesare can't be far behind. So we better hurry."

"Where are we going?"

She laughed. "Shopping, of course!"

CHAPTER 32

CESARE

I tapped my fingers on my knee as the helicopter made its descent onto the Diamanti headquarters helipad. Receiving word from Sebastian that Milana was indeed safe with my Aunt Gabriella had done nothing to allay my agitation. Nothing would, until I had her back in my arms and under my protection. Not even knowing Sebastian had several guards shadowing them as my Aunt Gabriella single-handedly made the quarterly sales quota of several grateful clerks as she flitted from designer store to designer store around Rome.

Not that I begrudged Milana her new purchases, far from it. I was pleased to know my aunt was taking her under her wing and finally giving my girl the luxury clothes she had always coveted.

I was annoyed I wasn't there for the fashion show.

I wanted to be there to see her face light up as the salesclerks from Versace, Cavalli, Valentino, Ferragamo, and the like fawned over her like she deserved.

The corner of my mouth lifted as I unbuckled my harness and unlatched the helicopter door. I guessed I would just have to spoil her all over again with another shopping trip, except this one would be for her wedding dress and honeymoon wardrobe. Perhaps I would take her to Milan? To my knowledge, she had never been. I was going to enjoy showing my babygirl the world.

My smile faded. That was if I could convince her to return with me.

Convince was the wrong word. More like if I could persuade her to not be too furious when I hauled her over my shoulder and carried her back to Cavalieri and our home there whether or not she liked it.

I stepped out of the helicopter and bent low to run across the tarmac. Sebastian emerged from a pair of tinted glass doors etched with the Diamanti family crest of a rearing dragon and unicorn.

Crede nullis. Vince omnes.

Trust none. Conquer all.

I smirked. It was no coincidence our families were so closely aligned.

He held out his hand. The moment I clasped it, he pulled me in for a one-armed hug and patted my back. "Cesare, my friend, let's go inside, away from the noise," he called out over the still-spinning helicopter blades.

I nodded in response.

We entered through the tinted glass doors and walked down a long hallway. After riding in a private elevator, we emerged into a private conference room. I knew I needn't be concerned about being overheard or security. The diamond business was significantly more cutthroat than the wine business. Sebastian's offices were more secure than *Agenzia Informazioni e Sicurezza Interna*. They were swept not just daily, but every few hours for any form of listening device. In addition to the room being completely soundproof.

Sebastian unbuttoned his suit jacket as he gestured for me to grab a seat in one of the high-backed black leather executive chairs. "Caffe? *Aperitivo?*"

I waved him off. "I'm fine."

He nodded and took a seat. Leaning back, he studied me thoughtfully before speaking.

I accepted his scrutiny. Anyone who had spent any time in Sebastian's presence knew he weighed his words carefully and assumed those around him would patiently wait for him to speak. Or, more accurately, expected them to wait.

He rubbed his index finger over his lower lip. He then leaned forward, placing his forearms on the highly polished mahogany surface of the conference table. "I have to congratulate you on your choice of bride, Cesare. Milana is a stunning creature. Graceful and beautiful. Met my gaze straight on, despite clearly being alarmed at my appearance. Have to admire that. There are many men who don't have the same courage. A fitting wife for a Cavalieri."

If those words had been uttered by any other man, I might have gotten possessively jealous, but Sebastian was like a brother. He would never steal what was mine. I accepted the compliment on Milana's behalf. "It gets better. She's fucking brilliant."

Sebastian pulled an oxblood leather portfolio toward him and opened it. He looked over a file and raised an eyebrow. "Judging by what I found out, she's definitely smarter than your dumb ass."

I threw my head back and laughed. "A man doesn't have to be smart to succeed in life. He only has to be smart in who he chooses to marry."

"Speaking of stupid fucking choices in wives, how's your brother doing?"

All levity forgotten, my lips thinned. "Just when we think it can't get any worse with that woman, she exceeds our expectations. We are both more than a little concerned she might be mixed up in this mess with Milana."

Sebastian hissed air through his teeth. "Fuck. That bad?"

"Depends on what you found out."

He gave the leather portfolio a slight shove. It slid across the table to me. "Not much. Ask me if the head of the American CIA has a mistress or if the King of England prefers butter or jam on his toast and I can tell you, but finding out the inner details of a vicious school prank seven years ago?"

My fingers curled into a fist. "It wasn't just a fucking prank. They gave her a concussion. They almost broke her nose. They threatened to rape her. They locked her in a dark room with barely any air and left her there. And they did all of it claiming they were following *my orders.*"

"No one is questioning the severity of the attack. Or its aftermath. The problem is, because it happened between teenagers and wasn't reported to the authorities, for all intents and purposes, it is considered an ugly prank. Boys will be boys and all the bullshit that goes with it. In other words, there is no paper trail. No documents. No emails."

"So you didn't find anything?"

He smirked. "I didn't say that." He nodded toward the file. "I think your instincts are correct. Romolo Castiglione's assets disappeared right before his divorce and yet his lifestyle remained the same. My people traced them to several shell companies linked to the Agnello crime family."

I frowned as I flipped through the file in front of me. It was filled with land documents, building plans, and permits all listed under foreign companies. "The Agnellos tried to get a foothold in the region last month through a warehouse owned by Renata's father, Bruno Moretti."

Sebastian shook his head. "Owned on paper only."

I leaned back. "I'm not going to like this, am I?"

"No. I only wish I hadn't destroyed the file my father prepared for Bruno and Renata before her and Enzo's wedding. I'd have more information for you."

"You thought you were doing the right thing. We both know your father would not be using that information to help me right now."

"Oh, he'd be helping you. For a price."

"Yes, and that price was usually your soul."

Sebastian shrugged. "Business the old-school way. So as far as I can tell, Romolo Castiglione had connections to the Agnellos. I believe he helped finesse paperwork regarding land purchases and other money laundering bullshit. At some point, Romolo's divorce made him a liability because he moved most of his assets overseas to hide them from his ex-wife. This caused problems because with the current political climate, the government isn't allowing foreign companies to purchase land and development properties as easily."

I rubbed my forehead. "So Romolo introduced Bruno Moretti to the Agnellos."

Sebastian pointed to me. "Exactly. For a price, Bruno allows the Agnellos to use his name, reputation, and company to purchase property around the Abruzzo region. It's the new McMafia. They don't just want a piece of the drug and gun trades. They want real estate and legitimate development projects for the long-game money. There's more political power in owning land, especially land in the resource-rich Abruzzo region."

I shook my head. This was why the cap rate appraisal Milana did on the project Romolo was bringing to me was so off. The figures were based on inflated numbers and false investors to hide the money chain.

I sighed. So Enzo's father-in-law was mixed up in some dirty land investment deals with the mafia.

And possibly Renata, since we still didn't know her level of involvement in her father's business dealings.

Sebastian continued. "Before he did everyone a favor and blew his damn head off, you told me Romolo referenced a man he was afraid of. I think that mystery man is an enforcer for the Agnellos. The man charged with keeping both Romolo and Bruno in line. In order for this scheme to work, significant amounts of money have to be transferred into their names for the sales transactions. The Agnellos will not let tens of millions of euro leave their hands on trust alone."

"And you think that man was the second man who attacked Milana all those years ago?"

Sebastian nodded.

"It makes sense. The way Romolo reacted to my accusation, the man was clearly connected to both his past and present. In order to keep Romolo and Bruno in line, the man would have to remain close, which means he would have to be someone who wouldn't raise suspicion. A local."

Sebastian's brow knitted. "Problem is, we can't find out his name. He's a ghost."

The man could be anyone.

Eventually, the Agnellos were going to become suspicious over Romolo's disappearance.

If Sebastian was able to draw a straight line to Milana, then so could they.

As if reading my mind, Sebastian said, "I've already reached out to your father. I'm sending him some men."

"We have our own security."

"Mine have bigger guns."

I couldn't argue with that. If Italy ever went to war, I half suspected they would come to the Diamantis for arms.

Wealthy people *fought* over expensive bottles of wine.

They *killed* one another over diamonds.

We both stood. I reached out my hand to shake his. "I have to get to— "

He finished for me. "Milana. Of course. I have a car already waiting for you."

"With a couple of guards as well, I hope. I'll need them if I'm going to drag Aunt Gabriella to Abruzzo in winter for her own safety."

Sebastian rolled his shoulders and lifted his chin. "The key with women is to establish early on your dominant authority and your expectations of obedience."

I paused with my hand on the doorknob and just looked at him. I then shook my head, swallowing a laugh. "I wonder if I sound as obnoxiously foolish to Milana when I say shit like that, too."

"What?"

"Nothing, old friend. I have a feeling you'll learn what I'm talking about soon enough."

CHAPTER 33

MILANA

I never in a million years would have thought it was possible to do *too much shopping*, but Gabriella proved me wrong. Now I saw why Amara kept describing her afternoon shopping spree with her as overwhelming and borderline alarming.

There was no telling the woman no!

There was no telling her enough!

There was no telling her I'm fine, I don't need a *fifth* cocktail dress!

Here this whole time, I thought Cesare got his stubborn, domineering personality from his father.

Nope.

It clearly ran on the female side of the family, too.

I thought if ever given the chance, I would be different from Amara. At the time, I thought she had been crazy about objecting to Gabriella spending Barone's money. Unlike her, I would gleefully spend Cesare's money to get back at him. And why not? He had plenty of it. It wasn't like me spending a thousand euro, or two, on a couple of dresses and maybe a new purse was going to break his bank account.

As I trudged up the central staircase to the guest bedroom with not even a tenth of my purchases weighing my arms down as they dangled from fancy bags, I marveled at the obscene amounts of money that was spent on me today in a whirlwind, as if it all meant nothing.

I thought Gabriella had bypassed *a couple thousand euro* within her first few steps inside the *very first* boutique. Each time I tried to object or, at the very least, *slow her down*, she would tell me that Cesare would want me to have something or that I was going to need a particular item as his future wife.

No matter how many times I told her I would not marry Cesare, she blissfully ignored me.

Each time, she would just raise a perfectly manicured hand in the air and rattle her heavy gold bracelets, waving off my protests as merely a lover's quarrel. She would then talk about how wonderful it was that Cesare had found himself a woman of intelligence and passion and how happy she was for both of us.

After that, she would tell me some endearing story about him as a boy.

She wasn't fooling me for one second.

I saw the sly looks she would cast me after each heart-warming story, hoping she was making an impression. I wouldn't put it past her to be embellishing the stories, or to be outright lying, just to sway me to Cesare's cause.

It was clear Gabriella wanted both Amara and me as

nieces. And the feeling was mutual. We both adored her. I meant, she was lovely, and everything we would ever want in an aunt. She was fun, vivacious, and fashionable. She was like a living, breathing bottle of prosecco. Pretty, bubbly, and made you feel just a little drunk and unstable if you stayed too long in her presence.

I walked into the bedroom and dropped the packages on the chaise under the window.

I turned when I heard the door slam shut behind me.

"Cesare!"

He reached behind him and turned the brass key in the lock.

I pressed a hand to my throat, but then lowered it when I remembered my Gemini chain was not there. I backed further into the room. If I screamed, that would bring Gabriella, and I had already involved her in my drama too much as it was. My gaze skittered over all the designer bags. I waved a shaking hand over them. "I can take them all back. I was just humoring Gabriella. And your car is fine. I was just... borrowing it. It's parked just outside."

He strolled over to the bags and glanced at them. He pulled on the outside edge of the *Federica Parmeggiani* lingerie bag. There was a delicate rustle of tissue paper. Then he lifted his arm. Hooked over his index finger was their hand-embroidered Nicole white bodysuit in tulle and white lace. It screamed *sexy bride on her wedding night*, which was why Gabriella insisted I buy it.

He lowered his head and fixed his heated gaze on me. "Put this on."

I blurted out, "It's crazy-expensive lingerie. I can't return it if I put it on."

His shoulders shook slightly as he chuckled. He shook his head. "Oh, my beautiful, stubborn, *piccola gattina selvaggia*. You still don't get it, do you?"

He tossed the lingerie onto the bed and advanced on me.

For once... I didn't move.

Not one step.

I didn't even move my head to look around for an escape.

I was tired of running from him.

I was tired of fighting him.

Tired of fighting my feelings for him.

Tired of denying him.

Tired of denying us.

Tired of pretending I hated him....

My eyes filled with tears.

If I allowed myself to finally, truly be honest, I had desperately missed him over the years. I missed his smile, and the silly way he'd wink at me when he was trying to charm me into agreeing with him. I missed smelling his cologne on my clothes. I missed how, when we were in a crowd, he would always put his arm protectively around my waist and tilt his shoulders toward me. I missed the easy way we would laugh together at our stupid inside jokes that only we thought were funny.

I missed how to him I was, and always had been, just Milana, not the daughter of a disgraceful mother, not the unwanted bastard of an unknown man, nor the disappointing granddaughter of a hateful grandmother. Just Milana.

And after spending just these few hours away from him,

all I had wanted to do was run back into his arms and say that I had made a mistake.

Cesare wrapped his arm around my middle and pulled me close as he delved his fingers into my hair and tilted my head back. He towered over me as he stared down at me, studying my face.

I opened my mouth to speak.

He stopped me. "Don't. Please, don't. I just want a moment to hold you."

He pulled my head to his chest. Placing my ear over his heart as his hand cupped my jaw. He tightened his arms around me.

I closed my eyes and inhaled a deep breath, then let it go in a long sigh.

His embrace felt like *home*. The first I had ever known.

I wrapped my arms around his waist to hold him back. It was only then that I felt the tension from his body release.

He hugged me even tighter before picking me up and carrying me to the bed.

He pulled back the covers and laid me gently on the powder blue silk sheets. Keeping his gaze on me, he stripped out of his clothes and joined me. Then, without saying a word, he carefully and slowly unbuttoned my jumpsuit and slid it over my arms and down my hips and off. He then lifted my shoulders and unhooked the heavy necklace Gabriella had given me.

He kissed the sensitive spot under my ear before whispering, "I meant what I said. From now on, my baby only wears jewels and clothes I bought her."

I moaned as he moved his lips along my jaw. "After my

ZOE BLAKE

dizzying shopping trip with your aunt today, I don't think that will be a problem."

He laughed as he pulled the covers over our bodies and moved between my thighs.

I really did love the sound of his laugh. It was a dark, rumbling chuckle that always started as a deep vibration in his chest.

He braced his forearms on either side of my head and raised his torso as he caged me in. His heavy cock rested against my inner thigh.

His gaze moved from my eyes to my lips and back. He then used his right hand to smooth back my hair before saying, "You really are the most beautiful woman I have ever laid eyes on."

I broke our gaze and opened my mouth to say something witty and sarcastic back, as was my way.

Cesare placed his finger over my lips, stopping me. "No. We're not doing that. Not now. Not in this moment."

His brow furrowed as he once more studied my face. He brushed my cheek with the backs of his fingers. "I owe you an apology."

My vision blurred as the tears came fast. I swallowed past the lump in my throat. "No. We are *definitely* not doing *that* either. *Not in this moment,*" I said, throwing his words back at him.

If we were going to have a future, I had to let the past go.

It wasn't fair to blame him for the actions of others.

It wasn't fair to blame him for not protecting me when I refused to even tell him what had happened.

Of course, what had happened to me wasn't fair either, but nothing in life was fair.

And I couldn't blame him for wanting to go all over-the-top protective alpha male now, either.

What had I expected after telling him what happened? Had I honestly thought he was just going to kiss me on the forehead and say that should make it all better? Of course the man was going to go seek revenge.

What also wasn't fair was me questioning my worthiness, based on the actions of my parents.

Or trying to prove anything to anyone other than myself.

Fuck all that kind of thinking.

For years, I had put on a boss bitch mask. It was time to own the persona, too.

He leaned down and kissed my forehead. Then the corner of my eye. Then my cheek. Then the corner of my mouth, before whispering against my lips, "I agree, but that is not what I'm apologizing for."

He shifted his hips.

I gasped as he pushed the thick head of his cock just inside my entrance.

I lifted my legs and wrapped them around his hips, intending to pull him fully inside of me.

He resisted. "Not yet."

I frowned. Then narrowed my eyes. I shimmied my hips while running my tongue over my lips, then raised an eyebrow. "Are you sure?"

He bared his teeth as he growled, "*La mia piccola gattina selvaggia*, behave. There is something we need to get straight between us first."

I thrust out my lower lip.

He leaned down and nipped at it with his teeth. "And pouting won't change my mind, minx."

Just to torture him, I raised my hips again and squeezed my inner thighs, loving how he threw his head back and groaned. "Fine," I huffed.

Starting again, he said, "I owe you an apology. I realize now that I have tried to get through that incredibly stubborn wall of yours by repeatedly reminding you of how beautiful, intelligent, and amazing I think you are. I have told you how much I admire your strength and spirit. And we both know you are annoyingly even better at property management than I am."

I snorted.

He raised an eyebrow.

I pulled my lips between my teeth and tried to look contrite.

With a warning look, he continued. "And I have shown you—repeatedly—just how irresistibly fucking sexy I think you are. There are times I have to restrain myself from just tossing you over any available surface and plowing into this sweet pussy regardless of where we are or who is watching."

It was my turn to look at him with raised eyebrows. "You have been showing *restraint* until this point?"

After another warning look from him, I pinched my fingers and motioned across my lips, zipping them shut.

He nudged his hips and pushed his cock inside of me, but only by a few teasing inches. "I have even told you how you are now—and always have been—mine and mine alone. How you are my *carissima*, my beloved, and how I already consider us bound for life as man and wife, and how there is nothing I want more in this life than to share a child with you."

A tear slipped out of the corner of my eye as my lower lip trembled.

He pushed deeper inside of me as he leaned down and pressed his lips to mine. For a moment we stayed like that, breathing each other's air. He thrust in again, filling me, as he shifted his arms to press his hands against the top of my head, enfolding me completely in his embrace as he claimed me completely.

His lips moved over mine as he said, "The one thing I neglected to say.... the one thing I should have been saying this whole time... is that *I love you, Milana.*"

I burst into tears and clasped my hands around his face, pulling him close as we kissed.

He pulled back slightly to stare into my eyes. "I love you, Milana. I have always loved you. I never stopped loving you. First as a friend, and now as my everything. And I hope soon as my wife. I love you, babygirl, and I don't expect you to say it back to me. I know it will take time to earn your trust and—"

"I love you, too!"

Cesare threw his head back. "Thank God!"

He claimed my mouth as he moved his hips in slow, methodical thrusts. I tightened my legs around his hips as I ran my tongue along his neck, tasting the tang of his cologne.

For the first time, we didn't fuck; we made love.

And it was... not us.

I shifted until I was on top of him, straddling his hips. I dropped my hands on either side of his head. He cupped my breasts as I leaned over him. "You know I love you now, right?"

He thrust up gently, being careful not to hurt me. "I'll never tire of hearing that."

I used the tip of my finger to trace his bottom lip as I lowered my voice to a seductive, husky whisper. "So I say this *with love*. I'm going to need you to stop with this sensitive 'making love' crap and *fuck me!*"

Cesare rolled me underneath him, snatched my wrists and pulled them over my head, growling, "God, I fucking love you." Right before he ruthlessly fucked me.

CHAPTER 34

MILANA

I snuggled deeper within Cesare's embrace. He was so nice and warm compared to the rest of the freezing bedroom.

Leaning up on one elbow, I lifted the silk sleeping mask that covered his eyes. "Time to wake up."

Although I hadn't had a night terror since that first night with him a few weeks ago, I still wasn't ready to give up sleeping with a light on and a window open. Cesare didn't seem to mind. He added some extra fluffy, warm blankets to our bed and wore a sleeping mask.

Since returning to the villa from Rome, we had taken a few days to just be alone at Cesare's house and adjust to the newness of our relationship. But it was Monday and time to get back to the real world.

Besides, I had a fabulous new wardrobe I was looking forward to showing off.

Amara and I had plans to meet in the village for lunch

after my morning meetings. She wanted to show me the latest round of drawings she had commissioned for the new Cavalieri wine labels, and I wanted to run an idea I had for a development project of some Cavalieri land to the north by her before presenting it to Cesare, since it was a bold, and slightly wild, idea. We were hoping Gabriella would join us since she had been less than pleased at Cesare's insistence that she return to the villa with us.

His arm wrapped around my waist as he pulled me on top of him. He took my hand and guided it between his legs to his already hard cock. "Since you are already awake, how about you amuse yourself by sucking my cock for a few minutes while I rest."

I slid down between his thighs and kissed his chest, then his abdomen.

Cesare threaded his fingers through my hair and let out a low groan. His cock bounced, hitting me below the jaw.

I giggled. "Nice try. My throat is still sore from the blow job I gave you last night," I said, before jumping off the bed and taking the blankets with me.

Cesare lunged for me, but the sleeping mask had fallen back into place, blocking his vision. So his arm swiped in an arc, catching only air. He called out as I ran into the dressing room we shared, "You can run and hide, but I think I've proven over and over again I'll still find you!"

CESARE ENTERED the dressing room and placed my latte macchiato on the vanity next to my makeup brushes.

He looked over at the vintage cream Chanel wool jacket and skirt I had pulled out. "A little dressy for hanging around the villa."

I leaned in closer to the mirror as I swept black eyeliner into a perfect cat eye. "But not too dressy for work and lunch with Amara and your aunt."

He paused in buttoning his white dress shirt. He crossed to me. I couldn't help but admire the glimpse of tan and muscled chest I caught between the open flaps of his dress shirt and the way his gray suit slacks hung low on his hips, exposing his flat abdomen. He caged me in, resting his hands on the edge of the vanity counter on either side of me as he leaned down.

He captured my gaze in the mirror. "I think there has been a miscommunication. You don't think you're going into the office, do you?"

My eyes narrowed as I slowly put down my eyeliner. "No, I don't *think* I'm going into the office. I *know* I'm going into the office."

He straightened and ran a hand through his hair. "Milana, I don't want to start an argument—"

"Then don't."

He let out a frustrated sigh. "I have no intention of keeping you from work, but until I figure out who the fuck the second man was who attacked you, it's not safe."

I turned in my chair and rested my forearm on the back. "You said yourself that it could be anyone."

"Yes."

"And that there has been no news about Romolo, which means he was such an unloved piece of shit that no one has even noticed he's missing yet, which also means no one is looking for him alive, let alone dead."

He placed his hands on his hips. "Also true."

"So for all we know, the Agnellos could spend months, maybe even years, looking for him abroad where all his shell companies are located, assuming he left the country before they even think that it might be a local issue."

His jaw tightened. "I don't like where this is going."

I raised my palms up innocently. "All I'm saying is that only Romolo knew that the Cavalieri family was coming after him for what he did to me, and that by extension you would eventually be going after the Agnellos when his involvement with them was exposed... and he took that information to his unmarked grave."

He rubbed his fingers over his eyes. "I'm definitely not liking where this is going."

I stood and wrapped my arms around his waist. "So there is no reason for the second man to be a danger to me. And it would make more sense for us to act normally while you continue to look for him. If we change things up, he might get suspicious." I shrugged as I batted my eyelashes. "And really... when you think about it... wouldn't I be safer spending my day with you, by your side at your office, then all alone here in the house?"

He pulled me close, placed a finger under my chin, and tilted my head back. "Don't think I didn't notice what you did just then."

I smiled. "Did it work?"

He sighed. "Yes. I hate when you're right."

I leaned up and gave him a quick kiss on the lips. "You should probably get used to it."

He gave me a quick spank on the ass in response before we both returned to getting dressed for work.

* * *

As we walked toward the receptionist's desk together, Liliana stood and held up a vase filled with yellow chrysanthemums. "*Buongiorno*, Milana. These are for you!"

Cesare's eyes narrowed. "Excuse me? Who is sending my fiancée flowers?"

Liliana's eyes widened at his intense glare. "Your sister-in-law."

We both said in unison, "Renata?"

Liliana nodded. "Yes. You just missed her. I'm surprised you didn't see her on the stairs. She said she had an appointment and couldn't wait but wanted to drop off these flowers for you."

I cast a glance at Cesare. I was fully aware of what an absolute, passive-aggressive, snobby bitch Renata had been to Amara from the moment she found out about Barone's intentions. There was absolutely no reason Renata would be inclined to be any nicer to me.

Cesare shrugged. "Maybe she's finally resolved to having you and Amara as sisters-in-law and is trying to turn over a new leaf?"

I smirked. Not likely. Mean girls like Renata rarely changed. It would also explain her odd choice of flowers, since everyone knew yellow flowers meant jealousy and betrayal, and chrysanthemums were usually only used for funerals.

Liliana nodded toward the vase. "She said you need to fill the vase with water so the flowers don't die."

"Thank you, Liliana."

Cesare and I walked a few steps away. "Did you want me to handle that for you?" he asked.

I shook my head. "No, I need to check my lipstick anyway."

He gazed at my mouth. "I checked. It's gone."

"That's because someone kissed it off in the car."

He gave me a kiss on the cheek and walked toward the hidden stairs that led to his upper-level office. "I will see you at lunch."

I called out, "I have plans with Amara and your Aunt Gabriella."

He turned and grinned. "I know. I'm coming with you. Just because I agreed to let you come back to the office doesn't mean I'm going to let you flit all over the village unprotected."

I opened my mouth to protest.

He lifted his hand up. "Nonnegotiable."

I stuck my tongue out at him. "Fine, but be prepared to be bored to death with talk of Gucci scarves and shades of lipstick."

He winked. "I'm good with that. I'll just be imagining that cute pink tongue of yours doing all kinds of naughty things while you are blindfolded with a Gucci scarf, leaving lipstick stains on my co—"

"Cesare!" I gasped, casting a scandalized look in Liliana's direction.

She was deliberately keeping her head down, shuffling papers on her desk, but her flaming red cheeks gave away that she had heard every word of our exchange.

He gave me an unrepentant grin. "You started it." Then turned and headed up the stairs, his laughter following him.

I adjusted my purse on my shoulder, picked up the vase, and headed across the upstairs lobby area to the ladies' room. It was to the right across from the central marble staircase.

As I crossed in front of the stairs, I saw a dark figure pass me out of the corner of my eye, like a fast-moving shadow. Before I could see what it was, there was a hard shove to my right shoulder. My torso jerked forward, throwing me off-balance. The vase slipped from my grasp. I watched in horror as it smashed against the edge of a marble stair, shattering. My arms windmilled as I tried to regain my balance, but the leather soles of my high heels slipped on the polished surface of the tile. My knee buckled and my body pitched toward the top of the stairs.

My vision seemed to move in slow motion, as if I were viewing things from underwater.

Everything was a blur of wavy, indistinct objects and colors as this weightless feeling overcame me. My arm caught on something. The pain was excruciating as it was twisted behind my back, before I saw with dawning horror the uneven edge of the top marble stair.

Then everything went black.

CHAPTER 35

MILANA

*C*haos and pain. It surrounded me. Chaos and pain. Pain and chaos.

Noise. Yelling. Pain.

Pain. Noise. Yelling. Chaos.

Pain. Aching. Throbbing. Pain.

I opened my eyes and quickly shut them again as a sharp stab of pure agony pierced my skull.

A warm hand cupped my cheek. "Milana, baby?"

I groaned.

"Baby, please. Open your eyes."

I didn't want to open my eyes. When I opened my eyes, there was only torture.

His arms wrapped around me tighter.

I could feel myself being lifted.

Cesare's words rumbled in his chest as he shouted out orders. "Get out of my way. Out of my fucking way! Where's the goddamn *ambulanza?*"

Someone else shouted, "Don Cavalieri says he and Amara will meet you at the *ospedale* and that he's called your family's physician and he's meeting you there as well."

My body was jostled as Cesare ran. He was breathless as he talked. "Hold on, Milana. Hold on, babygirl. It's going to be okay. I've got you."

I could hear the panic and fear in his voice. I wanted to tell him I was fine. I wanted to tell him not to worry, but I couldn't form the words. I tried to open my eyes again, but groaned and turned my head into his chest as the bright sunlight caused another shaft of pain when we exited the building and entered the piazza.

Hearing my whimper, his large hand covered my eyes, protecting them from the horrible light.

I felt the high-pitched sound of screeching tires like a physical blow.

Then I heard Enzo's voice. "The *ambulanza* is blocked down the lane by a double-parked car. Get in. We'll take her ourselves."

A voice I didn't recognize said, "Hand her to me."

Cesare ground out, "No fucking way."

"Sir, you have to get into the car. Please!"

My body was jostled as I was handed off briefly. I then felt the familiar warmth and strength of Cesare's embrace as I was nestled on his lap in the back seat of Enzo's car.

The last thing I remembered before unconsciousness claimed me again was the feel of Cesare's lips on my forehead and his voice whispering, "I love you, Milana."

* * *

"THE DOCTORS SAY I'M FINE!" I argued from my hospital bed several hours later.

Cesare, Barone, and Enzo stood at the end of the bed studying my medical chart as if all three suddenly had medical degrees.

Amara was holding my hand, while Gabriella rummaged in her purse looking for something to brighten me up after declaring I looked too pale.

Cesare shook his head. "I'm not comfortable with them just bandaging her up and handing us a couple *aspirina* and telling us to watch for cognitive symptoms over the next twelve hours."

Enzo crossed his arms over his chest as he stared at me thoughtfully. "Maybe we should insist on another opinion?"

I squeezed Amara's hand.

She sent Barone a pleading look. "Barone, we've already gotten five opinions and two MRIs. They've all said the same thing. She has a nasty bump on her head and a concussion, but she got really lucky."

Cesare's expression was stormy. There was a tic in his upper cheek as his jaw clenched. His right hand was curled into a fist. "Don't forget about the fifteen stitches in her neck from the cut that barely missed her jugular," he ground out.

Amara and I exchanged a look. We knew when we were beaten.

I had gotten lucky. Really lucky.

My purse strap had gotten hooked on the newel post, saving me from a nasty, and possibly fatal, fall down the entire marble staircase. My body had swung violently forward and then was jerked backward by the strap. I banged the back of my head on one of the stairs, but that was cushioned by my bulky purse. Thank God for bulging makeup bags!

The worse injury was caused by the shattered glass of the vase. A shard had pierced my neck, close to my jugular. At first I was worried about a scar, but I was told that Cesare had raised hell making sure the best surgeon sutured me up to lessen the chances of one.

Gabriella exclaimed, "Found it!" She pulled a scarf out of her purse and waved it in the air.

We all turned and looked at her.

Only Gabriella would be concerned about accessorizing a hospital gown, and I absolutely adored her for it.

She flicked her hair over her shoulder. "Don't you all give me those dirty looks. You are helping in your way. I'm helping in mine." She gently placed the brightly colored scarf around my neck and tied it in a fashionable knot, hiding the ugly bandage.

I patted her hand and gave her an encouraging smile to show my appreciation. She was hiding it behind her usual bravado, but from one diva to another, I could tell my near miss had rattled her as much as the rest of them. Her eyeliner was smeared at the edges of her eyes where she had clearly been wiping away tears, and the edges of her nose were red.

Enzo cleared his throat. "Benito wants to question her about the fall. There are a few employees who claim she may have been pushed but can't agree on what the person looked like because it all happened so fast."

Cesare cursed under his breath. "What the fuck is the point of having all this extra security if we can't protect our women? They are going to have to stay on Cavalieri grounds until we have this all figured out."

Gabriella huffed. "As usual, you are overreacting! Milana hasn't said she was pushed. Have you even bothered to ask *her* what happened before you go lock her and Amara up in towers like doomed maidens?"

Cesare threw his hands in the air. "Aunt Gabriella, I love you, but I'm not going to fucking risk Milana's safety again. I gave in once and let her go to the office and she almost fucking died."

Enzo then reasoned, "Well, if that's the case, then maybe we shouldn't leave her here? We can't secure the building. There are too many variables and unknowns. Maybe we should take her back to the villa with a team of doctors and nurses?"

I cast another silent, pleading look at Amara.

She squeezed my hand in understanding, then said, "Wait! Look, I'm more concerned for Milana than any of you—"

Cesare made an objecting growl.

Amara conceded and corrected, "... than *most* of you, and even I think a freaking team of doctors and nurses is a bit much. I'm worried we are going to overwhelm her with all this. Can't we just have Dr. Pontano stay at the villa? He treated me once, and he was very kind and efficient."

Cesare crossed to the other side of the bed, brushing Gabriella to the side and facing off with Amara. "She's not staying at the villa. She's staying with me, at our home."

"You can't look after her by yourself. She should be at the villa where Gabriella and Rosa and I can take turns watching

311

over her. She doesn't need a man right now. We will take care of her."

"She's my woman and I will be the one taking care of her!"

"Well, she's my best friend and —"

Enzo interrupted their argument before it got out of hand. "Regardless of who takes care of Milana, the villa is too big and the obvious place. If someone is truly trying to kill her, maybe we should stash her at the cottage. It's smaller and easier to secure."

Kill me.

Kill me?

Fuck, this was too much harsh reality for my pounding head to take in right now. I just wanted to curl up in bed and sleep.

Gabriella objected. "You are not *stashing* the girl anywhere. She's not contraband! I agree with Amara. She should be at the villa where we can all watch over her."

"Aunt Gabriella, you know I didn't mean it that way."

I winced as everyone raised their voices and talked over one another.

Barone held up his hand.

The entire room immediately became silent.

Blessedly, perfectly, beautifully silent.

He grasped the metal bar at the end of my bed and stared down at me. His voice was gentle but firm. "Milana, I want you to answer me honestly. Were you pushed?"

I twisted the bedsheet between my fingers as I looked from Cesare's strained and worried face to Amara's concerned one, then back to Barone. I didn't want to worry them, but I also knew this was too serious a matter to lie about. After swallowing past the dryness in my throat, I nodded. "I can't be certain. I think I might have been. It's all a bit fuzzy, but I'm pretty sure I remember a dark figure and the feeling of being shoved from behind. But I couldn't tell you who it was."

He exchanged a knowing look with Enzo and Cesare.

It was strange how the energy in the room immediately changed. It was like an ominous thundercloud had rolled down from the mountain to settle in over the valley. That was probably a pretty good analogy for what it was like when the Cavalieri gods descended from their mountaintop villa to punish the stupid humans for their behavior. If my head and body didn't ache so much, I might have found it amusing.

Even Gabriella seemed subdued.

Barone straightened and rolled his shoulders back. "It's settled then."

Cesare moved closer to me. He brushed his knuckles over my cheek as he looked down at me with love tinged with worry. "Agreed."

Enzo nodded as he uncrossed his arms and headed to the door. "I'll see to the arrangements."

Gabriella pulled out her mobile as she crossed the room to follow Enzo. "I'll call Alfonso and let him know what is happening, so he can start preparations."

Settled?

What the hell is settled?

I frowned as I looked at Amara to see if she understood what the hell was happening.

She met my gaze with equal confusion.

She turned to Barone. "Um, for those of us who aren't

Cavalieris, and who apparently cannot communicate tele-pathically, can you explain what just happened? What is settled?"

He gave her an indulgent smile as he wrapped an arm around her waist and pulled her close. He then gave her a kiss on the forehead. "Yet."

"What?"

"You're not a Cavalieri... *yet*."

Amara rolled her eyes. "Yet."

"*Brava ragazza*. I will explain outside. I think Cesare and Milana would like a moment."

Amara turned to me. "I'll be outside if you need me."

Cesare kept his gaze on me. "Thank you, Amara, but she won't. She has me."

Amara paused, but then smiled. She allowed Barone to lead her out of the room.

Cesare sat on the edge of the bed and reached over to smooth my hair back from my face.

I clasped his hand in mine. "So all that noise and chaos is what having a real family is like?"

He rubbed his thumb over the back of my hand. "Think you could get used to it?"

"I think so."

"You know you scared me to death today."

"I'm sorry."

"I don't know what I would have done if I'd lost you."

"Probably win more arguments."

"This isn't funny, Milana."

"I know. I'm just not used to so many people... I don't know... caring about me. It feels awkward."

He pulled the covers back and carefully lifted my legs to the side. "Well, that is something else you are going to have to get used to."

He pulled the blanket off the bed and wrapped it around my shoulders.

I looked around. "Where are my clothes and shoes?"

I didn't want to leave without them. That was a brand-new outfit, and it was expensive.

"Don't worry. Gabriella collected them. She was particularly annoyed about the shoes being scuffed but said she would take care of it, whatever that means."

I braced myself on the handrail on the side of the bed and prepared to stand.

Cesare frowned as he stood over me. His fists on his hips. "What do you think you're doing?"

I blinked up at him. "Getting up?"

He ran his hand through his hair and blew out a breath. "You're not walking, Milana! You just had a horrific fall. I'm going to carry you."

"That is unnecessary. I'm pretty sure I can walk."

Before I could argue further, Cesare swooped me up into his arms. "You are going to be a terrible patient, aren't you?"

I wrinkled my nose. "Probably."

As he carried me out of the room, he said, "There is something else you are going to have to get used to."

"What is that?"

"Saying I was right."

I leaned back and looked at him, my brow furrowed. "And what exactly were you right about?"

"About you not going into work."

My mouth fell open. "Oh no, you don't get to play that card. For all we know, I tripped, and this was all just an embarrassing accident. I do wear ridiculously high heels."

"Say it. Go on. Say it. Say, 'Cesare, you were right.'"

I softened my eyes as I put my fingertips to my temple. "I would, it's just that my head… it's starting to throb…."

Cesare chuckled. "Don't ever change, my love. Don't ever change."

As he carried me to the car where Barone and Amara were waiting, I tried to calm the frenetic, queasy feeling in my stomach.

I knew what Cesare was doing.

What we were both doing.

He was trying to tease and distract me. He was deliberately making light of the situation because he didn't want to worry me, but I wasn't fooled.

I had known him for too long.

We had too much history between us.

I could see it in his eyes.

The barely suppressed rage.

I had seen it a few days ago on the train when he learned the truth about my attack, and it was here now. He was doing his best to hide it, for me, and I loved him for trying, but I knew the truth.

What happened to me was no accident.

And judging by the looks exchanged by the Cavalieri men, someone was going to pay for it.

CHAPTER 36

ENZO

I was leaning against the wall of our darkened entryway, arms crossed, waiting, when she finally crept home.

"Good evening... *wife.*"

Renata's lips thinned, her nostrils flaring slightly with disdain before she schooled her features. Pasting a false smile on her heavily made-up face, she said, "Enzo, I didn't see you there."

I pushed off from the wall with my shoulders. "Come, have a drink with me."

She lifted one carefully manicured hand to her temple and fluttered her eyelids. "Actually, I'm quite tired. I think I'll just go to—"

I advanced on her.

Before she could escape, I wrapped a hand around her upper arm and dragged her across the hall into the parlor. "One drink with your husband, *wife.* I insist."

Like all the rooms in my once elegant home, it was garish and ugly. The only thing that could distract from the obscene Andy Warhol knockoff painting of Renata over the authentic sixteenth century hand-carved, white marble fireplace was the disgusting perversion of bright pink leather furniture accented with gold and glass tables.

I tossed her into a seat and crossed to the mirror-fronted bar, reaching for the bottle of Amaro liquor.

"Can I fix you one, *dear?*"

She adjusted the skirt of her dress as she lifted her chin and gave me a tight-lipped smile. "I'm pregnant. Remember, *honey?*"

"If I forget, it's probably because you so often do, *dearest.*"

Reaching for a fresh orange, I pulled out my pocketknife and opened the sharp blade, not missing Renata's slight gasp and the way her gaze flitted to the door and back to me. "I tried calling you several times today. You never answered your phone. I was worried, *darling.*"

I sliced two long strips of orange rind. I then set my knife aside and kept my gaze on her as I flicked open my sterling silver lighter and torched the rinds, sending the smoky scent of bittersweet orange into the air. I placed the charred, curled rinds into the glasses.

She looked down at her hands, pretending to examine her nails. "Sorry, my mobile ran out of charge." She smoothed out her skirt again. "Why, did something... happen?"

She looked up at me through a fan of fake eyelashes.

I poured a generous portion of Amaro into two glasses, covering the rinds with the bitter, dark amber liquor. I crossed the room and stood before her.

Towering over her, legs spread, I held out the glass.

She looked up at me, hesitating. Finally, she took it.

Maintaining my standing position over her, I said, "As a matter of fact, yes. Milana had a nasty fall at work."

She tried to stand. "Oh, no, is she—"

I pushed her back down by her shoulders. "Fortunately, she's fine."

Renata jerked her head to the side and down. "Really?" Her voice was tight and strained. "Well, she should be more careful in the future. She probably wasn't used to walking in vintage Chanel with high heels. Some women can find the skirt confining. It takes a special skill, especially on stairs," she rambled nervously, still avoiding eye contact. "I, of course, have no issues, but I was raised to have poise and sophistication."

I closed my eyes and took a deep breath as I tightened my abdominal muscles, resisting the urge to throw my head back and howl with outrage and pain. This was my fault. I had brought this venomous viper into my family. All out of a misplaced sense of honor. I should have listened to my father and brother when they begged me not to marry her.

But no, I'd had to punish myself for....

I took another breath and said through clenched teeth, keeping my voice deliberately calm, "Funny, *dearest*, I don't recall telling you it was a fall down the stairs."

Renata's head snapped up to meet my gaze. She blinked several times before responding with a laugh, the sound brittle and hard as she played with her earring. "Of course it was the stairs. How else would she fall? Unless the poor girl is so uncouth, she just trips over her own two feet on flat ground."

"You're right, of course." I nodded to her glass. "You're not drinking."

She stared at the glass but didn't lift it to her lips.

I knew what she was thinking.

I raised an eyebrow and leveled my gaze at her as I lifted my glass to my mouth and took a long, deliberate swallow before saying, "I *really* must insist that you do, *darling*."

I watched her throat move as she swallowed several times before hesitantly lifting the glass to her lips. She tried to take a small sip. I placed my finger under the bottom of the glass and tipped it up.

Renata choked as the bitter liquor dribbled out of the corner of her mouth.

I took another sip, taking strange solace in the acrid, herbal taste with its hints of bitter orange and clove. "Ironic that a liquor named Amaro is making you *choke*."

Renata glared at me as she swiped at her mouth with the back of her hand, smearing her lipstick.

"I understand you brought Milana flowers this morning?"

She set the glass aside and folded her hands in her lap as she straightened her back. "Since your brother and father seem determined to bring the Cavalieri name down with their choice of paramours, I thought I might as well make the best of it." She waved her hand in the air like some exiled, long-suffering monarch. "Perhaps they will see me as a guiding influence, someone they could emulate so they don't embarrass the family. But I was long gone before she tripped and fell, or I would, of course, have stayed to offer my help."

I crossed to the fireplace mantle, concerned about what I might do if I stayed within striking distance of her. "That's the worrying thing, *darling*. Milana is certain she didn't trip." I watched her closely. "She's certain she was pushed."

She picked up her glass and took another sip. Stalling. Finally, she said, "You don't believe her, do you?"

"Any reason why I shouldn't?"

"It's the oldest female trick in the book, *dearest*. Play the damsel in distress. First, she dredges up the past with some silly story about a harmless school prank, just to get Cesare's attention and sympathy, and when that doesn't get a marriage proposal out of him, she raises the stakes. Now there's some mysterious stranger out there trying to kill her? Seriously? Milana Carbone? Who would care about killing a nobody like her?"

I looked down at my drink, swirling the liquor. "Second oldest."

"What was that?"

I raised my head and leveled a glare at her. "*Second* oldest female trick. I believe the first is tricking a man into bed and getting pregnant."

She stood. Storming over to the bar, she slammed the glass onto the mirrored surface so hard I could hear it crack from across the room. "Don't pretend like you didn't want it."

I slammed my own drink onto the mantle and crossed to her. "You know damn well I thought you were your sister, Bianca."

She raked me over with a scathing glance. "It's not my fault you can't hold your liquor."

"And the text Bianca received that afternoon, supposedly

from me, telling her I wanted nothing to do with her? I guess you had nothing to do with that either?"

She lifted one shoulder. "I don't know what you're talking about. Now, if you're finished, I'm tired. I'm going to bed."

She crossed to the door, stopping on the threshold when I called out, "Pack your things. Tomorrow morning, I'm moving you to the cottage on the winery grounds... for your own protection... until we learn the truth about what happened to Milana."

And the truth about your involvement in this mess.

I would move her there and post a guard. At least that way, she wouldn't be able to cause any more harm until I could figure out what to do with her. Divorce was not an option. Obviously, neither were criminal charges. As Cavalieris, we preferred to handle these things within the family.

She swung on me, hands on her hips. "And if I refuse?"

The corner of my mouth lifted. "Go ahead. Refuse. And you'll see the dark side of all that Cavalieri money you so enjoy spending."

CHAPTER 37

MILANA

The villa kitchen was filled with laughter and warmth.

It had been a few days since my fall and the haunted look was still in Cesare's eyes. It didn't help that my night terrors had returned, but every night he was there to hold me and chase the monsters away. With each passing day they became less intense. He was my knight in shining armor, except his weapons were bright bedroom lights and passionate sex.

The men were still working on searching for my second attacker, but so far had come up empty-handed.

So tonight we were all gathered in the kitchen to have a meal together, if only for a few hours, to forget about the wolves at the door.

Thankfully, Renata had chosen not to join us.

We had seen little of her lately. Enzo had moved her to the cottage the day after my fall. Amara and I had braced ourselves for her being brought into the villa since the men seemed determined to keep us all close by and under protective guard, but I guessed she preferred the cottage. I was going to write her a note thanking her for the flowers and apologizing for ruining them, to at least be nice, but Cesare adamantly insisted I should rest and said he would pass along my message instead.

The men were all acting strangely about Renata, but then again, it couldn't be pleasant having her nearby all the time. I was pretty sure that not even Enzo, her own husband, liked her. Not that I blamed him one bit.

Rosa cupped her cheeks and exclaimed in despair, "You don't crush the eggs. You crack the eggs! Crack them! Look at all the shells! *Mamma mia!* Who taught you how to cook?"

Gabriella wiggled her ring-clad fingers in front of Rosa. "Do these look like the hands of a woman who does housework?"

Rosa waved her hands. "Out! Out! Out of my kitchen! Shoo!"

Gabriella grabbed her wineglass and moved around the kitchen island to where I was sitting on a padded bench along the kitchen table, since everyone was under strict orders from Cesare to not let me help cook. She sat down and sidled up next to me.

I put my head on her shoulder and said low enough so Amara and Rosa couldn't hear, "You did that on purpose, didn't you?"

Gabriella smirked. "Of course, darling. I'm not an idiot. I know how to crack a damn egg."

We clinked wineglasses as we watched Amara and Rosa dump out the bowl of ruined eggs.

324

Rosa cracked fresh eggs as Amara used her fist to create a well in the center of her mixture of flour and salt. Rosa carefully poured the eggs into the well as Amara kneaded the mixture into a smooth dough, then transferred it into a bowl and covered it.

Next, they started on the filling for the *ravioli di ricotta*. They were using Amara's mother's recipe. Just as they were finished mixing the ricotta cheese, chopped spinach, parmesan cheese, salt, and black pepper together, Barone walked in.

He crossed straight to Amara and wrapped his arms around her middle from behind. He gave her a kiss on the cheek. "Smells wonderful."

She laughed. "We haven't started cooking anything yet."

He nuzzled her neck. "I wasn't talking about the food."

Amara glanced up and around the room as her cheeks turned pink. It was nice seeing my best friend so happy and content. I was glad she didn't listen to my panicked rant about leaving Barone, the day after I slept with Cesare.

She and Barone were clearly madly in love and meant for one another.

I caught Cesare's intense gaze the moment he entered the kitchen. He looked at me as if I were the only person in the entire world.

It was thrilling and just a bit overwhelming... but I was getting used to it.

The moment he got close enough, he swept me up into his arms and onto his lap. He took the wineglass from my grasp and took a sip. "Hey, that was mine!"

"Get used to it. From now on, what's mine is yours, and what's yours is mine."

"Yes, but that hardly seems fair to you since you have lots and lots of money and stuff, and I have, well, nothing," I teased.

He pressed his forehead to mine. "Not true. As far as I'm concerned, money is nothing. You are the real treasure, so when you think about it, I'm getting the better deal out of this arrangement."

I took my glass back. "Shameless charmer."

He winked at me, and like Amara, I blushed.

We snuggled together as we watched Barone hook the pasta machine up to the kitchen island countertop while Amara and Rosa removed the dough from the bowl and started preparing it for the next step.

Barone cranked the pasta machine lever. It made a loud, cracking sound, and then jammed. It was Amara's mother's machine. The one her stepfather and stepbrother had broken. Barone had done his best to repair it, but it was still a little temperamental.

Just then, Alfonso walked in with Enzo.

Barone raised his arm. "Just in time, Alfonso, come help me with this thing."

"Sure, boss."

I turned to look at Gabriella and caught her fluffing her hair. Her cheeks had turned a pretty pink.

Alfonso and Barone fixed the machine, and soon there were sheets and sheets of thin dough ribboning out of it.

Barone opened a fresh bottle of the vineyard's best vintage of *Vino Nobile di Montepulciano d'Abruzzo dei Cavalieri* and poured everyone a fresh glass as we gathered around the kitchen island. As Enzo and Rosa used glasses to cut circles into the dough, Cesare and I used spoons to drop the filling into their centers.

Barone and Amara folded each circle of dough in half and sealed the edges with forks.

Gabriella even tried to help. At one point, Alfonso stood behind her, wrapped his arms around her, and placed his hand over the top of her right hand. He said, "You're pressing too hard. The dough just needs gentle pressure and a little patience."

Amara's eyes widened as she looked at me, shifted her eyes to Gabriella and Alfonso, then back to me.

She mouthed, "Oh my God!"

I mouthed back, "I know!"

Rosa broke the spell by admonishing us all. "You are going too slow. Go faster or get out of my kitchen!"

Barone gave her a mock salute, and we all got back to work.

It was an amazing night.

The kind of simple, carefree family night that most people took for granted.

The kind of night I never dreamed was in my future.

And I couldn't help having this awful feeling of dread, that this kind of blissful happiness wouldn't last... that eventually the other shoe would drop.

And I was right.

CHAPTER 38

MILANA

"I don't think this is a good idea," objected Cesare.

I pulled on his hand as I led him down the corridor in the villa that would take us to the spiral staircase which led down into the ancient part of the winery carved out of the mountain below.

In the end, to appease an anxious Amara, we had agreed to stay in the villa while I recovered from my fall. Except for the itchy stitches from the cut on my neck, and the occasional headache and muscle soreness, there had been little to recover from physically. Not that anyone would know that from the way Cesare had been acting all week. You would think I had broken every bone in my body.

Emotionally, it was a slightly different story, but unlike before, I had learned to give myself a little grace. Being pushed and almost dying from a fall down a flight of marble stairs was a scary thing, and I would not beat myself up over having a nightmare or two over it or getting a little twitchy when I thought about what could have happened. But unlike the last time, I wasn't alone now.

I had Cesare to hold me tight and chase away the monsters.

I had Amara and Rosa and Gabriella and even Barone and Enzo and Alfonso and the rest of the staff at the villa to comfort and support me. Even the staff from the office, who I had been worried would no longer respect me or would think I was just a slutty gold digger, had sent over get-well notes and flowers, telling me how much I was missed and that they hoped I would return to the office soon.

Matteo was even risking Cesare's wrath by slipping me email updates on all my projects.

Yesterday, I had sneaked away and called a few of my project managers who had been panicking from not being able to reach me. It felt good to be needed and to have such important responsibilities.

And tonight, Sal and his whole family were coming to the villa for dinner.

The strange feeling of impending doom that had twisted my stomach into knots was slowly easing.

I even hoped that by the end of this *fine settimana*, I could convince Cesare it was safe to return to the office for a few hours each day.

Life was good.

Life was getting back to normal.

"Come on. This is such an important part of your life. I want to see it."

He pulled me into his embrace and cupped my jaw. "The old wine vats are in the caves. It will be dark and enclosed."

I cocked my head to the side. "I'm not technically afraid of the dark or claustrophobic. It's just sometimes, in certain situations, those things can trigger me. I'll be fine, I promise. Besides, you'll be with me. Come on, you promised at dinner last night to take me. The whole family heard! They are my witnesses."

Although the Cavalieri winery had upgraded its facilities decades ago, they still made a very select, outrageously expensive batch of wines each year the traditional way, out of the original Cavalieri wine vats which were located inside caves carved out of the Apennine mountains. Since the villa was built on top of it, I had been down there before as a server during catering events. It was a maze of corridors and caves carved out by hand by the Etruscans who occupied the land before the Romans.

This select batch was personally supervised by the family and only a few trusted members of the staff.

I knew Cesare oversaw the property management portion of the family business out of necessity, but his first, true love was to the land and the vines. He truly loved the winemaking process and tending over this batch of wine each day was a special part of him, and I wanted to share it with him.

Cesare threw back his head and let out a dramatic sigh. "Fine, but the very first sign that you are the least bit agitated or stressed I'm pulling you out of there."

I smirked.

He narrowed his eyes. "Try not to look so smug at getting your way."

I shrugged. "I can't help it."

He playfully swatted my ass. "That's okay. Your payment for the concession will come later."

I gasped as I covered my butt and raced ahead of him down the corridor.

* * *

AS WE GOT CLOSER to the main cave, the atmosphere took on the reverent solemnity of a monastery.

Two massive, arched oak doors with hammered wrought iron bars flanked the entrance.

The moment we entered the room, Cesare pulled out a lighter from his pocket and moved from one iron candelabra to another, lighting ivory pillar candles. "This isn't just for light. It's also a precaution. There is no real ventilation in the cave. During the fermentation process, carbon dioxide can build up quickly. So we use the candles as an early warning system. If the candles go out, there is not enough oxygen in the room."

A frisson of fear raced up my spine as my gaze moved around the room, watching as the flickering candlelight cast eerie, dancing shadows onto the uneven surface of the rock walls.

Cesare crossed to me and placed his hands on my upper arms, staring down at me. "That's it. We're leaving."

I shook my head. "No! No, I'm okay. Really. Please keep going. This is interesting."

He stared at me a moment longer, then nodded. He continued lighting the rest of the candles until the room was ablaze with a warm, comforting glow.

"Although we now cheat a bit and use thermometers, in ancient times, they used to use the candles to measure the temperature of the wine as well."

I frowned. "Wait, what?"

"Fermentation causes heat. If the wine is fermenting too quickly, the temperature rises and the candles will melt faster, meaning the wine needs to be cooled. If the candles melt too slowly, the wine isn't generating heat, which means it's not fermenting enough. Either can impact the flavor and quality of the wine."

He walked over to the wall and selected a long wooden rod with a round base. "Are you ready to punch the wine?"

I put my hands on my hips. "Punch the wine? I'll give you the whole candles measuring the temperature of the wine thing, because that sounded pseudo-scientific, but now you're just making shit up."

He gestured with his head as he walked toward one of the vast vats of wine. It looked like an enormous whiskey barrel with its top cut off. I had to tilt my head back since it was so much taller than me.

Cesare ascended a small set of wooden stairs secured to the side of the vat. He swung the wooden tool over the vat and pressed down. "This is called a plunger. As the wine ferments, the crushed grape skins float to the top, creating a cap. Since the skins are essential to the fermentation process, we need to punch those skins down to make sure they are evenly dispersed throughout the juice."

I watched in awe as he methodically pressed the grape skins down.

Dressed in laborer attire of dark pants, work boots, and a

coarse, ivory tunic with the sleeves pulled up, showing off his muscular forearms, he could have easily passed for a turn-of-the-century winemaker.

An incredibly sexy, turn-of-the-century winemaker.

There was just something super-hot about a man who knew how to work with his hands. He was handsome as hell in a suit, but damn, it was nothing compared to him in a pair of worn jeans and work boots.

My gaze ran over his form as my tongue skimmed my lower lip.

"Keep looking at me like that, babygirl, and I'm going to fuck you standing right up against one of these rock walls," growled Cesare.

I blinked, not realizing he had caught me staring at him. "I was just… studying your form, so I knew what to do when it was my turn."

He raised an eyebrow. "Sure you were."

I cleared my throat. "My turn."

He climbed down and led me to the next vat.

We climbed the stairs and stood together on the landing, with him behind me.

His breath tickled my ear, sending a delicious shiver of awareness between my legs, when he said, "First, you need to hold the plunger firmly."

I wiggled my ass against his crotch before replying, "So you need me to grasp the long, hard wooden rod?"

"Behave," he growled. As he pushed his hips forward, his already hard cock pressed against my lower back. "Now you gently push down the cap." He kept his grip on the plunger as he demonstrated the motion.

I leaned forward, pushing my hips back seductively. "So I just press down nice and slow, using my body weight?"

He moved his hands to my waist, digging his fingers into my flesh as he growled in my ear, "Just wait until I get you back upstairs."

I giggled as I continued to rhythmically push down on the grape skins, watching as the dark purple mass bobbed and weaved with the motion. There was something very soothing about the practice.

Cesare stood protectively over me as I continued the motion. "*Brava ragazza.*"

A rush of pride pooled in my stomach.

As we descended the stairs, preparing to move on to the next vat, a staff member I didn't recognize entered the cave. "Cesare, Don Cavalieri is looking for you. There's someone in the formal office he wants you to meet."

The formal office was the one they used to greet clients and for tastings. It was far down the maze of hallways in a carved-out cave like the wine room.

Cesare turned to look at me. I waved him off. "I'll be fine. Go."

"Don't do a punch down without me. You could lose your balance and fall into the vat."

I rolled my eyes. "I'm not an idiot."

He kissed me on the cheek. "I'll be right back."

Cesare and the staff member left.

I spun around, taking in the primal beauty of the candle-light and that strange, ethereal attachment to the past the atmosphere evoked. I was also more than a little proud of myself for conquering that small frisson of fear I'd felt in the beginning. It would have been a shame to have missed out on sharing such an amazing experience with Cesare, especially something that was so near and dear to his heart and legacy.

Seconds later, I heard the scrape of a boot heel.

I smiled without turning. "You don't have to check on me. I promised I wouldn't do a punch down by myself."

"Well, if it isn't the village slut."

I whirled around to see Renata standing at the entrance. She was hanging onto one of the arched oak doors which had swung closed on silent, well-oiled hinges.

My eyes narrowed. "What did you just call me?"

She drummed her fingers on the edge of the door as she raked her cold eyes over me. "You just couldn't leave well enough alone, could you? Had to fucking dredge up the past and play the victim."

I bristled. "I'm not playing the victim, and what business is it of yours, anyway?"

She snorted. "I knew you were a stupid whore."

What the hell was happening?

I took in her slightly disheveled appearance, which was uncharacteristic of her, but there was something more. Her gaze was glassy and unfocused, but that wasn't it either. My mouth dropped open as my hand instinctively reached for the Gemini charm at my throat, which wasn't there. It was her belly. It was completely flat. While she never looked nearly as pregnant as she should have at the six or seven months along that she was supposed to be, she'd at least had a small belly. Now she had none.

I moved deeper into the cave, reaching behind me. I wrapped my hand around the smooth pole of the plunger.

"None of this would be happening if those idiots had just gotten a photo of you sucking cock like your whore of a mother."

My heart thumped madly in my chest as the blood rushed to my ears. Whereas before I had felt only a quick flash of fear upon entering the cave that had immediately been banished by Cesare's comforting strength, now paralyzing terror made my arms and legs tremble.

The stone walls seemed to breathe and move as they edged closer and closer, caging me in.

The past and present collided in my brain, meshing in a macabre dance of shadows as my vision darkened at the edges.

My jaw locked. I had to force the words out through clenched teeth. "It was you. You're the female."

My hand shook so badly I dropped my plunger weapon. It crashed to the floor.

I screamed at the sound and jumped to the side.

Renata threw her head back and cackled. "Of course it was me, you dumb bitch. The Cavalieri men were the only game in town, and I was going to make damn sure I had my pick."

Realization dawned. I frowned. "It was you who pushed me down the stairs."

She raised one shoulder and smiled. "Guilty." She gave me a scathing look as her upper lip lifted in a sneer. "Of course you had to be a pain in my ass and not break your stupid neck."

"But why? You married Enzo! You got what you wanted. I'm no threat to you now!"

"Like I said, you just couldn't leave the past alone. The

337

men have started asking questions. *Dangerous questions.* With you dead, the past will die with you, and eventually, after some time has passed, I can get back to my plan."

Her plan? I looked again at her flat belly. Fuck, what could be her plan?

"Renata, whatever you have planned—"

She looked sharply to her right. "I'd like to stay and chat, but you're not worth my time. And it wouldn't do for them to find me here when Cesare discovers your dead body."

She reached for the other oak door.

I screamed and raced for the exit.

The door slammed shut just as I reached it.

I heard the terrifying sound of the iron bolt sliding into place just as I pushed my shoulder against it. I pounded my fist on the door. "Renata! Renata! Open this door! Renata!"

I could barely hear her cackling laughter through the heavy oak as the sound of it receded down the hall.

I lifted both arms and pounded on the door, screaming for help until my lungs and throat were sore.

Using all my weight, I shoved against the doors with my shoulder, but they wouldn't budge.

It was only then I noticed the cave had gotten darker.

Swallowing past the lump of fear in my throat, I slowly turned to face the interior of the cave.

I watched with horror as, one by one, the candles snuffed out, leaving me in almost absolute darkness.

I slid down to the dirty stone floor and curled into a ball as a wave of dizziness hit me.

I tried to call out for Cesare, but my chest was so tight I couldn't pull in enough air.

My vision blurred.

I focused on the last remaining weak candle flame, forcing myself to remain conscious, praying that Cesare would return and find me in time.

Then the last flame flickered... and died.

CHAPTER 39

CESARE

*M*y father wasn't in the formal office. When I turned to ask the staff member where he was, he had disappeared, probably returning to his regular duties. Since I hadn't recognized him and didn't know his name to call him back, I moved further down the hall to the service kitchen and then through the doors and out to the veranda where I saw Vito, our winery foreman.

"Vito! Where is my father?"

Vito shrugged and gestured over his shoulder. "Probably in the warehouse. A shipment of bottles arrived and half of them are broken. Last I saw, he was helping the men sort through the mess to see what we could salvage."

I frowned. "So there isn't a client on site?"

He shook his head. "Not that I know of. Don Cavalieri cancelled all client meetings for the next few weeks. Said he didn't want any strangers on the property."

Fuck. That was right.

Milana.

Goddamn it.

Vito yelled after me, "What's wrong?"

I shouted over my shoulder, "Raise the alarm!"

I could be overreacting, but I didn't care. Feeling my heart pound in my chest, I raced through the twisting labyrinth of corridors until I reached the traditional wine cave corridor. From down the hall, I could see the oak doors were shut.

Dear fucking God.

I wrenched on the iron bar, pulled open the door and rushed inside the pitch-black cave.

Tripping over something the moment I crossed the threshold.

It was Milana's motionless body.

I fell to my knees and clutched her to me, howling with rage and fear.

I cried out her name over and over again. She didn't respond.

Pressing my ear to her chest, I couldn't hear or feel a heartbeat.

I placed my hand to her face.

Her skin was cool to the touch.

Her usually pretty pink lips were tinged with blue.

Desperately holding onto her, I swept her into my arms and ran down the corridor to reach the fresh air. I was met by staff and security guards. I didn't break my stride as I shouted at them to get an ambulance, then called out a description of the man who drew me away from Milana. "Find the bastard! No one gets off this property!"

I burst through the veranda doors in time to see Vito,

Enzo, and my father sprinting across the fields toward me. In the far distance I could hear the wail of the *ambulanza*.

I dropped to my knees, laid Milana on the soft grass and started CPR after frantically searching for any signs of life as I leaned over her. "Come on, babygirl. Come on, baby. Please, Milana. Please, baby. Don't leave me. Don't leave me, baby. Come on, Milana. Breathe, *carissima*. Breathe for me, baby."

Nothing.

She lay there. Motionless.

I pressed my ear to her chest then my fingers to her throat, but still couldn't detect a heartbeat.

My father laid a hand on my shoulder. "Cesare…."

I knew what he was trying to say but refused to accept it.

I shrugged him off violently. "Back off. She's not fucking dead."

I returned my attention to Milana and started compressions again. "Come on, baby. Fight! Goddamn it. Fight!" I yelled.

The *ambulanza* careened onto the property, rolling over several bushes and potted plants. Two *paramedici* came flying out of the back of the *ambulanza* before it had even come to a full stop. One was carrying a black medical duffel bag. The other had an oxygen tank.

As they neared us, an agonizing scream pierced the air.

Amara ran headlong from the villa toward us. Papà caught her before she reached Milana's motionless body. He could barely hold her back as she shrieked and despairingly stretched out her arms to try and reach her closest friend.

One of the *paramedici* tried to shove me out of the way. I let out a feral growl, refusing to budge. Enzo and Vito grabbed me under the arms and had to physically pull me from Milana's body.

Enzo pleaded with me. "Let them do their job, brother! Let them try to save her!"

I opened my mouth and let out a roar of anguish, forced to helplessly stand by and watch the life drain away from the woman I loved.

Time seemed to stand still as the *paramedici* checked for a pulse.

No one said a word.

No one moved.

No one breathed.

The very birds seemed to fall silent as we waited.

He looked up at his partner and... nodded.

My knees buckled.

If it hadn't been for the grip Enzo and Vito had on me, I would have fallen to the ground with relief.

The *paramedici* spoke. "It's weak, but we have a pulse. We have to move. Now!"

We couldn't even waste time getting the gurney. We all gently lifted her and raced to the back of the *ambulanza*. They strapped her into the bed as I hopped in and sat on the adjacent bench and clasped her hand in mine. I barely heard my father say they would all meet us at the hospital.

I leaned over Milana and smoothed her hair back as I studied her beautiful, deathly pale face that was mostly obscured by an oxygen mask.

The moment we got to the hospital, it was all controlled chaos.

A team of doctors and nurses were waiting at the emergency exit to meet the ambulance.

I ran alongside the gurney, refusing to let go of Milana's hand.

A nurse pleaded with me. "Signore Cavalieri, you must go. Signore. You must step aside. Signore?"

"I'm not leaving her," I growled.

There was a cacophony of sounds. It was so much worse than last week when she had fallen. At least then she had been conscious and smiling and reassuring me she was fine. Now she was lying motionless, close to death as nurses drew blood and hooked her up to machines. There was a volley of call outs from the doctors to the nurses and back for vital signs and tests.

And the whole time there was the relentless beeping of the medical machines.

"Her blood pressure is eighty-five over sixty, doctor."

"That's too low. Get me a blood oxygen test. We need to check organ function and electrolyte levels. She's a young female. Run the gamut."

"Yes, doctor."

"What's taking the ECG so long? Hurry!"

"Here. Hooking her up now."

"Do we know what she was exposed to, and for how long?"

"Order me a CT scan. We're going to need to check for lung damage."

"Yes, doctor."

"How the hell did this happen?"

"Where is this girl's family?"

My brother and father answered in unison as they placed

supportive hands on my shoulders. "Here."

I raised my chin. "We're her family. She was exposed to probably over 2500 ppm for carbon dioxide for approximately ten minutes."

As the doctor opened his mouth to respond, the horrible beeping stopped.

It became one long, devastating, steady beep.

The doctor's eyes widened. Without responding to what I said, he swung around and shouted, "Get them out of here!"

No one spoke.

I paced the small confines of the waiting room like a caged animal.

Papà had Amara on his lap, rocking her back and forth, soothing her as she continued to cry softly.

At one point, Vito came in. His shirt was torn, and he had a split lip.

Papà put Amara into Gabriella's care and we approached Vito.

Vito lowered his head and swiped at the back of his neck. "I'm not sure how to say this, boss."

It was obvious from his appearance that he found the staff member who'd lured me away from Milana under false pretenses.

I placed my left hand over my right fist. "Tell me."

Vito took a deep breath. "I guess your plans to go into the caves with Milana were discussed at dinner last night, so the person knew you would be there. They bribed a new staff member we brought on during the harvest who wasn't as loyal to the family. He swears he didn't know what they had planned."

Losing patience, I said, "Vito, who?"

He shifted from foot to foot. He glanced up between me, my father, and Enzo. After taking another fortifying breath, he blurted out, "Renata. It was Renata. I'm sorry, Enzo."

We both stared at Enzo. His face was a mask of stone. Without saying a word, he stormed out.

Papà raised his chin to Vito, who understood the silent command and followed Enzo.

I stood there staring straight ahead, trying to take the information in past all the pain and fear.

Renata.

It had been Renata. This whole time. How had I missed that?

"Don't."

I looked up at my father.

He shook his head. "Don't. There will be time for that later. Right now, we focus on Milana."

As though summoned by those words, the doctor entered the waiting room.

I rushed over to him, fear tightening my chest.

The doctor gave me a hesitant smile. "The good news is she's alive. She's going to pull through just fine."

I closed my eyes and sent a prayer up to God for saving her, as I heard an outburst of joy from the rest of the room.

The doctor continued. "Unfortunately...."

We fell silent as all eyes focused on the doctor.

".... it's too soon to tell if the baby will survive."

CHAPTER 40

BARONE

*T*he door to the cottage was splintered and hanging open on only one hinge. As I stepped over the threshold, the silence belied the wreckage. Furniture was upended. Glass from broken art frames lay in shattered fragments scattered over the tile floor.

Through the dark gloom, I found Enzo sitting on the edge of the bed in the main bedroom.

He was staring at the wall. His hands were bruised and bloodied.

Without looking up, he said, "She's gone."

I wasn't surprised. Word would have gotten to Renata that she had failed in killing Milana. She would have known it would be only a matter of time before we learned of her involvement.

I leaned against the doorjamb and crossed my arms. "Any thoughts on where?"

Enzo's hard gaze raised to mine. "Hopefully to hell."

"Milana survived."

Enzo's shoulders sagged as he closed his eyes. "Thank God."

I hated to cause my son more pain, but he deserved the whole truth. "She's pregnant."

He rubbed his eyes. "The baby?"

I swallowed past the lump in my throat. "Too soon to know."

In a flash, Enzo rose and punched the wall before turning and throwing his back against it and sliding down to the floor. He buried his head in his hands.

I joined him on the floor and placed my arm over his shoulders.

His voice was tortured when he spoke. "I should have listened to you. I brought that venomous bitch into our family."

"You couldn't have known."

He lifted his head and grimaced. "But I knew. I knew she was a cold, calculating bitch. I just... thought if there was a chance the baby was mine...."

"I know, son."

"I never thought she was capable of this."

"We all know that. No one blames you for this. *No one.*"

"That doesn't mean I don't blame myself."

We sat there in silence for several minutes.

Finally, he spoke. "What do I do now, Papà?"

I hugged him closer. "You come back to the hospital. You support your brother. We see Milana through this. And then we figure out the rest as a family."

I rose and held my hand out to him. After a moment's

pause, he took it and rose. "There's something I need to do first."

* * *

THE FLAMES SHOT high into the air as we stood and watched the cottage burn.

It was his first true architectural project.

He had poured his heart and soul into it.

My son loved that cottage.

Although he never said so, I knew he had built it with his future bride in mind.

And that woman had not been Renata.

CHAPTER 41

MILANA

*C*esare tucked a second blanket over my lap. "Are you sure you are warm enough?"

I gave him an indulgent smile. "You have a blanket wrapped around my shoulders and my lap *and* I'm sitting on one."

He disappeared, and I heard the trunk open and close. He returned seconds later with yet another folded blanket that he placed under my feet. With a nod of satisfaction, he pulled on the seat belt and reached around me to buckle it before closing the car door for me.

He got in on the driver's side and slowly pulled away from the hospital.

I leaned over and rested my head on his shoulder. "We've barely started dating and you've already turned me into a criminal. You Cavalieris are a bad influence."

He turned his head and kissed the top of mine. "Checking you out of the hospital is hardly a criminal offense, and don't forget, I was the one who kept watch when you shoplifted that DVD of *Pride and Prejudice* back when we were in school."

"If we aren't doing anything wrong, then why am I checking out in the middle of the night?"

"They can't take care of you as well as I can," grumbled Cesare.

I snuggled deeper into my insane number of blankets and closed my eyes.

The doctors told me that a few minutes longer in that cave and I would have surely died. Cesare saved me just in time. While I got better each day, I still tired easily and had some lingering headaches and brain fog, but overall, in time, I was told I should make a full recovery.

It had been a miserably traumatic week. I still hadn't processed everything that had happened.

Almost dying.

Renata being responsible for all of it.

The baby.

I pressed my palm to my abdomen.

It was still too soon to know anything for certain. I had to make an appointment with an obstetrician tomorrow to run more tests. Even then, the doctors warned me since the pregnancy was in the first trimester, I could still miscarry.

Cesare and I were determined to hold on to hope.

It was strange. I hadn't even known I was pregnant, hadn't even suspected it.

A few weeks earlier, I would have thought the world was ending if I had learned I was having a baby with Cesare Cavalieri. Now, all my love and energy were concentrated on willing our baby to survive, to fight and pull through.

I was so relieved to be going home with Cesare.

He hadn't left my side the entire week. Sleeping in an uncomfortable chair the nurses had dragged in from the waiting room for him. While the nurses were reluctantly fine with leaving the light on in the room for me, it had been a constant battle over leaving a window open.

The nurses and doctors feared the cold winter weather was unhealthy for me in my fragile state and that superseded my night terror fears. So, each night Cesare would open the window, and each night when both of us were asleep, they'd try to close it, and Cesare would wake up and open it again.

It was a constant battle of wills.

Until tonight.

Tonight, he showed up with a stack of blankets and a plan. He bundled me up and checked me out of the hospital. Declaring that what I really needed to recover was to be home, among family.

Family.

I had one now.

A real one.

After waving to the ominous-looking security guards who were now posted at the base of the mountain on the edge of Cavalieri land, we entered the drive that led to the winery.

As we drove closer to the villa, Cesare cut off his headlights and slowed the car down.

I frowned and sat up straight in my seat. "Why are we sneaking onto the grounds?"

"I don't want them to know you are here. I want you all to myself, at least for one night."

He pulled up to the grotto house and moved around the

car to help me out. As he was busy gathering up all the extra blankets, I looked across the wide drive to an upstairs balcony of the villa.

Amara and Gabriella were standing there.

Amara made an X with her arms over her chest and pointed at me. *Love you.*

Gabriella blew me a kiss.

Making sure Cesare couldn't see, I silently waved back.

They both moved back inside and turned out the light before Cesare noticed and would know his cover and big covert plans had been blown.

Even though Cesare had made sure to have all the lights on so we were met with a bright, welcoming glow, I hesitated as we approached the entrance to the house.

My stomach twisted as irrational fear tightened the muscles of my legs and arms.

I had barely put up with being inside the hospital room, but a lot of that had to do with the sedatives they had been giving me.

I could practically feel the walls closing in on me, and I hadn't even stepped inside yet.

Cesare placed a protective arm around my waist. "We're not going inside."

I looked up at him. "We're not?"

He kissed my forehead. "Come with me."

He led me down a small set of flagstone steps off to the side of the house that opened up into the partially hidden grotto pool area. The cabana was gone. In its place was a more permanent and sturdy structure. It had three sides, with the open wall facing the heated pool, and was made entirely of glass.

The small, open fire pit had been replaced by two larger tabletop gas fireplaces that flanked the structure, easily warming it, even in winter.

Inside the structure was our bed and even a few low bookshelves.

I stared at the mini glass bedroom in awe. "You did this for me."

"Haven't you learned yet, *carissima*. There is nothing... *nothing*... I wouldn't do for you."

He placed his hand at my lower back and led me to another, smaller building made entirely of flagstone and frosted glass that was set to the side. Inside was a luxurious spa bathroom, complete with an enormous white quartz tub, over which a massive skylight was centered.

Cesare walked over to the quartz tub and turned a silver knob.

It rained from the skylight.

I gasped in delight. The tub quickly filled with gloriously hot, steaming water.

He pulled the stopper off a crystal decanter and added a generous amount of clear bubble bath. The room filled with the fresh, clean scent of eucalyptus and lemongrass. After a week of inhaling the acrid stench of the antiseptic bleach and harsh chemicals used in the hospital, it was heavenly.

When the tub was full, he turned off the rain shower and gently pulled the blanket off my shoulders. He then slowly unzipped my Prada hoodie. His jaw clenched and his dark gaze hardened as the tips of his fingers traced the still healing cut from the glass shard that was now unbandaged since the stitches had been removed. He then moved to trace the faint scratch along my jaw that ended near my left ear, from where something had scratched my face in the chaos of the emergency room when they were hooking me up to machines and oxygen.

I reached up and clasped his hand and clutched it between my breasts so he could feel the steady beat of my heart. Several times over the last few days I had woken from a nap to the comforting touch of Cesare's hand on my heart. I finally realized he was also comforting himself with the sign of life.

He swallowed. "I should have let you run as far and as fast as you possibly could away from me." His brow wrinkled. "All I seem to do is hurt you."

I backed up a step as I raised the zipper to my hoodie. "You're right. We should just end this now." I turned and headed toward the door as I tossed over my shoulder, "Don't worry. I'll send you baby photos on their birthday and at Christmas."

Cesare grabbed me from behind. He spun me around and pressed me against the wall. Delving his fingers in my hair, he pulled my head back and growled, "You're not going anywhere," before claiming my mouth in a searing, possessive kiss that melted my bones.

We were both breathless when we broke free. I licked my lips as I stared at his mouth and then up into his stormy, dark eyes. "What happened to letting me go?"

His thumb caressed my jaw as his gaze wandered over my face, as if memorizing every detail. "I remembered what an arrogant, possessive, selfish bastard I am."

I grasped his hips. "Well, don't expect an argument from me on that point."

He rested his forehead against mine. "I can't do it, baby. I can't let you go. It would be like tearing off a limb, but fuck... I don't want to put you in danger."

I slid my hands up over his chest to wrap my arms around his neck. "If there is one lesson I've learned through this whole mess, it's that we are not to blame for the actions and choices of others. I'm not to blame for the choices my mother made, any more than you are for Renata's actions. The real mistake would be allowing *their* choices to affect *ours*. I don't want to give them that kind of power over our lives."

He tilted my chin up and looked down at me. "What did I do to deserve to be loved by such an amazingly intelligent and beautiful woman as you?"

I quirked my lips. For the barest of seconds, I thought about giving him a teasing retort, but decided to be honest. "You saw me. When others saw my mother's reputation or what I wanted them to see, you saw...me."

His mouth fell on mine again. As we kissed, he stripped us out of our clothes and lifted me into the tub, following me in. We sunk down into the silky, soapy water with me straddling his hips.

His hands cupped my ass as his cock pressed against my inner thigh.

My head fell back as he kissed my neck. "Fuck, baby. I need you so goddamn bad, but I don't want to hurt you. Your body's been through so much."

I reached between us and grasped his cock. I leaned up

and positioned him at my entrance. Capturing his gaze, I slowly lowered myself onto his shaft. Cesare threw his head back and groaned as his fingers tightened on my hips.

Bouncing me on top of his cock, he pulled one of my nipples deep inside of his mouth.

I rested my hands on his shoulders as I rocked my hips back and forth. "Oh, God! Yes!"

He reached over and turned the silver knob.

It rained down on us.

Cesare leaned up, wrapped his arms around me and held me close as he thrust his hips up harder and faster. Water sloshed over the edge of the tub in soapy waves as the water continued to pour down on us.

We climaxed together under the stars, in the rain, surrounded by an ethereal, silky cloud of soap bubbles.

AFTERWARD, I rested my head on his shoulder, clasped in his arms, his semi-hard cock still inside of me.

Cesare shut off the rain shower and stretched his arm out to a small bamboo table near the tub. "I have something for you."

I knelt up and sat back.

He held out a flat, black velvet case. "Milana Fiorella Carbone, I can say, honestly and truly, you are the only woman I have ever loved. I cannot imagine sharing my life with anyone else. Would you do me the very great honor of becoming my wife?"

The moment he opened the case, my mouth dropped open. "My necklace!"

Nestled inside the black velvet was my beloved Gemini charm necklace.

Cesare pulled out the necklace and set the box aside.

I lifted my wet hair as he wrapped his arms around my neck to secure it. "I realized you must have lost it on the train, so I had the conductor search for it. It's the original charm, but I had it re-plated in 24 karat gold and replaced the three star crystals with genuine diamonds."

I caressed the charm. "I love it!"

I stroked the inner curve of her breast near where the charm laid. "It may take me a few tries, but I'm learning. I knew better than to replace it outright, or to pick out an engagement ring without your input," he said with a wink.

As I shifted forward, intent on kissing him, Cesare pulled back. "Wait, you haven't given me an answer to my proposal yet."

CHAPTER 42

CESARE

"She said yes!"

Everyone at the breakfast table cheered.

Despite the winter chill, in deference to Milana, Amara had the staff set up a small breakfast feast out on the private balcony overlooking the Cavalieri vineyard. Wrought iron braziers were placed in the corners to warm the place with bright, cheery fire. The natural edge wood table was covered with overlapping ivory lace tablecloths held in place with silver platters of sliced oranges, melon, and berries, baskets of sweetened ricotta cheese *sfogliatelle*, jelly-filled *bombolone* dusted with powdered sugar, *focaccia dolce* with honey and lemon zest, and *cornetto alla cremas* bursting with vanilla pastry cream.

Of course, Aunt Gabriella made sure there were crystal vases of white roses strategically placed among the platters and bowls down the length of the table for an extra bit of flare.

Matteo was manning the copper espresso machine, handing out espressos and cappuccinos while Papà poured *Franciacorta Bellavista* into crystal flutes for a toast.

After Amara hugged Milana, Aunt Gabriella immediately started chatting about what size diamond she should get that would be impressive but not garish.

I pulled away to step over to Enzo, who hung back. I took in the dark circles under his eyes and his bruised knuckles. He laid a hand on my shoulder. "I'm very happy for you, brother. You have made an excellent choice in a wife." The inference hung between us.

I pulled him in for a hug. No one blamed him, but that didn't mean he didn't blame himself.

We were interrupted by Milana. "Am I allowed to hug my future brother-in-law?"

Enzo and I broke apart. Enzo looked from me to Milana. Although he had visited the hospital every day to check on us, he had stayed away from Milana's room, not wanting to upset her with his presence.

Milana stepped forward and wrapped her arms around his neck, pulling him close. She whispered something in his ear that I couldn't hear. When they pulled apart, Enzo blinked several times and looked to the side before nodding. "Thank you for that."

I placed a protective hand on her lower back and led her over to the breakfast table, but not before leaning down and asking, "What did you say to Enzo?"

She gave me a cheeky grin. "None of your business. That's between me and my new big brother."

I kissed the side of her head. "God, I love you."

She leaned her head against my chest as she wrapped her arm around my waist.

We all sat around the table chasing away the lingering fears of the future and what it would hold—about our baby, about Renata—with laughter and love. Whatever the future held, we knew we were stronger when we faced it together as a family. That was the true Cavalieri legacy.

* * *

OUR MERRIMENT WAS INTERRUPTED by Benito's arrival.

We could all tell by the solemn look on his face that it wasn't a social call.

My father rose from the table and spoke to him. Their heads dipped low in conversation. At one point, they both looked up to stare at Enzo.

All of our gazes followed.

Enzo stood. "Tell me."

My father pushed his shoulders back as he faced his eldest son, concern etched on his brow. "They've found Renata."

EPILOGUE

ENZO

Cesare pulled on his collar, clearly uncomfortable. "This is fucking ridiculous."

Father Luca cast us a dark look as he cleared his throat.

Cesare whispered, "Sorry, Father."

I flexed my fingers, resisting the urge to clench them into a fist as I stared across the church from my position near the altar to the first pew, where Renata's parents were glaring daggers at me. I then cast my gaze over the rest of the congregation, all dressed in somber black.

I let out a frustrated sigh. "I agree, but Papà is right. We need to keep up appearances. No matter that this is all just a fucking farce."

Father Luca cleared his throat again.

I leaned past Cesare and whispered, "Sorry, Father."

My gaze fell on Renata's coffin. The best my money could buy. Because of the extent of her injuries, we were forced to have a closed casket service. I took a sick pleasure in knowing that would have annoyed her. Her vanity would have wanted everyone to have one final look at her, so the *peasants* could marvel at her beauty, even in death.

Cesare rolled his head to ease the tension in his neck.

I couldn't blame him. While, as Cavalieris, we were used to the heightened scrutiny of those around us, this was different. Half the people seated in the pews were here to support me, the other half believed I was guilty of murdering my wife. There was a firm belief the only reason I hadn't been arrested yet was because of Cavalieri money and power. Arresting the eldest son and heir to one of the richest families in Italy was a tricky business.

Our father emerged from a side door and joined us at the base of the altar near Renata's coffin. "Security is in place to make sure the fucking vulture paparazzi don't interfere with the procession once we emerge from the church."

Father Luka thinned his lips and widened his eyes as he cleared his throat... again.

Papà raised his palm up. "Sorry, Father."

Cesare looked between us. "I don't care about the photos. I just want to make sure the girls are safe."

Papà nodded. "All taken care of. A small army will immediately surround them the second this fuckin"— he paused and cast a glance over his shoulder at Father Luca—"this *solemn service* is finished and take them to the villa."

I lifted the sleeve of my suit jacket and covertly checked the time. I was counting the seconds until this entire charade was over. "Can we get on with it?" I ground out.

Before anyone could respond, the doors to the church slammed open.

The glare from the afternoon sun created a white halo of light around a woman in a black dress that hugged her hourglass figure. Her high heels clacked against the ancient marble tile as she stormed down the center aisle, seeming not to notice the hundreds of eyes which turned to observe her entrance. Her face was obscured by a wide-brimmed hat pulled low, a black veil covering her face and wrapped around her throat.

She marched down the church aisle like a vengeful funeral bride intent on one purpose.

She then stopped directly in front of me... drew her arm back... and slapped me hard across the face.

The sound reverberated off the church walls.

Without a word, she turned on her heels and marched back down the aisle.

Papà asked, "Who the hell was that?"

Rubbing my jaw, I watched the sway of her hips as she walked away. "Bianca, Renata's sister."

To be continued....

Secrets of the Brother

Cavalieri Billionaire Legacy, Book Three

ABOUT THE AUTHOR

Zoe Blake is the USA Today Bestselling Author of the romantic suspense sagas *The Diamanti Billionaire Dynasty* & *The Cavalieri Billionaire Legacy* inspired by her own heritage as well as her obsession with jewelry, travel, and the salacious gossip of history's most infamous families.

She delights in writing Dark Romance books filled with overly possessive billionaires, taboo scenes, and unexpected twists. She usually spends her ill-gotten gains on martinis, travels, and red lipstick. Since she can barely boil water, she's lucky enough to be married to a sexy Chef.

ALSO BY ZOE BLAKE

CAVALIERI BILLIONAIRE LEGACY

A Dark Enemies to Lovers Romance

Scandals of the Father

Cavalieri Billionaire Legacy, Book One

Being attracted to her wasn't wrong... but acting on it would be.

As the patriarch of the powerful and wealthy Cavalieri family, my choices came with consequences for everyone around me.

The roots of my ancestral, billionaire-dollar winery stretch deep into the rich, Italian soil, as does our legacy for ruthlessness and scandal.

It wasn't the fact she was half my age that made her off limits.

Nothing was off limits for me.

A wounded bird, caught in a trap not of her own making, she posed no risk to me.

My obsessive desire to possess her was the real problem.

For both of us.

But now that I've seen her, tasted her lips, I can't let her go.

Whether she likes it or not, she needs my protection.

I'm doing this for her own good, yet, she fights me at every turn.

Refusing the luxury I offer, desperately trying to escape my grasp.

I need to teach her to obey before the dark rumors of my past reach her.

Ruin her.

She cannot find out what I've done, not before I make her mine.

Sins of the Son

Cavalieri Billionaire Legacy, Book Two

She's hated me for years... now it's past time to give her a reason to.

When you are a son, and one of the heirs, to the legacy of the Cavalieri name, you need to be more vicious than your enemies.

And sometimes, the lines get blurred.

Years ago, they tried to use her as a pawn in a revenge scheme against me.

Even though I cared about her, I let them treat her as if she were nothing.

I was too arrogant and self-involved to protect her then.

But I'm here now. Ready to risk my life tracking down every single one of them.

They'll pay for what they've done as surely as I'll pay for my sins against her.

Too bad it won't be enough for her to let go of her hatred of me,

To get her to stop fighting me.

Because whether she likes it or not, I have the power, wealth, and connections to keep her by my side

And every intention of ruthlessly using all three to make her mine.

Secrets of the Brother

Cavalieri Billionaire Legacy, Book Three

We were not meant to be together... then a dark twist of fate stepped in, and we're the ones who will pay for it.

As the eldest son and heir of the Cavalieri name, I inherit a great deal more than a billion dollar empire.

I receive a legacy of secrets, lies, and scandal.

After enduring a childhood filled with malicious rumors about my father, I have fallen prey to his very same sin.

I married a woman I didn't love out of a false sense of family honor.

Now she has died under mysterious circumstances.

And I am left to play the widowed groom.

For no one can know the truth about my wife...

Especially her sister.

The only way to protect her from danger is to keep her close, and yet, her very nearness tortures me.

She is my sister in name only, but I have no right to desire her.

Not after what I have done.

It's too much to hope she would understand that it was all for her.

It's always been about her.

Only her.

I am, after all, my father's son.

And there is nothing on this earth more ruthless than a Cavalieri man in love.

IVANOV CRIME FAMILY TRILOGY

A Dark Mafia Romance

Savage Vow

Gregor & Samara's story

I took her innocence as payment.

She was far too young and naïve to be betrothed to a monster like me.

I would bring only pain and darkness into her sheltered world.

That's why she ran.

I should've just let her go...

She never asked to marry into a powerful Russian mafia family.

None of this was her choice.

Unfortunately for her, I don't care.

I own her... and after three years of searching... I've found her.

My runaway bride was about to learn disobedience has consequences... punishing ones.

Having her in my arms and under my control had become an obsession.

Nothing was going to keep me from claiming her before the eyes of God and man.

She's finally mine... and I'm never letting her go.

Vicious Oath

Damien & Yelena's story

When I give an order, I expect it to be obeyed.

She's too smart for her own good, and it's going to get her killed.

Against my better judgement, I put her under the protection of my powerful Russian mafia family.

So imagine my anger when the little minx ran.

For three long years I've been on her trail, always one step behind.

Finding and claiming her had become an obsession.

It was getting harder to rein in my driving need to possess her... to own her.

But now the chase is over.

I've found her.

Soon she will be mine.

And I plan to make it official, even if I have to drag her kicking and screaming to the altar.

This time... there will be no escape from me.

Betrayed Honor

Mikhail & Nadia's story

Her innocence was going to get her killed.

That was if I didn't get to her first.

She's the protected little sister of the powerful Ivanov Russian mafia family - the very definition of forbidden.

It's always been my job, as their Head of Security, to watch over her but never to touch.

That ends today.

She disobeyed me and put herself in danger.

It was time to take her in hand.

I'm the only one who can save her and I will fight anyone who tries to stop me, including her brothers.

Honor and loyalty be damned.

She's mine now.

RUTHLESS OBSESSION SERIES

A Dark Mafia Romance

Sweet Cruelty

Dimitri & Emma's story

It was an innocent mistake.

She knocked on the wrong door.

Mine.

If I were a better man, I would've just let her go.

But I'm not.

I'm a cruel bastard.

I ruthlessly claimed her virtue for my own.

It should have been enough.

But it wasn't.

I needed more.

Craved it.

She became my obsession.

Her sweetness and purity taunted my dark soul.

The need to possess her nearly drove me mad.

A Russian arms dealer had no business pursuing a naive librarian student.

She didn't belong in my world.

I would bring her only pain.

But it was too late…

She was mine and I was keeping her.

Sweet Depravity

Vaska & Mary's story

The moment she opened those gorgeous red lips to tell me no, she was mine.

I was a powerful Russian arms dealer and she was an innocent schoolteacher.

If she had a choice, she'd run as far away from me as possible.

Unfortunately for her, I wasn't giving her one.

I wasn't just going to take her; I was going to take over her entire world.

Where she lived.

What she ate.

Where she worked.

All would be under my control.

Call it obsession.

Call it depravity.

I don't give a damn… as long as you call her mine.

Sweet Savagery

Ivan & Dylan's Story

I was a savage bent on claiming her as punishment for her family's mistakes.

As a powerful Russian Arms dealer, no one steals from me and gets away with it.

She was an innocent pawn in a dangerous game.

She had no idea the package her uncle sent her from Russia contained my stolen money.

If I were a good man, I would let her return the money and leave.

If I were a gentleman, I might even let her keep some of it just for frightening her.

As I stared down at the beautiful living doll stretched out before me like a virgin sacrifice,

I thanked God for every sin and misdeed that had blackened my cold heart.

I was not a good man.

I sure as hell wasn't a gentleman… and I had no intention of letting her go.

She was mine now.

And no one takes what's mine.

Sweet Brutality

Maxim & Carinna's story

The more she fights me, the more I want her.

It's that beautiful, sassy mouth of hers.

It makes me want to push her to her knees and dominate her, like the brutal savage I am.

As a Russian Arms dealer, I should not be ruthlessly pursuing an innocent college student like her, but that would not stop me.

A twist of fate may have brought us together, but it is my twisted obsession that will hold her captive as my own treasured possession.

She is mine now.

I dare you to try and take her from me.

Sweet Ferocity

Luka & Katie's Story

I was a mafia mercenary only hired to find her, but now I'm going to keep her.

She is a Russian mafia princess, kidnapped to be used as a pawn in a dangerous territory war.

Saving her was my job. Keeping her safe had become my obsession.

Every move she makes, I am in the shadows, watching.

I was like a feral animal: cruel, violent, and selfishly out for my own needs. Until her.

Now, I will make her mine by any means necessary.

I am her protector, but no one is going to protect her from me.

Printed in Great Britain
by Amazon

26452402R00216